QUOTABLE
STAR TREK®

Quotable
STAR TREK®

Jill Sherwin

P O C K E T   B O O K S

New York   London   Toronto   Sydney   Tokyo   Singapore

PHOTO CREDITS

DANNY FELD: 109

PETER IOVINO: 29, 51

COURTESY OF THE GREGORY JEIN COLLECTION: 1, 131, 183,
213, 261

ELLIOTT MARKS: 209

CRAIG T. MATHEW: 189

ROBBIE ROBINSON: 13, 21 41, 75, 81, 91, 141, 149, 155, 161,
167, 203, 221, 255

GREG SCHWARTZ: 179

BARRY SLOBIN: 243

An *Original Publication* of POCKET BOOKS

POCKET BOOKS, a division of Simon & Schuster Inc.
1230 Avenue of the Americas, New York, NY 10020

STAR TREK is a Registered Trademark of Paramount Pictures.

This book is published by Pocket Books, a division of Simon & Schuster
Inc., under exclusive license from Paramount Pictures.

ISBN: 0-671-02457-4

First Pocket Books trade paperback printing March 1999

10   9   8   7   6   5   4   3   2   1

POCKET and colophon are registered trademarks
of Simon & Schuster Inc.

Book design by Richard Oriolo

Printed in the U.S.A.

To my mother, Judith Sherwin
who encouraged my love of words

To Gene Roddenberry
who inspired the words

and
To DeForest Kelley
for his kind words

CONTENTS

Beam me up, Scotty.

It's the first quote everyone is going to look for, and I have to say—it's not here! I tried and I tried, I watched and I listened and I read, but I couldn't find the exact quote in any episode or movie. There seem to be several variations, but not that exact line. Never happened. Still, it wouldn't be a *Star Trek* quote book without it, so... what better way to begin?

Now, maybe you're wondering how I got to put this book together...

"Hard work, bribes, sucking up to the boss. Just like any job."
———Brunt to Rom
how he got his job with the F.C.A.
DS9 / "Family Business"

Okay, that, too.

But it also came about after a few years of being the unofficial researcher in the *Star Trek: Deep Space Nine* writers' offices. "Jill, read every script and find every reference to _____ for us." And silly me, I enjoyed doing it! Well, after you read through the entire script library over and over, you eventually start to notice some things. In my case I noticed that every time I read a script, I'd stop at the same point and think, "Gosh, that's a great line." And after the umpteenth or so time I did that, I thought to myself, "you know, someone should put these together in a book." And then I thought, "You know, *I* could put these together in a book!"

Having worked with some of the terrific people involved in making the *Star Trek* books (see where that "sucking up to the boss" part comes in?) while I was proofreading *Legends of the Ferengi*, I at least had a starting point of who to talk to about my idea. To my surprise and joy, they liked the idea, too. And *Quotable Star Trek* was born.

It's been a labor of love, and while I know that, inevitably (and mainly for reasons of space), a lot of material had to be left out that many people will wish had been included, I hope the book as it stands pleases the fans and offers something to people who never realized what they were missing by not watching *Star Trek*.

A quick reference key for your reading comprehension:

TOS = The Original Series   *DS9* = Deep Space Nine
TNG = The Next Generation   *VGR* = Voyager

When there is no series reference, the quote is from one of the movies. For example:

First Contact refers to the movie
TNG/"First Contact" refers to the episode

On the organization of the book... the first twenty-nine chapters include short quotes, bits of dialogue, and memorable speeches from the four live-action series and the first eight movies on various topics that require little or no knowledge of *Star Trek*, though I've added some commentary here and there where I thought it would help. These are the chapters you can put in front of your Uncle Shmullus's face and say "See there? *That's* what *Star Trek* is about!"

The last few chapters do require a stronger familiarity with the shows and their characters. In "Dramatis Personae," "For the Fans" and "Personal Favorites", I've tried to represent some of the special moments in *Star Trek*; things that made us sigh, cry, laugh, and BELIEVE. Because that's what *Star Trek* has always been about for me—that unshakable faith that there *are* heroes and there will continue to be, that life is worth living in all its ups and downs, and that...

"Even in the darkest moments, you can always find something that'll make you smile."

——Captain Benjamin Sisko's log
DS9 / "In the Cards"

——Jill Sherwin
Wonderland
August 1998

1. The Human Condition

"A man either lives life as it happens to him, meets it head on and licks it, or he turns his back on it and starts to wither away."

—Dr. Philip Boyce to Captain Christopher Pike
Star Trek: The Original Series / "The Cage"

"Charlie, there are a million things in this universe you can have and there are a million things you can't have. It's no fun facing that, but that's the way things are."
    "Then what am I going to do?"
"Hang on tight. And survive. Everybody does."

—Captain James T. Kirk and Charlie Evans
TOS / "Charlie X"

"In this galaxy, there's a mathematical probability of three million Earth-type planets. And in all of the universe, three million *million* galaxies like this. And in all of that...and perhaps more, only one of each of us."

—Dr. Leonard McCoy to Kirk
TOS / "Balance of Terror"

"Being a red-blooded human obviously has its disadvantages."
—Commander Spock to McCoy
TOS / "Miri"

"Here you stand…a perfect symbol of our technical society. Mechanized, electronicized, and not very human. You've done away with humanity, the striving of man to achieve greatness through his own resources…."

"We've armed man with tools. The striving for greatness continues."

—Anton Karidian and Kirk
TOS / "The Conscience of the King"

"We're a most promising species, Mister Spock, as predators go. Did you know that?"

"I've frequently had my doubts."

"I don't. Not any more. And maybe, in a thousand years or so, we'll be able to prove it."

—Kirk and Spock, on the Metron's judgment
TOS / "Arena"

"Sometimes pain can drive a man harder than pleasure."

—Kirk to McCoy
TOS / "The Alternative Factor"

"Improve a mechanical device and you may double productivity. But improve *man*, you gain a thousandfold."

—Khan Noonien Singh to senior staff
TOS / "Space Seed"

"Maybe we weren't meant for Paradise. Maybe we were meant to fight our way through, struggle, claw our way up, scratch for every inch of the way. Maybe we can't stroll to music of the lute, we must march to the sound of drums."

—Kirk to McCoy
TOS / "This Side of Paradise"

"We're the same. We share the same history, the same heritage, the same lives. We're tied together beyond any untying. Man or woman, it makes no difference. We're human. We couldn't escape from each other even if we wanted to. That's how you do it, Lieutenant. By remembering who and what you are, a bit of flesh and blood afloat in a universe without end and the only thing that's truly yours is the rest of humanity."

—Kirk to Lieutenant Carolyn Palamas
TOS / "Who Mourns for Adonais?"

"It's the custom of my people to help one another when we're in trouble."

—Kirk to Shahna
TOS / "The Gamesters of Triskelion"

"She seems very vulnerable."
    "We're all vulnerable in one way or another."

—McCoy and Kirk, on Dr. Miranda Jones
TOS / "Is There in Truth No Beauty?"

"How compact your bodies are. And what a variety of senses you have. This thing you call…language, though…most remarkable. You depend on it for so very much. But is any one of you really its master? But most of all…the aloneness. You are so alone. You live out your lives in this shell of flesh. Self-contained. How terribly lonely."

—Spock/Kollos
TOS / "Is There in Truth No Beauty?"

"Well, when the personality of a human is involved, exact predictions are hazardous."

—McCoy to Spock, on the long-term effects of the Zetarian possession of Mira
TOS / "The Lights of Zetar"

"But you can't deny, Captain, that you're still a dangerous, savage child-race."

—Q to Captain Jean-Luc Picard
Star Trek: The Next Generation / "Encounter at Farpoint"

"You see of all the species, yours cannot abide stagnation. Change is at the heart of what you are. But change into *what?* That's the question!"

—Q to Commander William Riker
TNG / "Hide and Q"

"I know Hamlet. And what he might say with irony I say with conviction. 'What a piece of work is man! How noble in reason! How infinite in faculty! In form, in moving, how express and admirable. In action, how like an angel. In apprehension, how like a god...'"

"Surely you don't see your species like that, do you?!"

"I see us one day *becoming* that, Q. Is it *that* which concerns you?"

—Picard and Q
Source: William Shakespeare, *Hamlet*, Act 2, scene 2
TNG / "Hide and Q"

"You humans are puny. Weak."

"But our spirit is indominatable."

—Armus and Picard
TNG / "Skin of Evil"

"A lot has changed in the past three hundred years. People are no longer obsessed with the accumulation of 'things.' We have eliminated hunger, want, the need for possessions. We've grown out of our infancy."

—Picard to Ralph Offenhouse
TNG / "The Neutral Zone"

"It's a blessing to understand that we are special...each in his own way."

—Woman to Lieutenant Geordi La Forge
TNG / "Loud as a Whisper"

"Haven't we grown beyond the point where we resolve our problems with physical conflict?"

—Dr. Katherine Pulaski to Riker
TNG / "The Icarus Factor"

"You see, lad, every moment of pleasure in life has to be purchased by an equal moment of pain."

—Danilo Odell to Lieutenant Worf
TNG / "Up the Long Ladder"

"They're so different."

"It is the differences that have made us strong."

—Prime Minister Granger and Picard, on the group of people about to join Granger's colony
TNG / "Up the Long Ladder"

"Different in appearance, yes. But we are both living beings—we are born, we grow, we live, and we die. In all the ways that matter, *we are alike!*"

—Picard to Nuria. The captain tries to convince Nuria that though he is an alien to her world, his people are no different from her people
TNG / "Who Watches the Watchers?"

"There are creatures in the universe who would consider you the ultimate achievement, android. No feelings, no emotions—no pain. And yet you covet those qualities of humanity. Believe me, you're missing nothing. But if it means anything to you…you're a better human than I."

—Q to Lieutenant Commander Data, on Q's punishment to live as a human
TNG / "Déjà Q"

"Being afraid all of the time of forgetting somebody's name. Not…not knowing what to do with your hands…I mean, I am the guy who writes down things to remember to say when there's a party. And then when he finally gets there, he winds up alone in the corner trying to look comfortable examining a potted plant."

—Lieutenant Reginald Barclay to La Forge
TNG / "Hollow Pursuits"

"All this magnificent technology, we still find ourselves susceptible to the ravages of old age. The loss of dignity, the slow betrayal of our bodies by forces we cannot master."

—Picard to Data
TNG / "Sarek"

"Is that not part of the human experience—growth and change?"

—Data to Wesley Crusher
TNG / "Ménage à Troi"

"When the Borg destroyed my world, my people were scattered throughout the universe. We survived. As will humanity survive. As long as there's a handful of you to keep the spirit alive. You *will* prevail. Even if it takes a millennium."

—Guinan to Picard
TNG / "The Best of Both Worlds, Part I"

"You know what the worst part of growing old is? So many of the people you've known all your life are gone...and you realize you didn't take the time to appreciate them while you still could...."

—Dr. Dalen Quaice to Dr. Beverly Crusher
TNG / "Remember Me"

"There is something to be learned when you're not in control of every situation."

—Counselor Deanna Troi to Riker
TNG / "The Loss"

"If being human is not simply a matter of being born flesh and blood...if it is instead a way of thinking, acting...and feeling...then I am hopeful that one day I will discover my own humanity. Until then, Commander Maddox, I will continue... learning, changing, growing...and trying to become more than what I am."

—Data's log
TNG / "Data's Day"

"You know, almost everyone has a moment in their lives when they exceed their own limits...achieve what seems to be impossible...."

—Troi to Barclay
TNG / "The Nth Degree"

"We should not discount Jean-Luc Picard yet. He is human...and humans have a way of showing up when you least expect them."

—Sela to Toral
TNG / "Redemption"

"Poverty was eliminated on Earth a long time ago. And a lot of other things disappeared with it: hopelessness...despair...cruelty..."

—Troi to Samuel Clemens
TNG / "Time's Arrow, Part II"

"Young lady, I come from a time when men achieve power and wealth by standing on the backs of the poor...where prejudice and intolerance are commonplace...and power is an end unto itself....And you're telling me...that isn't how it is anymore?"

—Clemens to Troi
TNG / "Time's Arrow, Part II"

"You see, one of the most important things in a person's life is to feel useful."

—Picard to La Forge
TNG / "Relics"

"Part of being human is learning how to deal with the unexpected...to risk new experiences even when they don't fit into your preconceptions."

—La Forge to Data
TNG / "Inheritance"

"They say, time is the fire in which we burn...right now, Captain, my time is running out. We leave so many things unfinished in our lives...."

—Dr. Tolian Soran to Picard
Source: Delmore Schwartz, "For Rhoda"
Star Trek Generations

"You know, Counselor...recently, I've become very much aware that there were fewer days ahead than there are behind....But I took some comfort from the fact that the family would go on."

—Picard to Troi
Generations

"It unites humanity in a way that no one ever thought possible...when they realize they're not alone in the universe."

—Troi to Zefram Cochrane
Star Trek: First Contact

"The acquisition of wealth is no longer the driving force in our lives. We work to better ourselves and the rest of humanity."

—Picard to Lily Sloane
First Contact

"Someone once said...'Don't try to be a *great* man...just be a man. And let history make its own judgments.'"
—Riker, quoting Zefram Cochrane
First Contact

"In my century we don't succumb to...revenge. We have a more evolved sensibility."
—Picard to Lily
First Contact

"Every choice we make has a consequence...."
—Commander Benjamin Sisko to wormhole alien
Star Trek: Deep Space Nine/ "Emissary"

"Doctor, most people in my experience wouldn't know reason if it walked up and shook their hand."
—Security Chief Odo to Dr. Julian Bashir
DS9 / "Emissary"

"It's not your fault that things are the way they are."
    "Everybody tells themselves that...and nothing ever changes...."
—Bashir and Lee
DS9 / "Past Tense, Part II"

"I wasn't aware that humans saw growing old as a negative experience. On Cardassia, advanced age is seen as a sign of power and dignity."
—Elim Garak to Bashir
DS9 / "Distant Voices"

"Being an outsider isn't so bad. It gives one a unique perspective."
—Odo to the female shape-shifter
DS9 / "The Search, Part II"

"I finally realized that it wasn't Starfleet I wanted to get away from. I was trying to escape the pain I felt after my wife's death. I thought I could take the uniform, wrap it around that pain, and toss them both away. But it doesn't work like that. Running may help for a little while, but sooner or later the pain catches up with you. And the only way to get rid of it is to stand your ground and face it."
—Sisko to Worf
DS9 / "The Way of the Warrior, Part II"

"In the meantime let me give you some free advice, just to show you I'm on your side. You people should take better care of yourselves. Stop poisoning your bodies with tobacco and atom bombs. Sooner or later, that kind of stuff will kill you."

—Quark to General Denning. Having traveled back in time to twentieth-century Earth, Quark resolves to form a business relationship with the humans using what little knowledge he has of the time period
DS9 / "Little Green Men"

"'There comes a time in every man's life when he must stop thinking and start doing.'"

—Benjamin Sisko to Joseph Sisko, quoting his father's words back to him
DS9 / "Paradise Lost"

"We all have scars. Of one kind or another."

—Kira Nerys to Kira Meru
DS9 / "Wrongs Darker Than Death or Night"

"My people taught me a man does not own land. He doesn't own anything but the courage and loyalty in his heart. That's where *my* power comes from."

—Commander Chakotay to Kar
Star Trek: Voyager / "Initiations"

"The past is a part of you, no matter how hard you try to reject it."

—Kolopak to young Chakotay
VGR / "Tattoo"

"The human fascination with 'fun' has led to many tragedies in your short but violent history. One wonders how your race has survived having so much 'fun.'"

—Ensign Tuvok to Dmitri Valtane
VGR / "Flashback"

"In my time, Mister Starling, no human being would dream of endangering the future to gain advantage in the present...."

—Captain Kathryn Janeway to Henry Starling
VGR / "Future's End, Part II"

"Families, societies, cultures—wouldn't have evolved without compassion and tolerance—they would have fallen apart without it."

—Kes to the Doctor
VGR / "Darkling"

"When your captain first approached us, we suspected that an agreement with humans would prove impossible to maintain. You are erratic...conflicted...disorganized. Every decision is debated...every action questioned...every individual entitled to their own small opinion. You lack harmony...cohesion...greatness. It will be your undoing."

—Seven of Nine to Chakotay
VGR / "Scorpion, Part II"

"We all have a past. What matters is *now*."

—Lieutenant Tom Paris to Seven of Nine
VGR / "Day of Honor"

"I realize it may be difficult for you to help save this creature's life...but part of becoming human is learning to have compassion for those who are suffering...even when they're your bitter enemies."

—Janeway to Seven of Nine, on a member of Species 8472
VGR / "Prey"

"A single act of compassion can put you in touch with your own humanity."

—Janeway to Seven of Nine
VGR / "Prey"

"Your people have faced extinction many times. But you've always managed to avoid it....You seem to recognize the need for change."

—Alpha-Hirogen to Janeway
VGR / "The Killing Game, Part II"

2. The Quality of Life

"When dreams become more important than reality, you give up travel, building, creating."
—Vina to Pike, on the Talosians' decaying society
TOS / "The Cage"

"She has an illusion and you have reality. May you find your way as pleasant."
—the Keeper to Pike, on Vina's choice to stay with the Talosians
TOS / "The Cage"

"To all mankind: May we never find space so vast, planets so cold, heart and mind so empty that we cannot fill them with love and warmth...."
—Dr. Tristan Adams to Kirk and Dr. Helen Noel, a toast
TOS / "Dagger of the Mind"

"Make the most of an uncertain future, enjoy yourself today. Tomorrow...may never come at all."
—Trelane to Kirk
TOS / "The Squire of Gothos"

"Now I don't pretend to tell you how to find happiness and love, when everyday is just a struggle to survive. But I do insist that you *do* survive. Because the days and the years ahead are worth living for. One day, soon, man is going to be able to harness incredible energies, maybe even the atom, energies that could ultimately hurl us to other worlds in…in some sort of spaceship. And the men that reach out into space will be able to find ways to feed the hungry millions of the world and to cure their diseases. They will be able to find a way to give each man hope and a common future. And those are the days worth living for…."

—Edith Keeler to her mission's poor, New York City, 1930
TOS / "The City on the Edge of Forever"

"There are many who are uncomfortable with what we have created. It is almost a biological rebellion, a profound revulsion against the planned communities, the programming, the sterilized artfully balanced atmospheres. They hunger for an Eden…where spring comes."

—Spock to Kirk, on those who reject modern convenience for a simpler life
TOS / "The Way to Eden"

"I feel pity for you. Your existence must be a kind of walking purgatory—neither dead nor alive, never really *feeling* anything. Just existing. Just existing. Listen to me—a dying man takes the time to mourn a man who will never know death. Funny, isn't it?"
    "Funny?…I have had…great difficulty determining what funny is."
"I've had the same difficulty most of my life. We're much alike."

—Dr. Ira Graves and Data
TNG / "The Schizoid Man"

"Without heart, a man is meaningless."

—Data/Graves to Picard
TNG / "The Schizoid Man"

"For some, security is more important than comfort."

—Worf to Troi
TNG / "The Dauphin"

"To survive is not enough…to simply *exist* is not enough…."

—Roga Danar to Nayrok
TNG / "The Hunted"

"Why do you resist? We only wish to raise…quality of life…for all species."
    "I like my species the way it is."

—Locutus of Borg and Worf, on the threat of assimilating the Klingon Empire
TNG / "The Best of Both Worlds, Part II"

"You always reach for the future. And your brother for the past."
    "There should be room for both in this life."

—Louis and Picard
TNG / "Family"

"As you examine your life, do you find you have missed your humanity?"
    "I have no regrets."
"'No regrets.' That is a human expression."
    "Yes. Fascinating."

—Data and Spock, on Spock's life as a half-vulcan, suppressing his human half.
TNG / "Unification, Part II"

"They've given away their humanity with this genetic manipula-tion.…Many of the qualities that they breed out—the uncer-tainty, the self-discovery, the *unknown*—these are many of the qualities that make life worth living…well, at least to me. I wouldn't want to live my life knowing that my future was writ-ten, that my boundaries had been already set. Would you?"

—Picard to Troi, on a genetically engineered society
TNG / "The Masterpiece Society"

"It was the wish of our founders that no one have to suffer a life with disabilities…"
    "Who gave them the right to decide whether or not I should be here? Whether or not I might have something to contribute…"

—Hannah Bates and La Forge, on La Forge's blindness
TNG / "The Masterpiece Society"

"Seize the time, Meribor.…Live now. Make 'now' always the most precious time. 'Now' will never come again."

—Picard to Meribor
TNG / "The Inner Light"

"Just because something's old doesn't mean you throw it away."
—La Forge to Captain Montgomery Scott
TNG / "Relics"

"Her belly may be full...but her spirit will be empty."
—Picard to Gul Madred. In Cardassian society, Madred's daughter reaps the benefits of the military, but loses the rewards of peace
TNG / "Chain of Command, Part II"

"*That* Picard never had a brush with death...never came face to face with his own mortality...never realized how fragile life is...or how important each moment must be...so his life never came into focus."
—Q to Picard; analyzing a potential alternate lifepath for Picard
TNG / "Tapestry"

"I would rather die as the man I was...than live the life I just saw."
—Picard to Q, on choosing to return to his dying body, proud of the life he lived rather than the safe but stagnant other lifepath Q showed him
TNG / "Tapestry"

"You are a culture of *one*. Which is no less valid than a culture of one billion."
—Picard to Data
TNG / "Birthright"

"They don't know how to do anything else but die—they've forgotten how to live."
—Kai Opaka to Kira, on the warring Ennis and Nol-Ennis
DS9 / "Battle Lines"

"Too many people dream of places they'll never go, wish for things they'll never have...instead of paying adequate attention to their real lives...."
—Odo to Quark
DS9 / "If Wishes Were Horses"

"...There's more to life than profit."
—Lieutenant Jadzia Dax to Pel
DS9 / "Rules of Acquisition"

"The old Klingon ways are passing. There was a time when I was a young man, the mere mention of the Klingon Empire made worlds tremble. Now, our warriors are opening restaurants and serving *racht* to the grandchildren of men I slaughtered in battle. Things are not what they used to be. Not even a blood oath."

—Kang to Dax
DS9 / "Blood Oath"

"I'm no writer, but if I were, it seems to me I'd want to poke my head up every once in a while and take a look around...see what's going on. It's *life*, Jake; you can miss it if you don't open your eyes."

—Benjamin Sisko to Jake Sisko
DS9 / "The Visitor"

"But what you're asking me to do is wrong. You can't go around making people prove they are who they say they are. That's no way to live and I'm not gonna go along with it."

—Joseph Sisko to Benjamin Sisko, on enforcement of blood screenings to test for changeling infiltrators
DS9 / "Homefront"

"A man's got to live. And sometimes living is messy."

—Jake to Nog
DS9 / "The Ascent"

"Now, nothing is certain."
    "Makes life interesting, doesn't it?"

—Kai Winn and Kira
DS9 / "Rapture"

"He used to say 'When you overindulge the body—'"
    "'—you starve the soul.'"

—Kira and the mirror Bareil, quoting the late Vedek Bareil
DS9 / "Resurrection"

"Captain, you are an explorer. What if you had nothing left to explore? Would you want to live forever under those circumstances?"

—Quinn to Janeway
VGR / "Death Wish"

"As the Q have evolved, we've sacrificed many things along the way. Not just manners. But mortality, and a sense of purpose, and a desire for change, and a capacity to grow. Each loss is a new vulnerability, wouldn't you say?"
—Quinn to Tuvok
VGR / "Death Wish"

"Q, now that you're mortal, you have a new existence to explore…an entirely new state of being…filled with the mysteries of mortal life…pleasures you've never felt before.…I like this life, Q. You might too. Think hard before you give it up."
—Janeway to Quinn
VGR / "Death Wish"

"Sometimes I think my people spend so much time trying to save lives they don't know how to live anymore."
—Danara Pel to the Doctor, on the disease ravaging her world
VGR / "Lifesigns"

"Before I met you, I was just a disease.…But now, everything's different.…When people look at me, they don't see a disease anymore.…They see a *woman*…a woman *you* made…a woman you love…a woman you're not afraid to touch.…"
—Danara to the Doctor, on his transference of her personality into a hologram, as her body lies dying from the phage
VGR / "Lifesigns"

"You said before you knew me, that you were…just a disease. Well, before *you*, I was just…a projection of photons held together by force fields…a computerized physician…doing a job…doing it exceptionally well, of course.…But still, it was just a profession, not a life.…But now that you're here, and my programming has adapted.…I'm not just working anymore, I'm *living*…learning what it means to be with someone…to love someone.…I don't think I can go back to the way things were either.…Danara, please, don't die."
—the Doctor to Danara
VGR / "Lifesigns"

"There's nothing sadder than a missed opportunity."
—Kes to Danara
VGR / "Lifesigns"

"One can pursue one's creative urges…spiritual urges…and physical urges. All have a place in the well-lived life."
—Lord Byron hologram to the Doctor
VGR / "Darkling"

3. Simple
Pleasures

"Sam Cogley asked me to give you something special. It's not a first edition or anything, just a book. Sam says that makes it special, though."
—Areel Shaw to Kirk
TOS / "Court Martial"

"On my planet, to rest is to *rest*, to cease using energy. To me it is quite illogical to run up and down on green grass, using energy instead of saving it."
—Spock to Kirk
TOS / "Shore Leave"

"The more complex the mind, the greater the need for the simplicity of play."
—Kirk to Lieutenant Hikaru Sulu
TOS / "Shore Leave"

"But I've never stopped to look at clouds before. Or rainbows. Do you know I can tell you exactly *why* one appears in the sky. But considering its beauty has always been out of the question."
—Spock to Leila Kalomi. Affected by the spores of an alien plant life, Spock is able to relax and enjoy himself
TOS / "This Side of Paradise"

"I see no practical use for them."

"Does everything have to have a practical use for you?
They're nice, they're soft, and they're furry, and they make
a pleasant sound."

"So would an ermine violin, Doctor, but I see no advantage in
having one."

—Spock and McCoy, on tribbles
TOS / "The Trouble with Tribbles"

"'All I ask is a tall ship and a star to steer her by.' You could feel
the wind at your back in those days, the sounds of the sea
beneath you and even if you take away the wind and the water,
it's still the same. The ship is yours, you can *feel* her. And the
stars are still there, Bones. . . ."

—Kirk to McCoy
Source: John Masefield, "Sea Fever"
TOS / "The Ultimate Computer"

"It's a song, you green-blooded Vulcan. You sing it. The words
aren't important. What's important is that you have a good time
singing it."

"Oh. I am sorry, Doctor. Were we having a good time?"

—McCoy and Spock
Star Trek V: The Final Frontier

"You've not experienced Shakespeare until you have read him in
the original Klingon."

—Gorkon to Spock
Star Trek VI: The Undiscovered Country

"Sometimes we must allow the surroundings to flow over us. To
dwell on each separate part. How it feels. To allow it to fill you."

—Warrior/Adonis to Troi
TNG / "Loud as a Whisper"

"I'll have ten hot fudge sundaes."

"I have never seen anyone eat ten chocolate sundaes."

"I'm in a really bad mood. And since I've never eaten before, I
should be very hungry."

—Q and Data. Newly made mortal, Q follows Data's suggestion of Troi's remedy for
feeling bad: chocolate
TNG / "Déjà Q"

"Humans like to touch each other. They start with the hands and go on from there."
—Guinan to Lal
TNG / "The Offspring"

"You know, Jean-Luc, it's lucky for you we met. If it wasn't for me…if it wasn't for me you'd still be back there sitting in the sun…relaxing."
—Vash to Picard
TNG / "Captain's Holiday"

"You know, there's nothing wrong with a healthy fantasy life, as long as you don't let it take over."
—Troi to Riker
TNG / "Hollow Pursuits"

"I never met a chocolate I didn't like."
—Troi to Riker
TNG / "The Game"

"Chocolate is a serious thing."
—Troi to Riker
TNG / "The Game"

"I would gladly risk feeling bad at times…if it also meant that I could taste my dessert."
—Data to Timothy, on the advantages of being human
TNG / "Hero Worship"

"That's the problem I see here…all this technology…only serves to take away life's simple pleasures. You don't even let a man open the door for a lady."
—Clemens to Troi
TNG / "Time's Arrow, Part II"

"That's the wonderful thing about crayons…they can take you to more places than a starship."
—Guinan to young Ro
TNG / "Rascals"

"No man should know where his dreams come from. It spoils the mystery...the fun."
—Dr. Noonien Soong to Data
TNG / "Birthright"

"For humans, touch can *connect* you to an object in a very personal way...make it seem more *real*."
—Picard to Data, on touching the *Phoenix*
First Contact

"But it's not going to be the same without you. When I look at a gas nebula, all I see is a cloud of dust, but seeing the universe through your eyes I was able to experience...wonder. I'm going to miss that."
—Q to Vash, on Vash's refusal to continue traveling with him
DS9 / "Q-Less"

"It's good to want things."
    "Even things you can't have?"
"*Especially* things I can't have."
—Quark and Odo
DS9 / "The Passenger"

"When it comes to picnics, the only thing that really matters is the company."
—Lwaxana Troi to Odo
DS9 / "The Forsaken"

"The Bajorans call that constellation the Runners. I can never figure out if they're running toward something or away from something."
    "Does that matter? Sometimes it just feels good to run."
—Sisko and Fenna
DS9 / "Second Sight"

"We all work for our supper. You'll be surprised how much sweeter it tastes when you do."
—Alixus to Sisko
DS9 / "Paradise"

"Anything worth doing in a holosuite can be done better in the real world."

"You obviously haven't been in the right holosuite program."

—Kira and Quark
DS9 / "Second Skin"

"Actually, I've lost my taste for beetle snuff. It might be fun for you and me, but it's no fun for the beetles."

—Grand Nagus Zek to Quark
DS9 / "Prophet Motive"

"Well you should tell your friend to live a little....Life's too short to deprive yourself of the simple pleasures...."

—Bashir/Torias to Dax, on diets
DS9 / "Facets"

"I savored those stories; I read them slowly, one each day. And when I was done, I wished I hadn't read them at all. So I could read them again...like it was the first time."

—Melanie to old Jake
DS9 / "The Visitor"

"There's only one 'first time' for everything, isn't there? And only one last time, too. You think about such things when you get to be my age. That today may be the last time you...sit in your favorite chair...or watch the rain fall...or enjoy a cup of tea by a warm fire."

—old Jake to Melanie
DS9 / "The Visitor"

"The one good thing about going away...is coming home."

—Keiko O'Brien to Chief Miles O'Brien
DS9 / "Accession"

"You know, you can tell a lot about people's moods just by watching them walk on the Promenade. When things are going good, people take their time, window-shop, talk to their friends."

—Jake to Bashir
DS9 / "Apocalypse Rising"

"Worf? My love…? Let me make this *very* clear—I do *not* want to spend my honeymoon climbing, hiking, sweating, bleeding, or suffering in any way."
—Dax to Worf
DS9 / "Change of Heart"

"Room service. I want to be pampered. I want a staff to cater to our every whim. I want to be embarrassed by the size of our room. I want a balcony with a view that would make you want to break down and cry from the sheer beauty of it all. And I don't want to spend one moment of our honeymoon suffering from anything except guilt about our complete self-indulgence."
—Dax to Worf, on her preference for their honeymoon
DS9 / "Change of Heart"

"Ah, real sunshine, fresh air…you and the kids. Life doesn't get any better than this."
—O'Brien to Keiko
DS9 / "Time's Orphan"

"It is…a tempting prospect. But when I hold it up against the prospect of seeing the sunrise over the Arizona Desert…or swimming in the Gulf of Mexico on a summer's day, there's just no comparison. I want to go home."
—Chakotay to Janeway, on staying in the Delta Quadrant
VGR / "The 37's"

"Frankly, it's refreshing to take myself out of the twenty-fourth century every now and then. And a little…disorganization can be very encouraging to the imagination. You might want to try it sometime."
—Janeway to Seven of Nine, on why she enjoys the holographic simulation of Leonardo da Vinci's workshop
VGR / "The Raven"

"I'll complain if I want to. It's comforting."
—the Doctor to Seven of Nine
VGR / "One"

"This journey certainly hasn't lacked excitement. I can't complain about being bored."

"Since you find it comforting, you'll undoubtedly find something else to complain about."

—the Doctor and Seven of Nine
VGR / "One"

4. Human Nature

"Has it occurred to you that there's a certain inefficiency in constantly questioning me on things you've already made up your mind about?"

"It gives me emotional security."
—Spock and Kirk
TOS / "The Corbomite Maneuver"

"The intelligence, the logic—it appears your half has most of that. And perhaps that's where man's essential courage comes from. For you see, he was afraid and you weren't."
—McCoy to Kirk. Split in two by a transporter malfunction, the "good" Kirk seeks the strengths within him
TOS / "The Enemy Within"

"Your Earth people glorify organized violence for forty centuries, but you imprison those who employ it privately."
—Spock to McCoy
TOS / "Dagger of the Mind"

"Do you know that you're one of the few predator species that preys even on itself?"
—Trelane to Kirk
TOS / "The Squire of Gothos"

"Oh, how absolutely typical of your species—you don't under-stand something so you become fearful."

—Trelane to Kirk
TOS / "The Squire of Gothos"

"Your violent intent and actions demonstrate that you are not civilized."

—Metron to McCoy
TOS / "Arena"

"By sparing your helpless enemy who surely would have destroyed you, you demonstrated the advanced trait of mercy, something we hardly expected. We feel that there may be hope for your kind, therefore you will not be destroyed. It would not be…civilized."

—Metron to Kirk
TOS / "Arena"

"Jim, madness has no purpose…or reason. But it may have a goal."

—Spock to Kirk
TOS / "The Alternative Factor"

"A killer first, a builder second. A hunter, a warrior and let's be honest—a murderer. That is our joint heritage, is it not?"

—Anan 7 to Kirk
TOS / "A Taste of Armageddon"

"Superior ability breeds superior ambition."

—Spock to Kirk on the genetically enhanced people of the twentieth century
TOS / "Space Seed"

"We can be against him and admire him all at the same time."

—Kirk to Spock, on Khan
TOS / "Space Seed"

"We're nothing like you. We're a democratic body."
     "Come now, Captain, I'm not referring to minor ideologi-cal differences. I mean that we are similar as a species. Here we are on a planet of sheep, two tigers, predators, hunters, killers. And it is precisely that which makes us great."

—Kirk and Kor
TOS / "Errand of Mercy"

"We think of ourselves as the most powerful beings in the universe. It's unsettling to discover that we're wrong."
—Kirk to Spock
TOS / "Errand of Mercy"

"Where did your race get this ridiculous predilection for resistance, hmm? You examine any object, you question everything...is it not enough to accept what is?"
—Korob to Kirk
TOS / "Catspaw"

"It would be illogical for us to protest against our natures, don't you think?"
—Spock to Nurse Christine Chapel
TOS / "Amok Time"

"It was far easier for you as civilized men to behave like barbarians than it was for them as barbarians to behave like civilized men."
—Spock to Kirk, on identifying their mirror universe counterparts
TOS / "Mirror, Mirror"

"May I point out that I had an opportunity to observe your counterparts here quite closely. They were brutal, savage, unprincipled, uncivilized, treacherous. In every way, splendid examples of *Homo sapiens*, the very flower of humanity. I found them quite refreshing."
—Spock to Kirk and McCoy. While the "real" Kirk and McCoy were trapped in a mirror universe, their counterparts interacted with Spock and the *Enterprise* crew
TOS / "Mirror, Mirror"

"Your species is self-destructive. You need our help."
      "We prefer to help ourselves. We make mistakes, but we're human. And maybe that's the word that best explains us."
—Norman and Kirk
TOS / "I, Mudd"

"It is a human characteristic to love little animals, especially if they're attractive in some way."
—McCoy to Spock
TOS / "The Trouble with Tribbles"

"After all these years among humans…you still haven't learned to smile."

"Humans smile with so little provocation."

—Amanda and Spock
TOS / "Journey to Babel"

"When suddenly faced by the unknown or imminent danger, a human will invariably experience a split-second of indecision— he hesitates."

—Spock to Ensign Garrovick
TOS / "Obsession"

"What he's saying, Spock, is that a man who holds that much power, even with the best intentions, just can't resist the urge to play god."

—McCoy to Spock, on interfering with another culture
TOS / "Patterns of Force"

"You did not kill. Is this the way of your kind?"

"It is. We fight only when there's no choice. We prefer the ways of peaceful contact."

—Melkotian and Kirk
TOS / "Spectre of the Gun"

"Humans do have an amazing capacity for believing what they choose and excluding that which is painful."

—Spock to Kirk
TOS / "And the Children Shall Lead"

"In critical moments men sometimes see exactly what they wish to see."

—Spock to McCoy
TOS / "The Tholian Web"

"We learn by doing."

—Kirk to Lieutenant Saavik
Star Trek II: The Wrath of Khan

"Spock: these cadets of yours—how good are they? How will they respond under real pressure?"

"As with all living things, each according to his gifts."

—Kirk and Spock
The Wrath of Khan

"You know that pain and guilt can't be taken away with a wave of a magic wand. They're the things we carry with us—the things that make us who we are. If we lose them, we lose ourselves. I don't want my pain taken away. I need my pain."

—Kirk to McCoy, on Sybok's offer to remove Kirk's emotional baggage
The Final Frontier

"You've got a lot to learn about humans if you think you can torture us or frighten us into silence."

—Picard to Q
TNG / "Encounter at Farpoint"

"Humans constantly think one thing and say another."

—Troi to Lwaxana
TNG / "Haven"

"Wasn't it your own Hartley who said 'Nothing reveals humanity so well as the games it plays?' *Almost* right. Actually, you reveal yourselves best in *how* you play."

—Q to Riker
TNG / "Hide and Q"

"Sometimes it's more important to consider others before yourself."

"Yes. But sometimes the game is to know when to consider yourself before others, give yourself permission to be...selfish."

—Wesley and Guinan
TNG / "The Child"

"You seem to find no tranquillity in anything. You struggle against the inevitable. You thrive on conflict. You are selfish, yet you value loyalty. You are rash, quick to judge, slow to change. It's amazing you've survived. Be that as it may—as species, we have no common ground. You are too aggressive. Too hostile. Too militant."

—Nagilum to Picard, on its opinion of humanity
TNG / "Where Silence Has Lease"

"See, it's human nature to love what we don't have."

—La Forge to Data
TNG / "Elementary, Dear Data"

"Confidence is faith in oneself; it can't easily be given by another."

—Troi to Picard
TNG / "Loud as a Whisper"

"It's a human response, that inborn craving to gauge your capabilities through conflict."

—Pulaski to Data
TNG / "Peak Performance"

"Data, humans sometimes find it helpful to have an outsider set the standard by which they're judged."
     "To avoid deceiving oneself."

—Troi and Data
TNG / "Peak Performance"

"We deal with our pain in many different ways, but over the years, I've discovered it is in joy that the uniqueness of each individual is revealed."

—Troi to Picard
TNG / "The Bonding"

"It is at the heart of our nature...to feel pain...and joy...it is an essential part of what makes us what we are."

—Picard to Marla Aster/Alien
TNG / "The Bonding"

"The human race has an enduring desire for knowledge, and for new opportunities to improve itself...."

—Data to Q
TNG / "Déjà Q"

"But I know human beings. They're all sopping over with compassion and forgiveness. They can't wait to absolve almost any offense. It's an inherent weakness of the breed."

—Q to Picard
TNG / "Déjà Q"

"Human intuition and instinct—are not always right. But they do make life interesting."

—Guinan to Troi
TNG / "The Loss"

"...To many humans, a mystery is irresistible. It must be solved."

—Picard to Troi/Paxan
TNG / "Clues"

"Earth was once a violent planet, too. At times, the chaos threatened the very fabric of life. But like you, we evolved. We found better ways to handle our conflicts. But I think no one can deny that the seed of violence remains within each of us. We must recognize that...because that violence is capable of consuming each of us."

—Picard to Tarmin
TNG / "Violations"

"You made a mistake. There isn't a man among us who hasn't been young enough to make one...."

—Boothby to Picard, on the captain's conduct as a cadet
TNG / "The First Duty"

"Every one of us has a thousand different kinds of little people inside of us. And some of them want to get out and be wild; and some want to be sad, or happy, or inventive or even just go dancing. That's why we all have so many different urges at different times. And all those different little people inside us? We must never be afraid to take them with us wherever we go. I mean who knows when we may need one of them to pop up and rescue us from ourselves. Variety, my little Alex. The great secret is not the variety of life; it's the variety of *us!*"

—Lwaxana to Alexander Rozhenko
TNG / "Cost of Living"

"Your arrogant pretense at being the moral guardians of the universe strikes me as being hollow, Q. I see no evidence that you are guided by a superior moral code—or any code whatsoever. You may be nearly omnipotent—and I don't deny that your parlor tricks are very impressive—but morality? I don't see it. I would put human morality against the Q's any day. And perhaps that's the reason that we fascinate you so...? Because our puny behavior shows you a glimmer of the one thing that evades your omnipotence—a moral center. And if so, I can think of no crueler irony than that you should destroy this young woman whose only crime...is that she's too human."

—Picard to Q, on the question of whether Amanda Rogers may return to the Q Continuum or be killed outright
TNG / "True-Q"

"Sometimes it's healthy to explore the darker side of the psyche. Jung called it 'owning your own shadow.'"

—Troi to Riker
TNG / "Frame of Mind"

"I have found that humans value their uniqueness, that sense that they are different from everyone else."

—Data to Worf
TNG / "Second Chances"

"It can be argued that a human is ultimately the sum of his experiences."

—Sisko to wormhole alien
DS9 / "Emissary"

"The one thing I've learned about humanoids is that in extreme situations, even the best of you are capable of doing terrible things."
—Odo to Kira
DS9 / "The Collaborator"

"…When you treat people like animals, you're gonna get bit."
—Biddle Coleridge, on the news reports of the hostage situation in Sanctuary
DS9 / "Past Tense, Part II"

"I've found that when it comes to doing what's best for you, you humanoids have the distressing habit of doing the exact opposite."
—Odo to Sisko
DS9 / "Homefront"

"I don't care how many…enhancements your parents had done. Genetic recoding can't give you ambition or a personality or compassion or any of the things that make a person truly human."
—O'Brien to Bashir
DS9 / "Doctor Bashir, I Presume?"

"He wants to play *tongo*; I want to have a late night snack; you want to lie here feeling sorry for yourself—we all deal with stress in different ways."
—Ishka to Quark
DS9 / "Profit and Lace"

"So they brought you here to see your first human. Take a good look. You won't see any hate in my eyes.…I'm a gentle man from a gentle people who wish you no harm.…"
—Chakotay to Kazon children
VGR / "Initiations"

"Why does everyone say relax when they're about to do something terrible?"
—Ensign Harry Kim to Lieutenant Lasca
VGR / "Non Sequitur"

"Yeah…but I'm starting to realize that it's not other people's opinions I should be worried about…it's *mine*."
—Paris to Janeway
VGR / "Threshold"

"I am finding it a difficult challenge to integrate into this group. It is full of complex social structures that are unfamiliar to me. Compared with the Borg, this crew is inefficient and contentious…but it is capable of surprising acts of compassion."
—Seven of Nine to Janeway
VGR / "Day of Honor"

"Unexpected acts of kindness…are common among our group. That's one of the ways we define ourselves."
—Janeway to Seven of Nine
VGR / "Day of Honor"

"But you have to start learning the difference between having an impulse—and acting on it."
—Janeway to Seven of Nine
VGR / "Retrospect"

"Curious. I've never understood the human compulsion to emotionally bond with inanimate objects. This vessel has 'done' nothing. It's an assemblage of bulkheads, conduits, tritanium. Nothing more."
"Oh, you're wrong. It's much more than that…this ship has been our home…it's kept us together…it's been part of our family. As illogical as this might sound…I feel as close to *Voyager* as I do to any other member of the crew. It's carried us, Tuvok, even nurtured us…and right now, it needs one of us."
—Tuvok and Janeway
VGR / "Year of Hell, Part II"

"Sometimes you've got to look back, in order to move forward."
—Janeway to Seven of Nine
VGR / "Hope and Fear"

5. Making Sense
of the Universe

"You keep wondering if man was meant to be out here. You keep wondering and you keep signing on...."

—Kirk to Joe Tormolen
TOS / "The Naked Time"

"Even in this corner of the galaxy, Captain, two plus two equals four."

—Spock to Kirk, on seeing the obvious
TOS / "The Conscience of the King"

"Mister Scott, there are always alternatives."

—Spock to Scott
TOS / "The Galileo Seven"

"The sum of the parts cannot be greater than the whole."

—Spock to McCoy
TOS / "The Galileo Seven"

"It's difficult to control so many things in so little time."

—Korob to Kirk
TOS / "Catspaw"

"After a time, you may find that having is not so pleasing a thing after all, as wanting. It is not logical, but it is often true."

—Spock to Stonn
TOS / "Amok Time"

"Physical reality is consistent with universal laws. When the laws do not operate, there is no reality."
—Spock to McCoy
TOS / "Spectre of the Gun"

"We judge reality by the response of our senses. Once we are convinced of the reality of a given situation, we abide by its rules."
—Spock to Kirk
TOS / "Spectre of the Gun"

"The glory of creation is in its infinite diversity."
   "And the ways our differences combine to create meaning and beauty."
—Miranda and Spock
TOS / "Is There in Truth No Beauty?"

"Change is the essential process of all existence."
—Spock to Bele
TOS / "Let That Be Your Last Battlefield"

"It's hard to believe that something which is neither seen nor felt can do so much harm."
   "That's true. But an idea can't be seen or felt and that's what's kept the Troglytes in the mines all these centuries. A mistaken idea."
—Vanna and Kirk
TOS / "The Cloud Minders"

"Beauty is transitory, Doctor."
—Spock to McCoy
TOS / "That Which Survives"

"Beauty survives."
—Kirk to Spock
TOS / "That Which Survives"

"What is it like to feel pain?"
   "It is like…like when you see the people have no hope for happiness, Father…you feel great despair and your heart is heavy because you know you can do nothing. Pain is like that."
—Hodin and Odona
TOS / "The Mark of Gideon"

"What is loneliness?"

"It is thirst. It is a flower dying in a desert."
—Rayna Kapec and Flint
TOS / "Requiem for Methuselah"

"Each of us, at some time in our lives, turns to someone—a father, a brother, a god, and asks, 'Why am I here? What was I meant to be?'"
—Spock to Kirk
Star Trek: The Motion Picture

"For everything, there is a first time, Lieutenant."
—Spock to Saavik
The Wrath of Khan

"As your teacher Mister Spock is fond of saying: I like to think that there always are possibilities."
—Kirk to Saavik
The Wrath of Khan

"The bureaucratic mentality is the only constant in the universe."
—McCoy to Kirk
Star Trek IV: The Voyage Home

"You're a great one for logic. I'm a great one for...rushing in where angels fear to tread. We're both extremists. Reality is probably somewhere in between."
—Kirk to Spock
The Undiscovered Country

"When did he find time for a family?"

"Well, like you always say—if something's important, you make the time."
—Kirk and Scott
Generations

"All life, Wyatt, all consciousness...is indissolubly bound together. Indeed it is all part of the same thing."
—Lwaxana to Wyatt Miller
TNG / "Haven"

"You do understand, don't you, that thought is the basis of all reality?"

—the Traveler to Picard
TNG / "Where No One Has Gone Before"

"The quest for youth, Number One…so futile. Age and wisdom have their graces, too."

"I wonder if one doesn't have to *have* age and wisdom to appreciate that, sir."

—Picard and Riker
TNG / "Too Short A Season"

"You can't rescue a man from a place that he calls his home."

—Ramsey to Troi
TNG / "Angel One"

"Things are only impossible, until they're not."

—Picard to Data
TNG / "When the Bough Breaks"

"How can a chemical substance provide an escape?"

"It doesn't. But it makes you think it does."

—Wesley and Lieutenant Natasha Yar
TNG / "Symbiosis"

"If there is a cosmic plan, is it not the height of hubris to think that we can, or should, interfere?"

—Riker to Picard, on interfering with a planet's course toward destruction
TNG / "Pen Pals"

"If there is a cosmic plan, are we not part of it? Our presence at this place at this moment in time could be a part of that fate."

—Troi to senior staff, on interfering with a planet's course toward destruction
TNG / "Pen Pals"

"…It is possible to commit no mistakes—and still lose. That is *not* a weakness. That is *life*."

—Picard to Data
TNG / "Peak Performance"

"If you drop a hammer on your foot, it's hardly useful to get mad at the hammer."

—Riker to Picard
TNG / "Shades of Gray"

"...Our function is to contribute in a positive way to the world in which we live."

—Data to Lal, on Lal's question of her purpose
TNG / "The Offspring"

"Is that the purpose of existence? To care for someone?"

—Data to Tam Elbrun
TNG / "Tin Man"

"Some days you get the bear, and some days the bear gets you."

—Riker to Picard
TNG / "Data's Day"

"It is interesting that people try to find meaningful patterns in things that are essentially random. I have noticed that the images they perceive sometimes suggest what they are thinking about at that particular moment."

—Data to Guinan
TNG / "Imaginary Friend"

"But...who knows—our reality may be very much like theirs. And all this...might just be an elaborate simulation running inside a little device...sitting on someone's table...."

—Picard to Troi, on subjective vs. objective perception of reality
TNG / "Ship in a Bottle"

"Someone once told me that time was a predator that stalked us all our lives. But I rather believe time is a *companion*...who goes with us on the journey, reminds us to cherish every moment...because they'll never come again."

—Picard to Riker
Generations

"The rules aren't important...what's important is—it's *linear*. Every time I throw this ball a hundred different things can happen in a game....He might swing and miss, he might hit it....The point is you never know....You try to anticipate, set a strategy for all the possibilities as best you can...but in the end it comes down to throwing one pitch after another...and seeing what happens. With each new consequence, the game begins to take shape...."

—Sisko to wormhole alien, on comparing baseball and life
DS9 / "Emissary"

"I believe in coincidences. Coincidences happen every day. But I don't trust coincidences."

—Garak to Bashir
DS9 / "Cardassians"

"Jake, the only time you should be in bed is if you're sleeping, dying, or making love to a beautiful woman. I'm not tired, I'm not dying, and the truth is, I'm too old for beautiful women, so I might as well be here."

—Joseph Sisko to Jake Sisko
DS9 / "Homefront"

"Time, like latinum, is a highly limited commodity."

—Brunt to Quark
DS9 / "The Bar Association"

"Everything's tidy when someone else is doing the cleaning."

—Sisko to Garak
DS9 / "Things Past"

"If you're happy, there's something very wrong in the world...the center cannot hold."

—Quark to Odo
Source: William Butler Yeats, "The Second Coming"
DS9 / "The Begotten"

"You win some, you lose some."
    "You always had problems with the 'lose some' part of that."

—Sisko and Dax
DS9 / "For the Uniform"

"Two days ago, this station felt like a tomb. I'd never seen so many of my crew depressed at the same time. But for some reason, it now seems as though a new spirit has swept through the station…as if someone had opened a door and let a gust of fresh air blow…through a musty old house. Why this is happening frankly is…a mystery to me. After all, nothing has really changed. The Dominion is still a threat, the Cardassians are still threatening to retake the station, and I can still see the clouds of war gathering on the horizon. So why do I sense a newfound sense of optimism in the air? But maybe I'm overthinking this. Maybe the real explanation is as simple as…something my father taught me a long time ago. Even in the darkest moments, you can always find something that'll make you smile."

—Sisko's log
DS9 / "In the Cards"

"You're always telling me that space is big. That it's an endless frontier, filled with infinite wonders."
    "It's true."
"Well if that's the case, you would think it would be more than enough room to allow people to leave each other alone."
    "It just doesn't work that way. It should. But it doesn't."

—Joseph Sisko and Benjamin Sisko
DS9 / "A Time to Stand"

"You can pulp a story but you cannot destroy an idea."

—Benny Russell to Douglas Pabst
DS9 / "Far Beyond the Stars"

"I believe that even in the worst of times, we can still find moments of joy and kindness. If you can find that kindness, hold on to it."

—Taban to Meru
DS9 / "Wrongs Darker than Death or Night"

"Have you ever had a moment of pure clarity? A moment when the truth seems to just leap up and grab you by the throat?"

—Kira to Dax
DS9 / "His Way"

"Only two moments of clarity in seven lifetimes?"

"Nerys, total clarity is a very rare thing."

—Kira and Dax
DS9 / "His Way"

"This may not make much sense to you now...a young man at the beginning of his career. But one of the things you learn as you move up the ranks and get a little older, is that you wish you had more time in your youth to really...*absorb* all the things that happen to you. It goes by so fast....It's so easy to become jaded...to treat the extraordinary as just another day at the office. But sometimes there are experiences which transcend all that. You've just had one, Mister Kim. And I want you to live with it for a little while. Write about it if you feel like it...paint...express yourself in some fashion. The bridge will still be there in two days."

—Janeway to Kim
VGR / "Emanations"

"I do believe there is more within each of us than science has yet explained."

—Tuvok to Elani
VGR / "Innocence"

"I don't know what happened to you, but there can be any number of explanations. Hallucination...telepathic communication from another race...repressed memory...momentary contact with a parallel reality...take your pick. The universe is such a strange place."

—the Doctor to Tuvok, on Tuvok's "vision"
VGR / "Flashback"

"I've found that when you don't think about a problem...sometimes the solution comes to you."

—Chakotay to Tuvok
VGR / "Flashback"

"Nothing's impossible if you want it badly enough."

—Lieutenant B'Elanna Torres/Korenna to Dathan
VGR / "Remember"

"Sometimes radical problems require radical solutions."

—Riley to Chakotay
VGR / "Unity"

"There are times, Catarina, when I find myself transfixed by a shadow on the wall, or the splashing of water against a stone....I stare at it, the hours pass....The world around me drops away, replaced by worlds being created and destroyed by my imagination....A way to focus the mind."

—Leonardo da Vinci hologram to Janeway
VGR / "Scorpion"

"Well, whatever happens, I try to keep in mind that things could be worse."

—Neelix to Chakotay
VGR / "Scientific Method"

"Species that don't change...die."

—Alpha-Hirogen to Hirogen SS Officer
VGR / "The Killing Game"

"When faced with desperate circumstances...we must *adapt*."

—Seven of Nine to Chakotay
VGR / "Demon"

"You don't feel anger toward a storm on the horizon...you just avoid it."

—Arturis to Janeway
VGR / "Hope and Fear"

"'Impossible' is a word that humans use far too often."

—Seven of Nine to Janeway
VGR / "Hope and Fear"

6. The Search for
Knowledge

"Do you realize the number of discoveries lost because of superstition...of ignorance...of a layman's inability to comprehend?"

—Dr. Roger Korby to Kirk
TOS / "What Are Little Girls Made Of?"

"Insufficient facts always invite danger, Captain."

—Spock to Kirk
TOS / "Space Seed"

"Knowledge, sir, should be free to all."

—Harry Mudd to Spock
TOS / "I, Mudd"

"How do you know so much?"
    "I asked them."

—McCoy and Spock, on the androids' plans
TOS / "I, Mudd"

"All your people must learn before you can reach for the stars."

—Kirk to Shahna
TOS / "The Gamesters of Triskelion"

"This crew has been to many places in the galaxy. They've been witness to many strange events. They are trained to know that what seems to be impossible often is possible given the scientific analysis of the phenomenon."

—Spock to Kirk, Dr. Janice Lester
TOS / "Turnabout Intruder"

"Why is any object we don't understand always called a 'thing'?"

—McCoy to Kirk
The Motion Picture

"It knows only that it needs, Commander. But like so many of us…it does not know what."

—Spock to Executive Officer Will Decker on V'ger's search to find its creator
The Motion Picture

"Come, come, Mr. Scott. Young minds, fresh ideas. Be tolerant."

—Kirk to Scott, on Scott's scoffing at a new technology
Star Trek III: The Search for Spock

"…The *unknown* is what brings us out here!"

—Picard to Q
TNG / "Encounter at Farpoint"

"The search for *knowledge* is always our primary mission."

—Picard to Beverly
TNG / "Lonely among Us"

"Captain, the most elementary and valuable statement in science…the beginning of wisdom…is: 'I do not know.'"

—Data to Picard
TNG / "Where Silence Has Lease"

"We can't protect ourselves against the unknown."

—Picard to La Forge
TNG / "Unnatural Selection"

"Scientists believe no experiment is a failure—that even a mistake advances the evolution of understanding….But all achievement has a price."

—Pulaski's log
TNG / "Unnatural Selection"

"China was thought to be a myth until Marco Polo traveled there."

—Picard to Wesley
TNG / "Contagion"

"Picard, you are about to move into areas of the galaxy containing wonders more incredible than you can possibly imagine...and terrors to freeze your soul."

—Q to Picard
TNG / "Q Who?"

"If you can't take a little bloody nose—maybe you ought to go back home and crawl under your bed. It's not safe out here. It's wondrous—with treasures to satiate desires both subtle and gross—but it's not for the timid."

—Q to Picard
TNG / "Q Who?"

"You know, some of our greatest advances have come from analyzing failure."

—Troi to Data
TNG / "Peak Performance"

"You can handle defeat in two ways. You can lose confidence or you can learn from your mistakes."

—Troi to Data
TNG / "Peak Performance"

"You have taught us there is nothing beyond our reach."
    "Not even the stars."

—Nuria and Picard
TNG / "Who Watches the Watchers?"

"Because you just can't rely on the plain and simple facts....Sometimes they lie...."

—La Forge to Data
TNG / "The Defector"

"There's theory...and then there's application. They don't always jibe."

—La Forge to Dr. Leah Brahms
TNG / "Galaxy's Child"

"You never really look for something until you need it."
—La Forge to Hannah
TNG / "The Masterpiece Society"

"When we look at Michelangelo's *David* or Symnay's *Tomb*...we don't ask, 'What does this mean to other people?' The real question is, 'What does it mean to us?'"
—Picard to Data
TNG / "Birthright"

"Questions are the beginning of wisdom...the mark of a true warrior."
—Worf to Kahless
TNG / "Rightful Heir"

"There are things we do not understand, yet they exist nonetheless."
—Worf to Troi
TNG / "Eye of the Beholder"

"For that one fraction of a second, you were open to options you had never considered. That is the exploration that awaits you...not mapping stars and studying nebula...but charting the unknown possibilities of existence."
—Q to Picard
TNG / "All Good Things..."

"Look for solutions from within, Commander...."
—Opaka to Sisko
DS9 / "Emissary"

"That may be the most important thing to understand about humans. It is the unknown that defines our existence. We are constantly searching...not just for answers to our questions... but for new *questions*. We are explorers....We explore our lives day by day...and we explore the galaxy, trying to expand the boundaries of our knowledge. And that is why I am here. Not to conquer you with weapons or with ideas. But to coexist and learn."
—Sisko to wormhole alien
DS9 / "Emissary"

"Ah! An open mind. The essence of intellect."

—Garak to Bashir
DS9 / "Past Prologue"

"I'm a teacher. My responsibility is to expose my students to knowledge. Not hide it from them."

—Keiko to Winn, refusing to edit the content of her teaching to satisfy Winn
DS9 / "In the Hands of the Prophets"

"I'm beginning to think that the scientific method and police method have a lot in common."
    "I never thought of it that way. Perhaps they do."
"In science we look for the obvious. We track in a straight line. If something looks too good to be true, it usually isn't true. If there appears to be more to something than meets the eye, there usually *is* more. We take it step by step."

—Dr. Mora Pol and Odo
DS9 / "The Alternate"

"Oh, you'd be surprised at the things you can learn when you're doing alterations."

—Garak to Odo
DS9 / "The Way of the Warrior, Part I"

"How can I know someone who doesn't know himself?"

—wormhole alien to Sisko
DS9 / "Accession"

"A dead man can't learn from his mistakes."

—Sisko to Omet'iklan
DS9 / "To the Death"

"If I were captain, I'd open every crack in the universe and peek inside just like Captain Janeway does."

—Kes to Neelix
VGR / "The Cloud"

"A nebula....What were we doing in a nebula? No wait...don't tell me. We were 'investigating.' That's all we do around here. Why pretend we're going home at all? All we're going to do is 'investigate' every cubic millimeter of this quadrant, aren't we?"
—the Doctor to Torres
VGR / "The Cloud"

"You're looking, but you're not seeing."
—Chakotay to Torres
VGR / "Emanations"

"It was a scientific inevitability—one discovery flowing naturally to the next. Something so enormous as Science will not stop for something as small as Man, Mister Neelix."
—Dr. Ma'Bor Jetrel to Neelix
VGR / "Jetrel"

"It's *good* to know how the world works. It is not possible to be a scientist unless you believe that all the knowledge of the universe, and all the power that it bestows, is of intrinsic value to everyone. And one *must* share that knowledge and allow it to be applied...and then, be willing to live with the consequences."
—Jetrel to Neelix
VGR / "Jetrel"

"...You've always been curious about other societies. And that is why I allowed you to read about them because I believe that ignorance is our greatest enemy."
—Kolopak to young Chakotay
VGR / "Tattoo"

"Focus on the *goal*...not the task."
—Tanis to Kes
VGR / "Cold Fire"

"What your eyes show you is only the surface of reality. Look deeper."
—Tanis to Kes
VGR / "Cold Fire"

"Studying it and knowing it are two different things. Aren't they…?"
—Lon Suder to Tuvok, on violence
VGR / "Meld"

"Mathematics. I can see why you enjoyed it. Solve a problem, get an answer. The answer's either right or wrong. It's very absolute."
—Guide to Janeway
VGR / "Sacred Ground"

"I know that self-sufficiency is very important to a Vulcan, but there is nothing shameful in getting a little guidance every once in a while."
—the Doctor to Vorik
VGR / "Blood Fever"

"What you're doing isn't self-defense, it's the exploitation of another species for your own benefit. My people decided a long time ago that that was unacceptable—even in the name of scientific progress."
—Janeway to Alzen, on using *Voyager*'s crew as test-subjects
VGR / "Scientific Method"

"You make contact with alien species without sufficient understanding of their nature. As a result, *Voyager*'s directive to 'seek out new civilizations' often ends in conflict."
—Seven of Nine to Neelix
VGR / "Random Thoughts"

"What you call ignorance…we call *exploration*. And sometimes it means taking a few risks.…"
—Neelix to Seven of Nine
VGR / "Random Thoughts"

"We seek out new races because we *want* to…not because we're following protocols. We have an insatiable curiosity about the universe.…"
—Janeway to Seven of Nine
VGR / "Random Thoughts"

"Ah, what the old philosophers say is true: 'Monstrous and wonderful are the peoples of undiscovered lands.'"

—Leonardo hologram to Janeway
VGR / "Concerning Flight"

"Seven, what you call a threat, I call an opportunity…to gain knowledge about this species. And in this case, maybe even show some compassion."

—Janeway to Seven of Nine, on the Hirogen
VGR / "Prey"

"I won't risk half the quadrant to satisfy our curiosity. It's arrogant, and it's irresponsible. The 'final frontier' has some boundaries that shouldn't be crossed…."

—Janeway to Tuvok
VGR / "The Omega Directive"

7. Life and Death

"Mister Spock, life and death are seldom logical."
—McCoy to Spock
TOS / "The Galileo Seven"

"I am frequently appalled by the low regard you Earthmen have for life."
—Spock to Lieutenant Boma and Lieutenant Gaetano
TOS / "The Galileo Seven"

"Gentlemen, I have no great love for you, your planet, your culture. Despite that, Mister Spock and I are going to go out there and quite probably die, in an attempt to show you that there are some things worth dying for."
—Kirk to the Organian Council of Elders
TOS / "Errand of Mercy"

"Believe me, Captain, immortality consists largely of boredom."
—Cochrane to Kirk
TOS / "Metamorphosis"

"You said you're prepared to die. Does that mean that you prefer to die?"
—Kirk to Eleen
TOS / "Friday's Child"

"He gave his life in an attempt to save others. Not the worst way to go."
—Kirk to Spock, on Commodore Matt Decker
TOS / "The Doomsday Machine"

"I've noticed that about your people, Doctor. You find it easier to understand the death of one than the death of a million."
—Spock to McCoy
TOS / "The Immunity Syndrome"

"Suffer the death of thy neighbor, eh, Spock? Now, you wouldn't wish that on us, would you?"
    "It might have rendered your history a bit less bloody."
—McCoy and Spock
TOS / "The Immunity Syndrome"

"The most cooperative man in this world is a dead man. And if you don't keep your mouth shut, you're gonna be cooperating."
—Bela Oxmyx to Spock
TOS / "A Piece of the Action"

"Jim…I can't destroy life. Even if it's to save my own."
—McCoy to Kirk, refusing to accept Gem's sacrifice
TOS / "The Empath"

"Four thousand throats may be cut in one night by a running man."
—Klingon to Kang
TOS / "Day of the Dove"

"To us, killing is murder, even for revenge."
—Kirk to Parmen
TOS / "Plato's Stepchildren"

"You're entitled to your own life, but not another's."
—Kirk to Zetarian
TOS / "The Lights of Zetar"

"Surely it is more logical to…to *heal* than kill."
—Surak to Kirk
TOS / "The Savage Curtain"

"How we deal with death is at least as important as how we deal with life, wouldn't you say?"
—Kirk to Saavik
The Wrath of Khan

"As a matter of cosmic history, it has always been easier to destroy than to create—"
—Spock to McCoy
The Wrath of Khan

"We are assembled here today to pay final respects to our honored dead. And yet, it should be noted, that in the midst of our sorrow, this death takes place in the shadow of new life, the sunrise of a new world, a world that our beloved comrade gave his life to protect and nourish. He did not feel this sacrifice a vain or an empty one—and we will not debate his profound wisdom at these proceedings. Of my friend, I can only say this...of all the souls I have encountered in my travels, his was the most—human."
—Kirk to crew, on Spock
The Wrath of Khan

"Lieutenant Saavik was right: you never have faced death."
    "No. Not like this. I haven't faced death, I've cheated death. I've tricked my way out of death and patted myself on the back for my ingenuity. I know nothing."
—David Marcus and Kirk, on the death of Spock
The Wrath of Khan

"He's really not dead. As long as we remember him."
—McCoy to Kirk, on Spock
The Wrath of Khan

"My God, Bones. What have I done?"
    "What you had to do. What you always do. Turn death into a fighting chance to live."
—Kirk and McCoy, on the destruction of the *Enterprise*
The Search for Spock

"You mean I have to die to discuss your insights on death?"
—McCoy to Spock, on lacking a common frame of reference
Star Trek IV: The Voyage Home

"Human life is far too precious to risk on crazy stunts."

—McCoy to Kirk
The Final Frontier

"Would you choose one life over one thousand, sir?"
"I refuse to let arithmetic decide questions like that!"

—Data and Picard
TNG / "Justice"

"How did they die?"
"They died well."

—K'nera and Worf, on the renegade Klingons
TNG / "Heart of Glory"

"My thoughts are not for Tasha, but for myself. I keep thinking how empty it will be without her presence. Did I miss the point?"
"No, you didn't, Data. You got it."

—Data and Picard, on the memorial for Tasha
TNG / "Skin of Evil"

"Some see it as a changing into an indestructible form...forever unchanging. They believe that the purpose of the entire universe is to then maintain that form in an Earthlike garden which will give delight and pleasure through all eternity. On the other hand there are those who hold to the idea of our blinking into nothingness with all of our experiences and hopes and dreams merely a delusion."
"Which do you believe, sir?"
"Considering the marvelous complexity of the universe, its clockwork perfection, its balances of this against that...matter, energy, gravitation, time, dimension, I believe that our existence must be more than either of these philosophies, that what we are goes beyond Euclidean or other 'practical' measuring systems...and that, our existence is part of a reality beyond what we understand now as reality."

—Picard and Data/Nagilum, on Picard's beliefs about death
TNG / "Where Silence Has Lease"

"Life is like loading twice your cargo weight onto your space-craft....If it's canaries and you can keep half of them flying all of the time, you're all right."

—Thadiun Okona to Data
TNG / "The Outrageous Okona"

"Stories often have happy endings. It's life that throws you for a loop."

—Graves to Data
TNG / "The Schizoid Man"

"What the hell. Nobody said life was safe."

—Riker to Picard
TNG / "Peak Performance"

"Deanna, facing death is the ultimate test of character. I don't want to die—but if I have to, I'd like to do it with a little pride."
    "And a lot of impudence."
"You bet. Dying is bad enough—but to lose my sense of humor? Forget it."

—Riker and Troi
TNG / "Shades of Gray"

"This is just a thing, and things can be replaced. Lives cannot."

—Data to Gosheven
TNG / "The Ensigns of Command"

"We feel a loss more intensely when it's a friend."
    "But should not the feelings run just as deep regardless of who has died?"
"Maybe they should, Data. Maybe if we felt any loss as keenly as we felt the death of one close to us, human history would be a lot less bloody."

—Riker and Data
TNG / "The Bonding"

"In my tradition, we do not grieve the loss of the body...we celebrate the releasing of the spirit."

—Worf to Jeremy Aster
TNG / "The Bonding"

"It is part of our life cycle that we accept the death of those we love. Jeremy must come to terms with his grief, he must not cover it or hide away from it. You see, we are mortal. Our time in this universe is finite. That is one of the truths that all humans must learn."

—Picard to Marla/Alien
TNG / "The Bonding"

"Guinan says I died a senseless death in the other timeline. I didn't like the sound of that, Captain. I've always known the risks that come with a Starfleet uniform. If I am to die in one, I'd like my death to count for something."

—Tasha to Picard
TNG / "Yesterday's *Enterprise*"

"When a man is convinced he's going to die tomorrow, he'll probably find a way to make it happen."

—Guinan to Riker
TNG / "The Best of Both Worlds, Part II"

"Do you believe...that we are in some way alike, sir?"
    "In many ways, I'd like to believe."
"Then it is all right for you to die...because I will remain alive."

—Data and Dr. Soong. The android conveys a sense of immortality to his dying creator
TNG / "Brothers"

"I just can't accept that fate would allow me to meet him like this...and then take him away. I mean, he's not ill. He hasn't had a tragic accident. He's just going to die...and for no good reason...because his society has decided that he's too old...so they just dispose of him. As though his life no longer had any meaning. You can't possibly understand at your age...but at mine...sometimes you feel tired. And afraid."

—Lwaxana to Troi, on the euthanasia of the elderly on Timicin's planet
TNG / "Half a Life"

"Will, if you were dying...if you were terminally ill with an incurable disease...and facing the remaining few days of your life in pain. Wouldn't you come to look on death as...a release?"

—Picard to Riker, on Worf's point of view, paralyzed after an accident
TNG / "Ethics"

"Suicide is *not* an option."

—Beverly to Picard, on Worf's desire to die rather than live with his paralysis
TNG / "Ethics"

"I've been studying this ritual of yours. Do you know what I've decided? I think it's despicable. I hate everything about it…the casual disregard for life, the way it tries to cloak suicide in some glorious notion of honor.…I may have to respect your beliefs…but I don't have to like them."

—Riker to Worf, on the ritual suicide being contemplated by the paralyzed Klingon
TNG / "Ethics"

"…How many men and women—how many *friends* have we watched die? I've lost count. Every one of them—every single one—fought for life until the very end."

—Riker to Worf
TNG / "Ethics"

"I am very *happy* for Commander La Forge. He has crossed over to…that which is beyond. For a Klingon, this is a joyful time…a friend has died in the line of duty…and he has earned a place among the honored dead. It is not a time to mourn."

—Worf to Data, on the presumed death of La Forge
TNG / "The Next Phase"

"You do not kill an animal unless you intend to eat it."

—Toq to Tokath
TNG / "Birthright, Part II"

"You cannot put a price on a life."

—Picard to Daimon Bok
TNG / "Bloodlines"

"You know there was a time when I wouldn't hurt a fly. Then the Borg came…and they showed me if there is one constant in this whole universe, it's death. Afterwards, I began to realize it didn't really matter. We're all going to die sometime, it's just a question of how and when. You will too, Captain. Aren't you beginning to feel time gaining on you? It's like a predator. It's stalking you. Oh, you can try and outrun it with doctors…medicines…new technologies…but in the end, time is going to hunt you down…and make the kill."

—Soran to Picard
Generations

"It's our mortality that defines us, Soran. It's part of the truth of our existence."

—Picard to Soran
Generations

"What we leave behind is not as important as how we've lived. After all, Number One…we're only mortal."
    "Speak for yourself, sir. I plan to live forever."

—Picard and Riker
Generations

"…The game wouldn't be worth playing if we knew what was going to happen."

—Sisko to wormhole alien, on baseball and life
DS9 / "Emissary"

"Dying gets you off the hook. Question is—are you willing to live for your people? Live the role they want you to play. That's what they need from you right now."

—Sisko to Li Nalas; Li doesn't wish to play the hero for his people
DS9 / "The Siege"

"Art should be an affirmation of life."

—Professor Gideon Seyetik to Sisko
DS9 / "Second Sight"

"My mind keeps going back to the Borg…how I despised their…indifference as they tried to exterminate us. And I have to ask myself…would I be any different if I destroyed another universe to preserve my own?"
—Sisko's log
DS9 / "Playing God"

"When you take someone's life, you lose a part of your own as well."
—Kira to Dax
DS9 / "Blood Oath"

"I think you Klingons embrace death too easily. You treat death like a lover. I think living is a lot more attractive. I think an honorable *victory* is better than an honorable defeat."
—Dax to Kang
DS9 / "Blood Oath"

"No one is expendable."
—Bashir to Subcommander T'Rul
DS9 / "The Search, Part I"

"I think you'll find that random and unprovoked executions will keep your workforce alert and motivated."
—Intendant to the mirror Garak
DS9 / "Through the Looking Glass"

"You had a choice. And you chose to disobey orders, override my judgment, and condemn those men to death."
    "Yes, I did. Because I thought it was the only way to save *your* life."
—Bashir and O'Brien
DS9 / "Hippocratic Oath"

"A man with a death wish is a danger not only to himself, but to the rest of his team."
—Odo to Worf
DS9 / "Sons of Mogh"

"I've found that nothing keeps me alert quite like a healthy fear of death."
—Sisko to Weyoun
DS9 / "To the Death"

"I am First Omet'iklan. And I am dead. As of this moment we are all dead. We go into battle to reclaim our lives. This we do gladly, for we are Jem'Hadar. Remember…victory is life."
—Omet'iklan to Jem'Hadar soldiers
DS9 / "To the Death"

"I threatened to kill you, but you were willing to sacrifice your-self to save my life."
"Looks that way."
"Why?"
"If you have to ask, you'll never understand."
—Omet'iklan and Sisko
DS9 / "To the Death"

"It may sound cruel, but we both know that ship out there was worth it. Those five deaths may save five thousand lives…or maybe even five million. And if I had to make the same trade all over again, I would. But five people are dead…fine men and women who deserved a lot more than to die on some lonely planet fifty thousand light-years away from home."
—Sisko to Dax, on obtaining vital military intelligence at the cost of his crew
DS9 / "The Ship"

"They chose a life in Starfleet. They knew the risks and they died fighting for something that they believed in."
"That doesn't make it any easier."
"Maybe nothing should."
—Dax and Sisko, on the crew members who died on their mission
DS9 / "The Ship"

"And I will not ask Kira to sacrifice her life, for eight thousand people, for eight million. No one has the right to ask that…."
—Sisko to Yedrin Dax
DS9 / "Children of Time"

"I don't have the freedom to kill you to save another. My culture finds that to be a reprehensible and entirely unacceptable act."

—Janeway to Motura
VGR / "Phage"

"Maybe I kill myself slowly because I don't have the courage to do it quickly."

—Lidell Ren to Paris, on smoking
VGR / "Ex Post Facto"

"It may mean something to you to die a violent death, but I'd like to get out of this without killing or being killed."

—Chakotay to Kar
VGR / "Initiations"

"You once told me that you used to treat life like one big game. Rules…players…winners…losers…you never took any of it seriously. Until you lost."

—Kim to alternate Paris
VGR / "Non Sequitur"

"Unfortunately, extinction is often the natural *end* of evolution…."

—Janeway to Torres
VGR / "Prototype"

"All this time, I thought I was so lucky…no family back home…nobody to miss. Now it seems kind of sad not to leave anybody behind…."

—Ensign Bennet to Tuvok, on dying
VGR / "Innocence"

"I cannot protect you from the natural conclusion of life…nor would I try. Vulcans consider death to be the completion of a journey. There is nothing to fear."

"I won't be afraid. Not if you're with me."

—Tuvok and Tressa
VGR / "Innocence"

"Waste nothing. That's one of the first rules of survival."

—Neelix to Hogan
VGR / "Basics, Part II"

"I offer you a Vulcan prayer, Mister Suder—May your death bring you the peace you never found in life."

—Tuvok to Suder, upon finding Suder's dead body
VGR / "Basics, Part II"

"Killing's the worst thing I've ever had to do."

—Chakotay to Namon
VGR / "Nemesis"

"You're trying to rationalize genocide. One species is significant. A single life is significant."

—Chakotay to Annorax
VGR / "Year of Hell, Part II"

"There seem to be countless rituals and cultural beliefs designed to alleviate their fear of a simple biological truth: all organisms eventually perish."

—Seven of Nine to Tuvok
VGR / "Mortal Coil"

"Excuse me if I can't feel terribly sorry for you. I learned this morning that a lot of my friends are dead. And I've gone from being so angry that I wanted to kill someone...to crying for an hour...and now I'm just trying to...to accept it and move on."

—Torres to Paris
VGR / "Hunters"

"It is wrong to sacrifice another being to save our own lives."

—Janeway to Seven of Nine
VGR / "Prey"

"I have observed that you have been willing to sacrifice your own life to save the lives of your crew."

"Yes, but that's different. That was *my* choice. This creature does not have a choice."

—Seven of Nine and Janeway, on a member of Species 8472
VGR / "Prey"

"...As long as you're alive...there's hope."

—Janeway to Arturis
VGR / "Hope and Fear"

8. Good and Evil

"Jim, you're no different than anyone else. We all have our darker side. We need it. It's half of what we are. It's not really ugly, it's human."

—McCoy to Kirk
TOS / "The Enemy Within"

"I object to you. I object to intellect without discipline. I object to power without constructive purpose."

—Spock to Trelane
TOS / "The Squire of Gothos"

"Are your faces alike? Can you tell from them which of you is good and which of you is evil?"

—Kirk to Cloud William, on judging someone based on appearance
TOS / "The Omega Glory"

"Does not your sacred book promise that good is stronger than evil?"

"Yes, it is written. Good shall always destroy evil."

—Kirk and Sirah
TOS / "The Omega Glory"

"Spock, I've found that evil usually triumphs...unless good is very, very careful."

—McCoy to Spock
TOS / "The Omega Glory"

"Evil does seek to maintain power by suppressing the truth."
  "Or by misleading the innocent."
—Spock and McCoy
TOS / "And the Children Shall Lead"

"Without followers evil cannot spread."
—Spock to Kirk
TOS / "And the Children Shall Lead"

"I see, Doctor McCoy, that you still subscribe to the outmoded notion promulgated by your ancient Greeks that what is good must also be beautiful."
  "And the reverse of course, that what is beautiful is automatically expected to be good."
—Spock and Dr. Laurence Marvick
TOS / "Is There in Truth No Beauty?"

"It would seem that evil retreats when forcibly confronted."
—Yarnek to Kirk
TOS / "The Savage Curtain"

"A great poet once said 'all spirits are enslaved that serve things evil.'"
—Picard to Armus
Source: Percy Bysshe Shelley, "Prometheus Unbound"
TNG / "Skin of Evil"

"You say you are true evil? Shall I tell you what true evil is? It is to submit to you. It is when we surrender our freedom, our dignity, instead of defying you."
—Picard to Armus
TNG / "Skin of Evil"

"Captain, one of the things I've learned on these voyages and on this ship and from you...is that most life-forms act out of an instinct for survival—not out of malice."
—Riker to Picard
TNG / "Shades of Gray"

"Mister Worf, villains who twirl their mustaches are easy to spot. Those who clothe themselves in good deeds are well camouflaged."

—Picard to Worf
TNG / "The Drumhead"

"Doctor, the sperm whale on Earth devours millions of cuttlefish as it roams the oceans. It is not evil…it is feeding. The same may be true of the Entity."

—Picard to Dr. Marr, on the Crystalline Entity that has destroyed planets
TNG / "Silicon Avatar"

"You cannot explain away a wantonly immoral act because you think that it is connected to some higher purpose."

—Picard to Alkar
TNG / "Man of the People"

"Well, it may turn out that the moral thing to do…was not the right thing to do."

—Picard to Riker
TNG / "Descent Part I"

"It's easy to look back seven centuries and judge what was right and wrong."

—Benjamin Sisko to Jake Sisko
DS9 / "In the Hands of the Prophets"

"Causing people to suffer because you hate them is terrible…but causing people to suffer because you have forgotten how to care…that's really hard to understand."

—Bashir to Sisko
DS9 / "Past Tense, Part I"

"He wanted to protect the innocent…and separate the darkness from the light. But he didn't realize that a light only shines in the dark…and sometimes innocence…is just an excuse for the guilty."

—Kira to Odo
DS9 / "The Darkness and the Light"

"Everyone has their reasons. That's what's so frightening. People can find a way to justify any action, no matter how evil."
—Kira to Tora Ziyal
DS9 / "By Inferno's Light"

"One man's villain is another man's hero, Captain."
—Dukat to Sisko
DS9 / "By Inferno's Light"

"Evil must be opposed."
—Vedek Yassim to crowd
DS9 / "Rocks and Shoals"

"I should've killed every last one of them, I should've turned their planet into a graveyard the likes of which the galaxy had never seen! I should've killed them all."
     "And that...is why you're not an evil man?"
—Dukat and Sisko. Dukat's hatred of the Bajorans comes to the forefront as he attempts to justify himself
DS9 / "Waltz"

"You know, Old Man...sometimes life seems so complicated. Nothing is truly good or truly evil. Everything seems to be a shade of gray. And then you spend some time with a man like Dukat...and you realize that there is such a thing as truly evil."
     "To realize that is one thing...to do something about it is another."
—Sisko and Dax
DS9 / "Waltz"

"Without the darkness...how would we recognize the light?"
—Tuvok to Kes
VGR / "Cold Fire"

"Do not fear your negative thoughts. They are part of you. They are a part of every living being."
—Tuvok to Kes
VGR / "Cold Fire"

9. Theology and Faith

"Did you hear him joke about compassion? Above all else a 'god' needs compassion!"

—Kirk to Dr. Elizabeth Dehner, on Gary Mitchell and his newfound powers
TOS / "Where No Man Has Gone Before"

"Morals are for men, not gods."

—Mitchell to Elizabeth
TOS / "Where No Man Has Gone Before"

"A god cannot survive as a memory. We need love, admiration, worship as you need food."

—Apollo to Carolyn
TOS / "Who Mourns for Adonais?"

"Even for a god there's a point of no return."

—Apollo to Carolyn
TOS / "Who Mourns for Adonais?"

"I would've cherished you, cared for you. I would have loved you as a father loves his children. Did I ask so much?"
    "We've outgrown you. You asked for something we can no longer give."

—Apollo and Kirk, on Apollo's need for worshippers
TOS / "Who Mourns for Adonais?"

"Once, just once, I'd like to be able to land someplace and say, 'Behold, I am the Archangel Gabriel.'"
"I fail to see the humor in that situation, Doctor."
"Naturally. You could hardly claim to be an angel with those pointed ears, Mister Spock. But say you landed someplace with a pitchfork...."

—McCoy and Spock
TOS / "Bread and Circuses"

"Well, if you're speaking of worships of sorts, we represent many beliefs."

—McCoy to Septimus
TOS / "Bread and Circuses"

"Words of peace and freedom. It wasn't easy for me to believe. I was trained to fight. But the words, the words are true."

—Flavius to Kirk, on hearing the words of the Son
TOS / "Bread and Circuses"

"The Message of the Son, that all men are brothers, was kept from us. Perhaps I'm a fool to believe it. It does often seem that a man must fight to live."
"You go on believing it, Flavius. All men are brothers."

—Flavius and Kirk
TOS / "Bread and Circuses"

"Captain, thank heaven!"
"Mister Scott, there was no deity involved. It was my cross-circuiting to B that recovered them."
"Well, then, thank pitchforks and pointed ears."

—Scott, Spock, and McCoy on Kirk's safe transport back to the ship
TOS / "Obsession"

"And as you believe, so shall you do."

—Gorgan to children
TOS / "And the Children Shall Lead"

"We all create God in our own image."

—Decker to Kirk, on V'ger's assumption that its creator is a machine
The Motion Picture

"V'ger must evolve. Its knowledge has reached the limits of this universe and it must evolve. What it requires of its God, Doctor, is the answer to its question. 'Is there nothing more?'"

—Spock to McCoy
The Motion Picture

"Jim, you don't ask the Almighty for his ID."

—McCoy to Kirk, on encountering a being who claims to be God
The Final Frontier

"I doubt any God who inflicts pain for his own pleasure."

—McCoy to Being
The Final Frontier

"Cosmic thoughts, gentlemen?"
    "We were speculating…is God really out there?"
"Maybe he's not out there, Bones. Maybe he's right here…in the human heart."

—Kirk and McCoy
The Final Frontier

"You must have faith."
    "Faith…?"
"That the universe will unfold as it should."

—Spock and Valeris
The Undiscovered Country

"That's a problem with believing in a supernatural being…trying to determine what he wants."

—Troi to Liko
TNG / "Who Watches the Watchers?"

"We've learned, Administrator, that hope is a powerful weapon against anything."

—Batai to the Administrator
TNG / "The Inner Light"

"It is true I am acting on my personal beliefs. But I do not see how I can do otherwise."

—Data to Riker
TNG / "The Quality of Life"

"Kahless has been dead for a thousand years…but the idea of Kahless is still alive. Have you ever fought an idea, Picard? It has no weapon to destroy, no body to kill."
—Gowron to Picard
TNG / "Rightful Heir"

"The Starfleet officers who first activated me on Omicron Theta told me I was an android—nothing more than a sophisticated machine with human form. However I realized that if I were simply a machine, I could never be anything else—I could never grow beyond my programming. I found that difficult to accept. So I chose to believe that I was a person, that I had the potential to be more than a collections of circuits and sub-processors. It is a belief which I still hold."
—Data to Worf
TNG / "Rightful Heir"

"Like many of our people, they need something to believe in…just like I did…something larger than themselves…something that will give their lives meaning."
—Worf to Gowron, on members of Gowron's crew reacting to the return of the legendary Kahless
TNG / "Rightful Heir"

"Everything is sacred to us. The buildings…the food…the sky…the dirt beneath your feet…and you. Whether you believe in your spirit or not…we believe in it. You are a sacred person here, Wesley."
—Lakanta to Wesley
TNG / "Journey's End"

"So if you are sacred…then you must treat yourself with respect…to do otherwise is to desecrate something that is holy."
—Lakanta to Wesley
TNG / "Journey's End"

"Our culture is rooted in the past, but it's not limited to the past. The spirits of Klingon, the Vulcan, and Ferengi come to us just as the bear, and the coyote, the parrot. There's no difference."
—Lakanta to Wesley
TNG / "Journey's End"

"Our religion is the only thing that holds my people together."
—Kira to Sisko
DS9 / "Emissary"

"A Bajoran draws courage from his spiritual life."
—Opaka to Sisko
DS9 / "Emissary"

"In the eyes of the Prophets, we are all children...."
—Opaka to Kira, on the gods of Bajor
DS9 / "Battle Lines"

"Some might say 'pure science' taught without a spiritual context *is* a philosophy, Mrs. O'Brien."
—Kira to Keiko
DS9 / "In the Hands of the Prophets"

"My philosophy is that there is room for *all* philosophies on this station."
—Sisko to Kira and Keiko
DS9 / "In the Hands of the Prophets"

"It may not be what you believe, but that doesn't make it *wrong*."
—Benjamin Sisko to Jake Sisko
DS9 / "In the Hands of the Prophets"

"And without your faith, Nerys...what do you have left?"
—Vedek Yarka to Kira
DS9 / "Destiny"

"It's hard to work for someone who's a religious icon."
—Kira to Sisko, on his being the Emissary of the Prophets
DS9 / "Destiny"

"Then it seems to me you have a choice: You can either make your own decisions...or you can let these prophecies make them for you."
—Dax to Sisko
DS9 / "Destiny"

"I have fought against races that believe in mythical beings who guide their destinies and await them after death. They call them gods. The Founders are like gods to the Jem'Hadar…but our gods never talk to us…and they don't wait for us after death. They only want us to fight for them…and to die for them."

—Goran'Agar to Bashir
DS9 / "Hippocratic Oath"

"Oh, don't be ridiculous. The Divine Treasury is made of pure latinum. Besides…where's the Blessed Exchequer, where are the Celestial Auctioneers? And why aren't we bidding for our new lives, hmm?"

—Quark to Rom, refusing to believe they're dead
DS9 / "Little Green Men"

"Our gods are dead. Ancient Klingon warriors slew them a millennia ago. They were more trouble than they were worth."

—Worf to Kira, on Klingon theology
DS9 / "Homefront"

"That's the thing about faith…if you don't have it, you can't understand it. And if you do, no explanation is necessary."

—Kira to Odo
DS9 / "Accession"

"It is not for us to accuse a god of betraying heaven."

—Omet'iklan to Toman'torax on Odo's refusal to join his people
DS9 / "To the Death"

"It's an old Klingon tradition. When a warrior dies in battle, his comrades stay with the body to keep away predators. That allows the spirit to leave the body when it is time to make the long journey to *Sto-Vo-Kor*."

—Worf to O'Brien
DS9 / "The Ship"

"What I believe in is faith. Without it there could be no victory. If the captain's faith is strong, he will prevail."

—Worf to Dax
DS9 / "Rapture"

"Those of you who were in the Resistance—you're all the same. You think you're the only ones who fought the Cardassians...that you saved Bajor single-handedly. Perhaps you forget, Major, the Cardassians arrested any Bajoran they found to be teaching the word of the Prophets. I was in a Cardassian prison camp for five years...and I can remember each and every beating I suffered. And while you had your weapons to protect you, all I had was my faith...and my courage."

—Winn to Kira
DS9 / "Rapture"

"Gods don't make mistakes. Though sometimes I think it would be nice to be able to carry a tune."

—Weyoun to Kira, on the Founders not providing the genetically engineered Vorta with aesthetic sensibilities
DS9 / "Favor the Bold"

"You say you don't want me to sacrifice my life—well, fine, neither do I. You want to be gods—then be gods. I need a miracle. Bajor needs a miracle. Stop those ships."

—Sisko to wormhole aliens, on the Dominion reinforcements coming through the wormhole
DS9 / "Favor the Bold"

"I suppose it must be nice to have that kind of faith. I've always preferred to believe in nothing—that way I'm never disappointed."

—the mirror Bareil to Kira
DS9 / "Resurrection"

"It seems to me that if the Prophets want the Bajoran people to follow a given path, they should provide more specific directions."
    "It doesn't work like that."
"Maybe it should."

—Odo and Kira
DS9 / "The Reckoning"

"Besides, I do have faith in some things."
    "Such as?"
"You."
    "I'll try not to disappoint you."

—Odo and Kira
DS9 / "The Reckoning"

"I mean out of all the people on this station, the Prophets chose me. I'm not sure I know why I deserved that honor."

"Perhaps that's why you were chosen. You have faith and humility."

—Kira and Odo, on being a vessel for her gods, the Prophets
DS9 / "The Reckoning"

"Pah-wraiths and Prophets. All this talk of gods strikes me as nothing more than superstitious nonsense."

"You believe that the Founders are gods, don't you?"
"That's different."

"In what way?"
"The Founders *are* gods."

—Weyoun and Damar
DS9 / "Tears of the Prophets"

"*A-koo-chee-moya*...we are far from the sacred places of our grandfathers. We are far from the bones of our people. But perhaps there is one powerful being who will embrace this woman and give her the answers she seeks."

—Chakotay conducting a ritual to seek Janeway's animal guide
VGR/ "The Cloud"

"The wheel represents both the universe outside...and the universe inside our minds as well. They believe each is a reflection of the other. When a person is sleeping, or on a vision quest...it's said that his soul is walking the wheel. But if he's in a coma...or near death...it means that he's gotten lost. These stones are signposts to help point the way back."

—Torres to the Doctor, on Chakotay's medicine wheel
VGR / "Cathexis"

"It's said the Sky Spirits honored the land above all else. Maybe it's because this land yields so many different kinds of Life...maybe they *wanted* us to become friends with everything in nature, including the bugs!"

"Sorry, Sky Spirits, I will never make friends with bugs."
"Maybe that's why they keep biting you."

—Kolopak and young Chakotay
VGR / "Tattoo"

"Vulcans believe that a person's *katra*, what some might call a soul, continues to exist after the body dies."

—Tuvok to Corin
VGR / "Innocence"

"If you can explain everything, what's left to believe in?"

—Old Man #2 to Janeway
VGR / "Sacred Ground"

"I know it's an important part of your religion to trust the Spirits without question, but I wasn't brought up that way. It's hard for me to accept."

"So much for your tolerant, open-minded Starfleet ideals."

—Janeway and Old Man #1
VGR / "Sacred Ground"

"There's a difference between respecting the spiritual beliefs of other cultures and embracing them myself."

—Janeway to Old Man #1
VGR / "Sacred Ground"

"You'll find all the answers, eventually, with enough time and study, and the right sort of tools. That's what you believe, isn't it...as a scientist?"

—Old Woman to Janeway
VGR / "Sacred Ground"

"Even when her science fails right before her eyes, she still has full confidence in it. Now there's a *leap of faith*."

—Old Man #2 to Janeway
VGR / "Sacred Ground"

"When one's imagination cannot provide an answer...one must seek out a greater imagination. There are times, when even I find myself kneeling in prayer."

—Leonardo hologram to Janeway
VGR / "Scorpion"

10. Parents, Children, and Family

"I'm trying to make people like me. I want them to like me...."
    "Most seventeen-year-olds do."
—Charlie and McCoy
TOS / "Charlie X"

"Everything I do or say is wrong. I'm in the way. I don't know the rules. And when I learn something and try to do it, suddenly I'm wrong!"
—Charlie to Kirk
TOS / "Charlie X"

"He's a boy in a man's body, trying to be an adult, with the adolescent in him getting in the way."
—Kirk to Spock on Charlie
TOS / "Charlie X"

"I think children have an instinctive need for adults. They want to be told right and wrong."
—Kirk to Rand
TOS / "Miri"

"The Horta is intelligent, peaceful, mild. She had no objection to sharing this planet with you till you broke into her nursery and started destroying her eggs. Then she fought back in the only way she knew how. As any mother would fight when her children are in danger."

—Kirk to Chief Engineer Vanderberg
TOS / "The Devil in the Dark"

"Parents like stupid things."
    "Oh, I don't know about that. Parents like children."

—Don Linden and Chapel
TOS / "And the Children Shall Lead"

"Youth doesn't excuse everything, Doctor McCoy."

—Kirk/Lester to McCoy
TOS / "Turnabout Intruder"

"My logic is uncertain where my son is concerned."

—Sarek to High Priestess T'Lar
The Search for Spock

"Our children are not for sale at any price."

—Beverly to Radue
TNG / "When the Bough Breaks"

"You are trifling with the primal instincts of our species. I must warn you that human parents are quite willing to die for their children."

—Picard to Radue on the kidnapping of the Enterprise children
TNG / "When the Bough Breaks"

"Dad, I want to be an artist. But I don't want to take calculus anymore."
    "You can be anything you want, Harry. Anything. But you still have to take calculus."

—Harry Bernard, Jr. and Dr. Bernard
TNG / "When the Bough Breaks"

"The most dangerous animal is a mother protecting her young."

—Picard to Troi
TNG / "The Dauphin"

"You choose your enemies…you choose your friends…but family…that's in the stars."
—O'Brien to Riker
TNG / "The Icarus Factor"

"It's a funny thing about being a parent. There aren't any tech manuals, no quick read-outs to get you through the next set of variables. You've just got to wing it from day to day.…"
—Kyle Riker to Will Riker
TNG / "The Icarus Factor"

"You can't guide someone into adulthood. The experiences are unique to each person. Whether Wes succeeds or fails, he will learn from the experience."
—Troi to senior staff, on Wesley
TNG / "Pen Pals"

"He is a boy, not a sword."
    "Who will one day become a man and, to extend the metaphor, will need a fine edge that won't dull at the first touch of resistance."
—Pulaski and Picard on Wesley
TNG / "Pen Pals"

"A mother shapes her child in ways she doesn't even realize. Sometimes just by listening."
—Guinan to Beverly
TNG / "Evolution"

"There comes a time in a man's life that you cannot know… when he looks down at the first smile of his baby girl and realizes he must change the world for her…for all children."
—Alidar Jarok to Picard
TNG / "The Defector"

"I will never see my child smile again. She will grow up believing that her father was a traitor. *But she will grow up.*"
—Jarok to Picard, on preventing a war between the Federation and the Romulans regardless of personal cost
TNG / "The Defector"

"Why should biology rather than technology determine whether it's a child? Data has created an offspring…a new life out of his own being. To me that suggests a child. If he wishes to call Lal his child, then who are we to argue?"

—Troi to Picard
TNG / "The Offspring"

"I have observed that in most species, there is a primal instinct to perpetuate themselves. Until now, I have been the last of my kind. If I were to be damaged or destroyed, I would be lost forever. But if I am successful with the creation of Lal, my continuance is assured. I understand the risks, sir. And I am prepared to accept the responsibility."

—Data to Picard, having created an android "child"
TNG / "The Offspring"

"And it is interesting to note that as I observe Lal learning about her world…I share in her experience, almost as though I am learning things over again…."

—Data's log, describing what the child teaches the parent
TNG / "The Offspring"

"Just help her realize she's not alone. And be there to nurture her when she needs love and attention."

—Beverly to Data, on Lal
TNG / "The Offspring"

"There are many things that she can learn only from me. My lifetime of experiences, the mistakes I have made and what I have learned from them…."

—Data to Picard. As Starfleet threatens to take Lal away from her "father," Data wants her to remain with him
TNG / "The Offspring"

"It would seem you've actually improved upon yourself, Data."
    "Is that not the goal of every parent, sir?"

—Picard and Data, on the android Lal's behavior
TNG / "The Offspring"

"Admiral, when I created Lal, it was in the hope that someday she would choose to enter the academy and become a member of Starfleet. I wanted to give something back in return for all that Starfleet has given me. I still do. But Lal is my child. You ask that I volunteer to give her up. I cannot. It would violate every lesson I have learned about human parenting. I have brought a new life into this world. And it is my duty, not Starfleet's, to guide her through these difficult steps to maturity, to support her as she learns, to prepare her to be a contributing member of society. No one can relieve me from that obligation. And I cannot ignore it. I am her father."

—Data to Admiral Haftel
TNG / "The Offspring"

"Thank you…for…my…life."

—Lal to Data. As Lal the android is dying, she shows appreciation to her creator/father
TNG / "The Offspring"

"Mother, look. Perhaps some day I will marry. But you have to let me make my own choices…live my own life, and not the life that you would choose for me."

—Troi to Lwaxana
TNG / "Ménage à Troi"

"You know, Captain, almost no one is born being a good parent. Most people just have to muddle through and do the best that they can."

—Troi to Picard
TNG / "Suddenly Human"

"You know what Michelangelo used to say? That the sculptures he made were already there before he started, hidden in the marble. All he need to do was remove the unneeded bits. It wasn't quite that easy with you, Data. But the *need* to do it, *my* need to do it, was no different than Michelangelo's need."

—Soong to Data, on creating Data
TNG / "Brothers"

"So you believe that having children gives humans a sense of immortality, do you?"

—Soong to Data, on having Data answer his own question of why he was created
TNG / "Brothers"

"They're brothers, Data. Brothers forgive."

—Beverly to Data
TNG / "Brothers"

"Last time my old man was on board I found him chasing Nurse Stanton around a biobed in sickbay...."
    "I am not concerned about my father chasing nurses."
"Ah, well, it's always something with parents, isn't it...?"

—O'Brien and Worf
TNG / "Family"

"You're only a baby...but it's remarkable....I can see in your face all the people I've loved in my lifetime...your mother...my father and mother...*our family*. I can see me in you, too. And I can *feel* that you're *my* son. I don't know how to describe it....But there's this connection, this bond....I'll always be a part of you, Wesley...."

—Jack Crusher to Wesley. A message from father to son, recorded years before Jack Crusher's death
TNG / "Family"

"When I was your age...my own father...wasn't there for me. And I really needed him. I've often wondered what kind of father I'd be. I never felt quite ready. The idea even scared me a little."

—Riker to young "Jean-Luc"
TNG / "Future Imperfect"

"Young children are sometimes frightened of the world. That doesn't mean that their parents should let them stay in their cribs."

—Barclay to Troi
TNG / "The Nth Degree"

"We raise them, we care for them, we suffer for them, we keep them from harm their whole lives…now eventually, it's *their* turn to take care of us."

—Lwaxana to Timicin, on children's responsibilities to aging parents
TNG / "Half a Life"

"No parent should expect to be paid back for the love they've given their children."

—Timicin to Lwaxana
TNG / "Half a Life"

"Father and son…both proud, both stubborn…more alike than either of them are prepared to admit. A lifetime spent building emotional barriers. They're very difficult to break down. And now the time has come when it's too late. It's a difficult moment.…It's a lonely one."

—Picard to Data, on Spock and Sarek's unresolved relationship at the time of Sarek's death
TNG / "Unification, Part I"

"You must do what you think is best for him. That's all a parent can hope to do."

—Helena Rozhenko to Worf, on Worf's son, Alexander
TNG / "New Ground"

"Children don't have the experience to handle emotional crises. Instead of dealing with their feelings, they act on them."

—Troi to Worf
TNG / "New Ground"

"One day you're going to be glad your father cared enough about you to insist on rules. It may be hard to imagine right now…but eventually, most children come to appreciate their parents."

—Troi to Alexander
TNG / "Cost of Living"

"Well, of course he's unreasonable; he's a child. And such a child. You know, making little boys reasonable only gives them pimples."

—Lwaxana to Worf, on Alexander
TNG / "Cost of Living"

"I'm supposed to do everything right all the time. I don't know how!"

"To tell you the truth, little warrior, neither do I."

—Alexander and Lwaxana
TNG / "Cost of Living"

"Children are a lot stronger than you think. As long as they know you love them...they can handle just about anything life throws at them, you know?"

—La Forge to Ensign Sutter
TNG / "Imaginary Friend"

"As adults, we don't always stop to consider how everything we say and do shapes the impressions of young people. But if you're judging us as a people by the way we treat our children...and I think there can be no better criterion...then you must understand how deeply we care for them. When our children are young, they don't understand what might be dangerous. Our rules are to keep them from harm. Real or imagined. And that's part of the continuity of our human species. When Clara grows up, she will make rules for her children...to protect them...as we protect her."

—Picard to Isabella
TNG / "Imaginary Friend"

"I always believed that I didn't need children to complete my life...now, I couldn't imagine life without them."

—Picard to Eline, on their children
TNG / "The Inner Light"

"It's amazing, isn't it...the way they're able to sneak into your heart....I must admit, I was completely unprepared for the power she had over me...from the moment she was born."

—Madred to Picard, on Madred's daughter
TNG / "Chain of Command, Part II"

"When children learn to devalue others...they can devalue anyone. Including their parents."

—Picard to Madred
TNG / "Chain of Command, Part II"

"There were many parts of my youth that I'm not proud of...they were loose threads...untidy parts of me that I would like to remove. But when I pulled on one of those threads...it unraveled the tapestry of my life."

—Picard to Riker
TNG / "Tapestry"

"In the Klingon *MajQa* ritual, there is nothing more important than receiving a revelation about your father. Your father is a part of you...always. Learning about him teaches you about yourself...."

—Worf to Data
TNG / "Birthright"

"On Atrea there is a saying...that a child born from parents who love each other will have nothing but goodness in his heart. I guess that explains you...."

—Juliana Tainer to Data
TNG / "Inheritance"

"We have strong ties to our ancestors...we believe their actions guide us even now. Knowing more about your family might help me to better understand you."

—Anthwara to Picard
TNG / "Journey's End"

"You know, I don't think anyone is born knowing how to be a parent. You just sort of figure it out as you go. But the one quality that tends to be a requirement for parenthood is patience."

—Beverly to Picard
TNG / "Bloodlines"

"When I was very young...and afraid of monsters under my bed...he played for me. He said that the *klavion* had special powers. Monsters were afraid of it...and when they heard it they would disappear. When I listened to that music he played for me...I was never afraid to go to sleep. When he died...I realized...even he couldn't make all the monsters go away."

—Ensign Ro Laren to Macias, on her father
TNG / "Preemptive Strike"

"The sound of children playing. What could be more beautiful...?"
—Benjamin Sisko to Jennifer Sisko
DS9 / "Emissary"

"Going through my own adolescence was difficult enough. Surviving my son's is going to take a miracle."
—Sisko to Dax
DS9 / "The Nagus"

"On Cardassia, family is everything. We care for our parents and children with equal devotion. In some households, four generations eat at the same table. Family is...everything."
—Pa'Dar to O'Brien
DS9 / "Cardassians"

"It's your life, Jake. You have to choose your own way. There is only one thing I want from you. Find something you love...then do it the best you can...."
—Benjamin Sisko to Jake Sisko
DS9 / "Shadowplay"

"I never thought I'd hear myself saying this...but I miss taking care of Jake when he was a baby. I miss holding him...singing to him at night...feeding him...."
—Sisko to Dax, on his son growing up
DS9 / "The Abandoned"

"There are times when I would give almost anything for the days when I could make Jake happy...just by lifting him over my head."
—Sisko to Dax
DS9 / "The Abandoned"

"My son's happiness is more important to me than anything, even latinum. Remember that...*Brother*."
—Rom to Quark, on Nog
DS9 / "Facets"

"Wherever he goes, I go. He's the only family I have. And this is the only home I need."

—Ziyal to Kira, on traveling with her father, Dukat
DS9 / "Return to Grace"

"You know babies…every little thing they pick up goes straight into their ears. I used to love reading to him. You know, 'See Brak acquire. Acquire, Brak, acquire.'"

—Quark to O'Brien, on Nog
DS9 / "Accession"

"Seems just yesterday he was five years old…clinging to me because he'd just scraped his knee and I was the only one in the world who could make it better. I remember sometimes getting up in the middle of the night and slipping into his room just to make sure he was all right…and I'd sit there and watch him sleep…and I'd think to myself that no matter what, I wasn't going to let anything bad happen to this child. Now he's a sector away, in a war zone, and there's nothing I can do to protect him."

—Sisko to Odo, on Jake
DS9 / "Nor the Battle to the Strong"

"But Jake is eighteen years old. Does your father still worry about you?"

  "Oh, all the time."

—Odo and Sisko
DS9 / "Nor the Battle to the Strong"

"I know what it's like to worry about a child. Raifi put Tobin through hell. When Neema was six, she came down with Rugelan fever. Audrid spent two weeks in the hospital with her, and never left her side. It was hundreds of years ago, and I can still remember how helpless I felt. I read her all seventeen volumes of Caster's *Down the River Light*, even though I knew she couldn't hear me. It made me feel like I was doing *something*, that we were still connected. It wasn't until much much after that that I realized I was doing it as much for me as I was doing it for her."

—Dax to Sisko
DS9 / "Nor the Battle to the Strong"

"I remember the first time I held you in my hands. You were only a few minutes old…and I looked down at your face and it was almost as if I could see your whole life stretched out in front of you—all the joys it would bring…and the bruises. It was all there, hidden in that scrunched up little face. The baby that I'm holding in my hands now…is the universe *itself*. And I need time to study its face."

—Benjamin Sisko to Jake Sisko, on his visions from the Prophets
DS9 / "Rapture"

"It's always nice to have someone around to help change the diapers."

—Sisko to Odo
DS9 / "The Begotten"

"I think I finally understand how much I meant to you…and what you must've gone through when I left."
    "You had to find your own way in the world."

—Odo and Mora. Resolving their differences, Odo accepts the contributions of the man who helped him "grow up"
DS9 / "The Begotten"

"You've never had a child. You don't know what it's like to watch your son…to watch him fall a little further behind every day.…You know he's trying, but something's holding him back. You don't know what it's like to stay up every night worrying that maybe it's *your* fault. Maybe you did something wrong during the pregnancy, maybe you weren't careful enough, or maybe there's something wrong with you. Maybe you passed on a genetic defect without even knowing it."

—Amsha Bashir to Julian Bashir, explaining why his "slowness" to learn compelled his parents to have him genetically enhanced
DS9 / "Doctor Bashir, I Presume?"

"What are you telling me, my baby's just…sad?"
    "Perhaps he's become prematurely aware of life's existential isolation."
"You're sure it's not a rash?"
    "Look at the bright side: he'll probably be a great poet."

—O'Brien and Bashir, on Kirayoshi's constant crying
DS9 / "Business as Usual"

"There's only one person in my life who's always been there for me…who's never too busy to listen…who reassures me when I'm scared…comforts me when I'm sad…and who showers me with endless love, without ever asking anything in return."

—Rom to Quark, on their mother, Ishka
DS9 / "Ferengi Love Songs"

"This is very important to me. My father has never let me down…he's always been there for me when I needed him. And right now he needs me….I don't want to let him down."

—Jake to Nog, on getting a vintage baseball card to cheer Sisko up
DS9 / "In the Cards"

"You didn't raise me to be a liar."
    "I raised you to be a chef, for all the good it did me."

—Benjamin Sisko and Joseph Sisko
DS9 / "A Time to Stand"

"But she is my daughter. That may mean nothing to you, but it means everything to me."

—Dukat to Damar, on wanting to maintain good relations with his daughter, Ziyal
DS9 / "The Sacrifice of Angels"

"Family. You understand."
    "Not really. I was cloned."

—Quark and Yelgrun
DS9 / "The Magnificent Ferengi"

"I'm your mother. I can't leave you alone."

—Ishka to Quark
DS9 / "Profit and Lace"

"I am a Klingon warrior and a Starfleet officer. I have piloted starships through Dominion mine fields, I have stood in battle against Kelvans twice my size, I courted and won the heart of the magnificent Jadzia Dax. If I can do these things…I can make this child go to sleep."

—Worf to Dax, on babysitting Kirayoshi
DS9 / "Time's Orphan"

"Well, if you're going to do something, do it right—that's what my father used to say."

"Every father says that. Even I say that."

"That's why you're such a good parent—you know all the clichés by heart."

—Kasidy Yates and Sisko
DS9 / "The Sound of Her Voice"

"Bringing a child into the world…it's a huge responsibility. I know you'd want to be sure we're both up to the task….I mean…somebody would have to keep their eye on the little guy all the time…or he'd be off sticking his finger into an EM conduit…or playing with the plasma injectors…."

"That's right. That's called being a parent."

—Neelix and Kes
VGR / "Elogium"

"I can only tell you that if you have considerable doubts about fatherhood, it would not be wise to enter into the process. It is so much more overwhelming than one expects that I believe only the most committed should become parents."

—Tuvok to Neelix
VGR / "Elogium"

"However, I must point out that, as illogical as it seems—being a father can have infinite rewards—far more than would seem possible. My children occupy a significant portion of my thoughts—now, more than ever."

—Tuvok to Neelix
VGR / "Elogium"

"I don't have anything to teach a daughter…."

"Why would it be any different from what you would teach a son?"

—Neelix and Tuvok
VGR / "Elogium"

"But isn't that why we have minds? To look beyond biological urges...to consider their consequences? If I'm going to ask myself to look at those consequences...then I have to ask myself some questions. Am I really ready to have a child? Am I prepared to give that child the attention and devotion it deserves? Am I capable of taking on such a huge responsibility? There's so much I haven't done....There's so much I want to study and learn. I'm not sure *I'm* finished growing....How could I help a child grow?"

—Kes to the Doctor
VGR / "Elogium"

"We weren't on very good terms when he died. Once he was gone, I didn't know how to reconcile our differences...how to heal our old wounds. I returned to my colony and continued the fight in his name. I took the mark that he wore to honor his ancestors."

—Chakotay to alien, on his father, Kolopak
VGR / "Tattoo"

"I have learned that pregnancy and patience go hand-in-hand."

—Tuvok to Kim
VGR / "Deadlock"

"My attachment to my children cannot be described as an emotion. They are part of my identity, and I am...incomplete without them."

—Tuvok to Elani
VGR / "Innocence"

"I have never understood the practice in some cultures of describing ferocious creatures in an attempt to lull children to sleep."

—Tuvok to Corin
VGR / "Innocence"

"How do you take a child into your heart who is forced upon you...by a mother's deception...?"

     "He knows nothing of deception. He is innocent."

—Chakotay and Kolopak, on the child Seska believed she conceived by stealing a DNA sample from Chakotay
VGR / "Basics, Part I"

"Raising children of my own made me appreciate what my parents experienced raising me…and I came to realize that the decisions I made as a young man were not always in my best interests. I understood their decision to send me to the academy…and that there were many things I could learn from humans and other species."

—Tuvok to Janeway, on returning to Starfleet
VGR / "Flashback"

"Those 'best qualities of humanity' you talked about aren't a simple matter of genetics. Love…conscience…compassion… they're attributes that mankind has developed over centuries, values that have passed from one generation to the next, taught by parents to their children. Creating a new kind of Q is a noble idea. But it will take more than impregnating someone and walking away. If you want your offspring to embrace your ideals, you're going to have to teach them yourself."

—Janeway to Q
VGR / "The Q and the Grey"

"Well, I'll admit, I look at the Universe in an entirely different way now. I mean, I can't go around causing temporal anomalies or subspace inversions without considering the impact it'll have on my son."

—Q to Janeway, on fatherhood
VGR / "The Q and the Grey"

"You make it sound like you're treating a sick patient. I'm not sure you can diagnose and cure a family."

—Paris to the Doctor, on coping with a computer simulation of a family
VGR / "Real Life"

"As husband and father, I believe it is my duty to set some parameters. It's part of good parenting."

—the Doctor to holo-family
VGR / "Real Life"

"Think about what's happened to us here on *Voyager*. Everyone left people behind…and everyone suffered a loss. But look how it's brought us all closer together. We found support here…and friendship. And we've *become* a family…in part because of the pain we shared. If you turn your back on this program, you'll always be stuck at this point. You'll never have the chance to say good-bye to your daughter…or to be there for your wife and son when they need you…and you'll be cheating yourself of the chance to have *their* love and support. In the long run…you'll miss the whole point of what it means to have a family."

—Paris to the Doctor, on the death of the Doctor's holographic "daughter," Belle
VGR / "Real Life"

"'We do not stand alone…we are in the arms of family. Father…mother…sister…brother…father's father…father's mother…father's brother…mother's brother….' Suffice to say, the list is extensive. 'We gather on this day to extol the warmth and joy of those unshakable bonds. Without them, we could not call ourselves complete. On this day, we are thankful to be together. We do not stand alone.'"

—Tuvok to crew, reciting the traditional welcome to the Talaxian Prixin ceremony
VGR / "Mortal Coil"

11. Love

"If I had the whole universe, I'd give it to you."

—Charlie to Rand
TOS / "Charlie X"

"What if you care for someone? What do you do?"
"You go slow. You be gentle. I mean, it isn't a one-way street, you know—how you feel and that's all. It's how the girl feels, too. Don't press, Charlie. If the girl feels anything for you at all, you'll know."

—Charlie and Kirk
TOS / "Charlie X"

"I've been good at my job. But I've never been in love. Never. What kind of a life is that? Not to be loved…never to have shown love."

—Commissioner Nancy Hedford to McCoy
TOS / "Metamorphosis"

"Love sometimes expresses itself in sacrifice."

—Kirk to McCoy
TOS / "Metamorphosis"

"Well, Cyrano Jones says that a tribble is the only love that money can buy."
—Lieutenant Uhura to Kirk
TOS / "The Trouble with Tribbles"

"Too much of anything, Lieutenant, even love, isn't necessarily a good thing!"
—Kirk to Uhura
TOS / "The Trouble with Tribbles"

"Love is the most important thing on Earth, especially to a man and a woman."
—Kirk to Shahna
TOS / "The Gamesters of Triskelion"

"On Earth, we select our own mate, someone we care for. On Earth, men and women live together, help each other, make each other happy."
—Kirk to Shahna
TOS / "The Gamesters of Triskelion"

"Well, among humans it's meant to express warmth and love."
    "Oh. You are trying to seduce me."
—Kirk and Kelinda, on kissing
TOS / "By Any Other Name"

"This business of love, you have devoted much literature to it. Why do you build such a mystique around a simple biological function?"
    "We enjoy it."
"Literature?"
—Kelinda and Kirk
TOS / "By Any Other Name"

"The sooner our happiness together begins, the longer it will last."
—Miramanee to Kirk
TOS / "The Paradise Syndrome"

"May I give you the love you want and make the time you have beautiful."

—Natira to McCoy
TOS / "For the World Is Hollow and I Have Touched the Sky"

"She loved you, Captain. And you, too, Mister Flint, as a mentor, even as a father. There was not enough time for her to adjust to the awful power and contradictions of her newfound emotions. She could not bear to hurt either of you. The joys of love made her human and the agonies of love destroyed her."

—Spock to Kirk and Flint, on the "death" of the android Rayna
TOS / "Requiem for Methuselah"

"You wouldn't understand that, would you, Spock? You see, I feel sorrier for you than I do for him because you'll never know the things that love can drive a man to: the ecstasies, the miseries, the broken rules, the desperate chances, the glorious failures, and the glorious victories. All of these things you'll never know simply because the word 'love' isn't written into your book."

—McCoy to Spock, on Kirk's loss of Rayna
TOS / "Requiem for Methuselah"

"Humans...young human males particularly...have difficulty separating platonic love and physical love."

—Troi to Riker
TNG / "Haven"

"Doesn't love always begin that way? With the illusion more real than the woman?"

"Oh, Jean-Luc, spoken like a true Frenchman."

—Picard and Minuet
TNG / "11001001"

"What about love?"

"The act or the emotion?"

"They're both the same."

"I believe that statement to be inaccurate, sir."

—Okona and Data
TNG / "The Outrageous Okona"

"There'll be others—but every time you feel love, it'll be different. Every time it's different."

"Knowing that doesn't make it any easier."

"It's not supposed to."

—Guinan and Wesley, on parting from the girl he loves
TNG / "The Dauphin"

"K'Ehleyr...I will not be complete without you."

—Worf to K'Ehleyr, at their parting
TNG / "The Emissary"

"Who needs rational when your toes curl up...?"

—Beverly to Troi, on Troi's irrational relationship with Devinoni Ral
TNG / "The Price"

"I fell in love in a day. It lasted a week. But *what* a week."

—Beverly to Troi, on a whirlwind romance
TNG / "The Price"

"I...love...you...father."

"I wish I could feel it with you."

"I...will...feel...it...for...both...of...us."

—Lal and Data. Overwhelmed by emotions data is incapable of experiencing, Lal uses her final moments to express her feelings
TNG / "The Offspring"

"Words come later. It is the scent that first speaks of love."

—Worf to La Forge
TNG / "Transfigurations"

"Human bonding rituals often involve a great deal of talking, and dancing, and crying."

—Worf to Data, on weddings
TNG / "Data's Day"

"Marriage is an agreement to share who you are with someone else...to spend your lives together...to grow old together."

—Troi to Data
TNG / "Data's Day"

"...You can't be open to love if you don't risk pain...."

—Troi to Beverly
TNG / "The Host"

"Perhaps...someday...our ability to love won't be so limited."

—Beverly to Kareel/Odan; unable to accept Odan the symbiont as a joined being
TNG / "The Host"

"Data, when you get involved with another person, there're always risks. Of disappointment. Of getting hurt."

—Riker to Data
TNG / "In Theory"

"Data, when it really works between two people, it's not like anything you've ever experienced—the rewards are far greater than simple friendship."

—Riker to Data on love
TNG / "In Theory"

"So...I'm just a small variable in one of your new computational environments?"

"You are much more than that, Jenna. I have written a subroutine specifically for you—a program within the program. I have devoted a considerable share of my internal resources to its development."

"Data, that's the nicest thing anybody's ever said to me."

—Lieutenant Jenna D'Sora and Data, discussing Data's way of expressing her importance in his life
TNG / "In Theory"

"The Book of Love, chapter four, paragraph seventeen: When your girlfriend arrives with a gift, stop whatever it is you're doing and give her your undivided attention."

—Jenna and Data
TNG / "In Theory"

"I am female. I was born that way. I have had those feelings…
those longings…all of my life. It is not unnatural. I am not sick
because I feel this way. I do not need to be helped, I do not
need to be cured. What I need—and what all of those who are
like me need—is your understanding and your compassion. We
have not injured you in any way. And yet we are scorned, and
attacked. And all because we are different. What we do is no
different from what you do. We talk and laugh…we complain
about work and we wonder about growing old…we talk about
our families, and we worry about the future…And we cry with
each other when things seem hopeless. All of the loving things
that you do with each other…that is what we do. And for that,
we are called misfits, and deviants…and criminals. What right
do you have to punish us? What right do you have to change us?
What makes you think you can dictate how people love each
other?"

—Soren to Noor. On a world where the people have evolved a gender-neutral mind-
set, Soren is an outcast for having a female orientation
TNG / "The Outcast"

"It's like the first time you fall in love…you don't ever love a
woman quite like that again."

—Picard to Scott, on the love of their first ships
TNG / "Relics"

"Relationships with coworkers can be fraught with consequences."

—Picard to Troi
TNG / "Lessons"

"I've lost people under my command…people who were very
dear to me…but never someone I've been in love with. And
when I believed that you were dead, I just began to shut
down.…I didn't want to think or feel. I was here, in my quarters, and…the only thing I could focus on was my music…and
how it would never again give me any joy."

—Picard to Neela Daren
TNG / "Lessons"

"Listen to me, Julian. You're the one who's always talking about adventure…adventure. Marriage is the greatest adventure of them all. It's filled with pitfalls and setbacks and mistakes, but it's a journey worth taking…because you take it together. I know Keiko's been unhappy…about us coming to the station.… We still argue about it…But that's all right…because at the end of the day, we both know we love each other. And that's all that matters."

—O'Brien to Bashir
DS9 / "Armageddon Game"

"The point is sometimes we don't see true love even when it's staring us right in the face."

—Dax to Odo
DS9 / "Shadowplay"

"What was I supposed to say? That I love her? That I would do anything for her? That without her, my life would be meaningless? Sure I could say those things, but what good would it do? How could I expect you to understand? You've never had those feelings. You don't know what it means to really care about another person. You've never been in love. You've got all the emotions of a stone. No offense."

—Quark to Odo, on his feelings for Professor Natima Lang
DS9 / "Profit and Loss"

"That's the thing about love. No one really understands it, do they?"

—Garak to Quark
DS9 / "Profit and Loss"

"Listen…there's nothing harder than knowing that the person you love is unhappy…and I know how important it is to do something about it."

—Sisko to O'Brien
DS9 / "The House of Quark"

"Well, it's been my experience that during any serious disagreement a smile and sweet words will buy you two hours…flowers will buy you a week…an arboretum—well, that's at least two months. But in the end, you still have to solve the underlying problem."

—Bashir to O'Brien, on helping out an unhappy Keiko
DS9 / "The House of Quark"

"I'll never forget the first time I saw you…that day you came to the station. You had such a serenity about you….I thought you had all the answers….It really got on my nerves for a while. But then I got to know you…and I realized you were just as confused as the rest of us…you had just accepted your confusion better than anyone I've ever known. That's when I realized I loved you…."

—Kira to Bareil
DS9 / "Life Support"

"And it's been my observation that you humanoids have a hard time giving up the things you love…no matter how much they might hurt you."

—Odo to Kira
DS9 / "Heart of Stone"

"I don't understand how two people who've fallen in love, and made a life together, can be forced to just…walk away from each other because of a…taboo."

—Kira to Bashir, on "reassociation" in Trill society—when a Trill resumes a romance with someone from a former host's life
DS9 / "Rejoined"

"If I were in your position…I'd probably be just as ready to throw away everything for the person I love. But I would also want to make sure that I was ready to pay the price."

—Sisko to Dax
DS9 / "Rejoined"

"Everyone is trying to…look out for us. Protect us from ourselves. But in the end, all that matters is how we feel…and what we do about it. Because either way, we're the ones who have to live with the consequences."

—Dax to Dr. Lenara Kahn, on their relationship, forbidden in Trill society
DS9 / "Rejoined"

"When you're not with me, when you're not around, it's like a part of me is missing. I want to be with you more than anything.…But I don't think that I can do this.…Dax, I am not like you.…I don't have a little Curzon inside me telling me to be impulsive…to ignore the rules…to give up everything that I've worked for.…"

—Lenara to Dax, on their forbidden relationship
DS9 / "Rejoined"

"You humanoids. You're all obsessed with these convoluted mating rituals."

—Odo to Garak
DS9 / "Broken Link"

"But do you think we'd waste so much time on something that wasn't worthwhile?"

—Garak to Odo on "mating rituals"
DS9 / "Broken Link"

"I…am a fool."
    "You're in love. Which I suppose is the same thing."

—Worf and Dax, on his behavior with Grilka
DS9 / "Looking for *par'Mach* in All the Wrong Places"

"If I were in your shoes, I would be looking for someone a little more entertaining…a little more fun…and maybe even a little more attainable."
    "You are not in my shoes."
"Too bad. You'd be amazed at what I can do in a pair of size eighteen boots."

—Dax and Worf, on looking for love
DS9 / "Looking for *par'Mach* in All the Wrong Places"

"True love should always win."

—Dr. Lewis Zimmerman to Leeta, on losing her to Rom
DS9 / "Doctor Bashir, I Presume?"

"But you can't go through life trying to avoid getting a broken heart. If you do, it'll break from loneliness, anyway. So you might as well take a chance. If you don't, she'll move on, and you'll never know what you might have had. And living with that is worse than having a broken heart, believe me."

—Bashir to Odo
DS9 / "A Simple Investigation"

"The way I see it, people are either meant to be together or they're not."

—Kira to Dax
DS9 / "Children of Time"

"I guess I'd rather believe that any relationship can work as long as both people really want it to."

—Dax to Kira
DS9 / "Children of Time"

"I can see our lives together will not be easy."
     "True. But they'll be fun."

—Worf and Dax
DS9 / "Sons and Daughters"

"I'm so vulnerable to her…all she has to do is smile at me and I'm happy beyond reason…a minor disagreement between us and I'm devastated. It's absurd. Sometimes I wish I could reach inside myself and tear out my feelings for her. But I can't."

—Odo to the female shape-shifter, on Kira
DS9 / "Behind the Lines"

"Blood, Pain, Sacrifice, Anguish, and Death."
"Sounds like marriage all right."

—Worf and Bashir, on the upcoming Klingon pre-wedding rituals
DS9 / "You Are Cordially Invited…"

"This is about more than just tradition. You and I have embarked on a spiritual journey, one that will bind us together through this life and into the next. You cannot turn back now."

—Worf to Dax, on marriage and wedding disagreements
DS9 / "You Are Cordially Invited…"

"We are not accorded the luxury of choosing the women we fall in love with. Do you think Sirella is anything like the woman I thought that I'd marry? She is a prideful, arrogant, mercurial woman who shares my bed far too infrequently for my taste. And yet…I love her deeply. We Klingons often tout our prowess in battle, our desire for glory and honor above all else…but how hollow is the sound of victory without someone to share it with. Honor gives little comfort to a man alone in his home…and in his heart."

—General Martok to Worf
DS9 / "You Are Cordially Invited…"

"I wasn't looking to fall in love. I was perfectly happy by myself. I had friends, a career, adventure…then one day, this Klingon with a bad attitude walked into my life. And the next thing I know, I'm getting married. After three hundred and fifty-six years and seven lifetimes…I still lead with my heart."
"You know, that is what I've always loved about you…and I think that's why Worf loves you, too."

—Dax and Sisko
DS9 / "You Are Cordially Invited…"

"I wouldn't want to bet against a man's wife."

—O'Brien to Worf, on Dax's game of *tongo*
DS9 / "Change of Heart"

"I would rather lose a bet on you than win on someone else."

—Worf to Dax, on her *tongo* game
DS9 / "Change of Heart"

"I am a married man. I have to make certain…adjustments in my lifestyle."

—Worf to Dax
DS9 / "Change of Heart"

"I had to go back…and it did not matter what Starfleet thought or what the consequences were. She was my wife and I could not leave her."

—Worf to Sisko, on choosing to save Dax's life over completing his mission
DS9 / "Change of Heart"

"You come first. Before career, before duty—before anything. I do not regret what I did. And I would do it again."

—Worf to Dax on failing in his duty in order to save her life
DS9 / "Change of Heart"

"It's love, baby. Nothing better than that."

—Vic Fontaine to Kira, on Odo's infatuation with her
DS9 / "His Way"

"Love's…a distraction. And a distracted policeman is…? An opportunity."

—Quark to Jake, on Odo being distracted by Kira
DS9 / "The Sound of Her Voice"

"We prefer permanence…the reward of relationships that endure…and grow deeper with the passing of time."

—Janeway to Gathorel Labin
VGR / "Prime Factors"

"Before I met *you*, eight or nine years seemed like an eternity. It never occurred to me that anyone could live longer. Now that we're together, no matter how many years we have left, it doesn't seem like enough. But the important thing is to cherish whatever time we have together—whether it's a day, or a decade."

—Kes to Neelix
VGR / "Jetrel"

"Jealousy is about the fear of losing someone we love. There's no pain greater than that."

—Chakotay to Neelix
VGR / "Twisted"

"Nothing makes us more vulnerable than when we love someone. We can be hurt very easily. But I've always believed that what you *get* when you love someone…is greater than what you risk."

—Chakotay to Neelix
VGR / "Twisted"

"You should consider it a high compliment. Throughout history, men have fought over the love of a woman. Why, I can quote you autopsy reports from duels as far back as 1538…."

—the Doctor to Kes, on Neelix and Paris fighting over her
VGR / "Parturition"

"Whenever you walk into the room, his respiration increases, his pupils dilate, and the coloration of his ears turns decidedly orange. Until I noticed the pattern, I thought he was suffering from Tanzian flu…."

—the Doctor to Kes, on Paris's attraction to Kes
VGR / "Parturition"

"Romance is not a malfunction."

—Kes to the Doctor
VGR / "Lifesigns"

"Of course, the first one is always the hardest to get over."

—Paris to the Doctor, on love
VGR / "Lifesigns"

"…Every now and then, even years later, something reminds you of her—a certain smell, a few notes of a song—and suddenly you feel just as bad as the day she told you she never wanted to see you again. If you want to know the honest truth, Doc, you never completely get over a woman you really cared about."

—Paris to the Doctor
VGR / "Lifesigns"

"Listen to me: nothing could ever change the way I feel about you...not a few scars...not some diseased skin...*nothing*...."

—the Doctor to Danara
VGR / "Lifesigns"

"I love you. Say something."
    "You picked a great time to tell me...."

—Torres and Paris, adrift in space with their oxygen running out
VGR / "Day of Honor"

"Commander...I don't think you can analyze love. It's the greatest mystery of all. No one knows why it happens, or doesn't. Love is a chance combination of elements...Any one thing might be enough to keep it from igniting...a mood, a glance, a remark. And if we could define love...predict it...it would probably lose its power."

—Neelix to Chakotay
VGR / "Unforgettable"

12. The Sexes

"I don't know what I am or what I'm supposed to be or even who. I don't know why it hurts so much inside all the time."
"You'll live, believe me. There's nothing wrong with you that hasn't gone wrong with every other human male since the model first came out."

—Charlie and Kirk
TOS / "Charlie X"

"Worlds may change, galaxies disintegrate, but a woman…always remains a woman."

—Kirk to Lenore Karidian
TOS / "The Conscience of the King"

"I've never understood the female capacity to avoid a direct answer to any question."

—Spock to Leila
TOS / "This Side of Paradise"

"You'll both grow old here and finally die."
"That's been happening to men and women for a long time. I've got the feeling it's one of the pleasanter things about being human…as long as you grow old together."

—Spock and Cochrane
TOS / "Metamorphosis"

"It's very hard for a working officer to shine as a woman every minute."
—the mirror Marlena Moreau to Kirk
TOS / "Mirror, Mirror"

"But we're strangers to each other."
        "But is not that the nature of men and women? That the pleasure is in the learning of each other?"
—McCoy and Natira, on asking the doctor to stay on Yonada
TOS / "For the World Is Hollow and I Have Touched the Sky"

"You may eliminate the symbols, but that does not mean death to the issues which those symbols represent. No power in the universe can hope to stop the force of evolution. Be warned. The execution of Mister Ramsey and his followers may elevate them to the status of martyrs. Martyrs cannot be silenced."
—Riker to Beata, on Ramsey and his followers being symbols of change toward equality in a matriarchal society
TNG / "Angel One"

"Men do not roar. Women roar. Then they hurl heavy objects. And claw at you."
        "What does the man do?"
"He reads love poetry. He ducks a lot."
— Worf and Wesley, on Klingon mating rituals
TNG / "The Dauphin"

"In spite of human evolution, there are still some traits that are endemic to gender."
        "You think that they're going to knock each other's brains out because…they're men?"
"Human males are unique. Fathers continue to regard their sons as children even into adulthood…and sons continue to chafe against what they perceive as their fathers' expectations of them."
—Troi and Pulaski, on Wil Riker and Kyle Riker
TNG / "The Icarus Factor"

"It's almost as if they never really grow up at all, isn't it?"
    "Perhaps that's part of their charm and why we find them
    so attractive."

—Pulaski and Troi, on men
TNG / "The Icarus Factor"

"You men draw a mug, and solve all the problems of the world
while the beer goes down. But when it comes to the practical
matters it always falls to the women to make your grand
dreams come true."

—Brenna Odell to Picard
TNG / "Up the Long Ladder"

"Competition seems to bring out the best in the human male."

—Lwaxana to Picard
TNG / "Manhunt"

"You are human, and among humans, females can achieve anything the males can."

—Worf to Jono
TNG / "Suddenly Human"

"…I would be delighted to offer any advice I can on understanding women. When I have some, I'll let you know."

—Picard to Data
TNG / "In Theory"

"Well, perhaps it is that complexity…which makes the differences in the sexes so interesting."

—Soren to Riker
TNG / "The Outcast"

"…When it comes to accumulating profit, women are as capable as men."

—Pel to Quark
DS9 / "Rules of Acquisition"

"You hew-mons, you never learn. You let your women go out in public, hold jobs, wear clothing, and you wonder why your marriages fall apart."
—Quark to O'Brien
DS9 / "Fascination"

"You hew-mons, all you want to do is please your women. You want them to be your friends. But we Ferengi know better. Women are the enemy. And we treat them accordingly. The key is to never let them get the upper hand. If she says she doesn't see you enough, threaten to see her even less. If she wants more gifts, take back the ones you've already given her. It's all about control."
—Quark to Sisko
DS9 / "Indiscretion"

"We consider Klingon women our partners in battle. They are the mothers of our children...."
    "And a lot of fun at parties, too."
—Worf and Dax
DS9 / "To the Death"

"It's as if I have to remind her that she's pregnant!"
    "Yeah. I guess the extra weight, the morning sickness, the mood swings, the medical examinations...they aren't reminders enough."
—O'Brien and Dax, on Keiko's adventurous behavior
DS9 / "Body Parts"

"Why does pregnancy always make men hysterical?"
—Dax to Kira
DS9 / "Nor the Battle to the Strong"

"All men are sentimental. They just cover it up with scowls and clenched jaws."
—Dax to Kira
DS9 / "You Are Cordially Invited..."

"She says it's because he's a pig-headed, stubborn man who puts tradition before everything else. He says it's because she's a frivolous, emotional woman who refuses to take him or his culture seriously. You can see the problem."

"They're both right."

—Quark and O'Brien, on Dax and Worf
DS9 / "You Are Cordially Invited…"

"Most men don't know how to defer gratification."

—Larell to Quark
DS9 / "Who Mourns for Morn?"

"Science fiction needs more strong women characters."

—Kay Eaton to Benny
DS9 / "Far Beyond the Stars"

13. Friendship and
Loyalty

"Did you do something wrong? Are you afraid of something? Whatever it is...let me help...."

"'Let me help.' A hundred years or so from now, I believe, a famous novelist will write a classic using that theme. He'll recommend those three words even over 'I love you.'"

—Edith and Kirk
TOS / "The City on the Edge of Forever"

"I owe him my life a dozen times over. Isn't that worth a career? He's my friend."

—Kirk to McCoy, on disobeying orders to get Spock home to Vulcan
TOS / "Amok Time"

"Are they enemies, Captain?"

"I'm not sure they're sure."

—Flavius and Kirk, on Spock and McCoy
TOS / "Bread and Circuses"

"You would really do that? You would extend welcome to invaders?"

"No. But we would welcome *friends*."

—Rojan and Kirk, on inviting Rojan's people to colonize within the Federation
TOS / "By Any Other Name"

"On what, precisely, is our friendship to be based?"
"Well, upon the firmest of foundations, Mister Spock—enlightened self-interest."

—Spock and Garth of Izar, on Garth's proposal of friendship
TOS / "Whom Gods Destroy"

"I am pleased to see that we have differences. May we together become greater than the sum of both of us."

—Surak to Kirk
TOS / "The Savage Curtain"

"I'm going to tell you something very...I never thought I'd ever hear myself say...But it seems I've missed you. I don't know if I could stand to lose you again."

—McCoy to Spock
The Search for Spock

"What I have done...I had to do."
"But at what cost? Your ship...your son."
"If I hadn't tried, the cost would have been my soul."

—Sarek and Kirk, on saving Spock
The Search for Spock

"My father says that you have been my friend....You came back for me."
"You would have done the same for me."
"Why would you do this?"
"Because the needs of the one outweighed the needs of the many."

—Kirk and Spock, on why Kirk returned to the Genesis Planet to save Spock
The Search for Spock

"As I recall, I opposed your enlistment in Starfleet....It is possible that judgment was incorrect. Your associates are people of good character."
"They are my *friends*."

—Sarek and Spock
The Voyage Home

"Understanding has made friends of many different people."

—Picard to Lutan
TNG / "Code of Honor"

"Friendship must dare to risk, Counselor, or it's not friendship."

—Picard to Troi
TNG / "Conspiracy"

"Remembrance and regrets, they too are a part of friendship."

—Picard to Data
TNG / "Pen Pals"

"As I experience certain sensory input patterns, my mental pathways become accustomed to them. The input is eventually anticipated and even missed when absent."

—Data to Ishara Yar, on his definition of friendship
TNG / "Legacy"

"There are many ways to help a friend…and sometimes the best way is to leave them alone."

—Troi to Data
TNG / "Data's Day"

"The loyalty that you would so quickly dismiss does not come easily to my people, Gul Macet. You have much to learn about us. Benjamin Maxwell earned the loyalty of those who served with him. You know, in war he was twice honored with the Federation's highest citation for courage and valor. And if he could not find a role for himself in peace, we can pity him, but we shall not dismiss him."

—Picard to Gul Macet
TNG / "The Wounded"

"You spend time with me when I'm lonely….You encourage me when I'm down. No man has ever been kinder to me….Those are the things that matter.…"

—Jenna to Data
TNG / "In Theory"

"A danger shared might sometimes bring two people together."

—Picard to Captain Dathon
TNG / "Darmok"

"Let me remind you of something…a Klingon does not put his desires above those of his family or his friends. How many people on this ship consider you a friend? How many owe you their lives? Have you ever thought about how you've affected the people around you? How we might feel about your dying?"

—Riker to Worf, on Worf's contemplated ritual suicide after being paralyzed in an accident
TNG / "Ethics"

"A warrior does not let a friend face danger alone."

—Worf to Riker
TNG / "The Outcast"

"But mostly a true friend is a person you can always tell the truth to without worrying about it."

—Lwaxana to Alexander
TNG / "Cost of Living"

"They're friends. They love contradiction.…They thrive on challenge.…They flourish in conflict.…"
    "Then why are they friends?"
"Who else are you going to fight with if not your friends?"

—Juggler and Alexander
TNG / "Cost of Living"

"In almost all societies it is traditional to say a ritual farewell to those you call friends. I never knew what a friend was until I met Geordi. He spoke to me as though I were human.…He treated me no differently from anyone else. He accepted me for what I am. And that, I have learned, is friendship. But I do not know how to say good-bye."

—Data to Worf, on La Forge's presumed death
TNG / "The Next Phase"

"But then again, 'Before you can be loyal to another, you must be loyal to yourself.'"

—Bashir to Garak, creating a quote to fit his needs
DS9 / "Profit and Loss"

"There's an old saying on Cardassia, 'Enemies make dangerous friends.'"

—Garak to Bashir
DS9 / "The Search, Part II"

"I guess I just forgot you were a Ferengi."
     "You forgot? To most people, the lobes are a dead give-away."
"What I mean is...we spend so much time together...and we seem so much alike...I sometimes forget we're different."

—Jake and Nog
DS9 / "Life Support"

"Before I met her, my world was a much smaller place. I kept to myself. I didn't need anyone else...and I took pride in that. The truth is...I was ashamed of what I was...afraid that if people saw how truly different I was...they would recoil from me. Lwaxana saw how different I was...but she didn't recoil. She wanted to see *more*. For the first time in my life, someone wanted me *as I was*. And that changed me...forever. The day I met her, is the day I stopped being alone."

—Odo to gathered friends, on Lwaxana
DS9 / "The Muse"

"Look at them, Brother. And you thought you had no assets."
     "Sisko...Dax...Bashir...Morn...they're my assets?"
"To name a few."

—Quark and Rom, on friendship
DS9 / "Body Parts"

"Because I'm exiled, and alone, and a long way from home. And when I'm with you...it doesn't feel so bad."

—Garak to Ziyal
DS9 / "In Purgatory's Shadow"

"Our loyalty is demonstrated by our actions, not our words."

—Kudak'Etan to Lamat'Ukan
DS9 / "One Little Ship"

"I'm going to take care of you. I don't forget my friends. 'Cause friends—they're like family—nothing's more important. Nothing."

—Liam Bilby to O'Brien
DS9 / "Honor Among Thieves"

"We've grown apart, the lot of us. We didn't mean for it to happen—but it did. The war changed us…pulled us apart. Lisa Cusak was my friend. But you are also my friends. And I want my friends in my life. Because some day we're going to wake up and we're going to find that someone is missing from this circle.. and on that day we're gonna mourn…and we shouldn't have to mourn alone."

—O'Brien to crowd. A eulogy for Captain Lisa Cusak
DS9 / "The Sound of Her Voice"

"I don't need anyone to choose my friends for me."

—Kim to Paris
VGR / "Caretaker"

"You are one of my most valued officers…and you are my friend. It is vital that you understand me here. I need you. But I also need to know that I can count on you. You are my counsel…the one I turn to when I need my moral compass checked. We have forged this relationship for years, and I depend on it. I realize you made a sacrifice for me…but it's not one I would have allowed you to make."

—Janeway to Tuvok
VGR / "Prime Factors"

"I think maybe you're beginning to realize I'm not your enemy. And only a fool would kill a friend."

—Chakotay to Kar
VGR / "Initiations"

"Harry, Harry, Harry…never ever play with anyone, not even your best friend, if he says, 'Let's make it interesting.…'"

—Paris to Kim
VGR / "Meld"

"You'll find that more happens on the bridge of a starship than just carrying out orders and observing regulations. There's a sense of loyalty to the men and women you serve with…a sense of family. Those two men on trial…I served with them for a long time. I owe them my life a dozen times over. And right now, they're in trouble…and I'm going to help them. Let the regulations be damned."

—Sulu to Tuvok, on disobeying orders in order to save Kirk and McCoy
VGR / "Flashback"

"You want to know what I remember? Someone saying, 'This man is my friend. Nobody touches him.' I'll remember that for a long time."

—Paris to Kim, recalling the way Kim protected him
VGR / "The Chute"

"I'm your friend, and I have to watch out for you when your judgment's been impaired. If you let these instincts take over now, you'll hate yourself—and me, too, for taking advantage of you. I won't do that."

—Paris to Torres, while she is under the influence of the mating time of *Pon farr*
VGR / "Blood Fever"

"Three years ago…I didn't even know your name. Today…I can't imagine a day without you."

—Janeway to Chakotay
VGR / "Scorpion, Part I"

"I'll tell you when we lost control of this situation…when we made our mistake. It was the moment we turned away from each other. We don't have to stop being individuals to get through this. We just have to stop fighting each other."

—Janeway to Chakotay
VGR / "Scorpion, Part II"

"I can't give you back to the Borg. But you're not alone. You're part of a *human* community, now…a human collective. We may be individuals, but we live and work together. You can have some of the unity you require…right here on *Voyager*."

—Janeway to Seven of Nine
VGR / "The Gift"

"Abandon ship? The answer's no. I'm not breaking up the family, Chakotay. We're stronger as a team...one crew, one ship. The moment we split apart, we lose the ability to pool our talents...we become vulnerable...we'll get picked off one by one. Now I say we make our stand...*together*."

—Janeway to Chakotay
VGR / "Year of Hell, Part I"

"I won't ask the crew to risk their lives because of my obligation."

"'My obligation.' That's where you're wrong. *Voyager* may be alone out here, but you're not. Let us help you."

—Chakotay to Janeway
VGR / "The Omega Directive"

14. Honesty and Trust

"What is the greater morality—open honesty or a deception which may save our lives?"

—Anan to High Council
TOS / "A Taste of Armageddon"

"If I can have honesty, it's easier to overlook mistakes."

—Kirk to Lieutenant Marla McGivers
TOS / "Space Seed"

"I don't trust men who smile too much."

—Kor to Council of Elders
TOS / "Errand of Mercy"

"A lie is a very poor way to say hello."

—Edith to Kirk
TOS / "The City on the Edge of Forever"

"It is not a lie to keep the truth to oneself."

—Spock to Romulan commander
TOS / "The *Enterprise* Incident"

"Is truth not truth for all?"

—Natira to Oracle
TOS / "For the World Is Hollow and I Have Touched the Sky"

"You lied."
    "I exaggerated."
—Saavik and Spock
The Wrath of Khan

"Your honor, a courtroom is a crucible. In it we burn away irrelevancies, until we're left with a pure product—the truth—for all time."
—Picard to Captain Phillipa Louvois
TNG / "The Measure of a Man"

"Candor seems to be a trait he admires."
    "Honesty is the trait he admires most."
—Kyle Riker and Troi, on Will Riker
TNG / "The Icarus Factor"

"We have good reason to mistrust one another. But we have even better reason to set those differences aside. Now of course, the question is who will take the initiative? Who will make the first gesture of trust? The answer is—*I* will."
—Picard to Tomalak
TNG / "The Enemy"

"In all trust there is the possibility of betrayal."
—Riker to Data
TNG / "Legacy"

"Without trust, there's no friendship, no closeness. None of the emotional bonds that make us who we are."
—Riker to Data
TNG / "Legacy"

"Trust is earned, not given away."
—Worf to Troi
TNG / "The Wounded"

"That's the problem with being such a well-known liar. Even when I'm telling the truth no one believes me."
—Vash to Picard
TNG / "QPid"

"Lies must be challenged."

—Picard to Worf
TNG / "Redemption"

"I believe truth is in the eye of the beholder."
    "Isn't that supposed to be 'beauty'?"
"'Truth,' 'beauty'…works for a lot of things."

—Guinan and Ro
TNG / "Ensign Ro"

"When you lie or steal, you not only dishonor yourself, but your family. You dishonor *me*."

—Worf to Alexander
TNG / "New Ground"

"Oh, you told the truth…up to a point. But a lie of omission is still a lie."

—Picard to Wesley
TNG / "The First Duty"

"The first duty of every Starfleet officer is to the truth…whether it's scientific truth, or historical truth, or personal truth. It is the guiding principle on which Starfleet is based. Now if you can't find it within yourself to stand up and tell the truth about what happened…you don't deserve to wear that uniform."

—Picard to Wesley
TNG / "The First Duty"

"Contracts are usually between people who don't really trust one another."

—Lwaxana to Troi
TNG / "Cost of Living"

"A child who is trusted becomes worthy of that trust."

—Lwaxana to Worf
TNG / "Cost of Living"

"When you tell the truth, you never have to remember later what you lied about."

—Lwaxana to Alexander
TNG / "Cost of Living"

"You've taught me to pursue the truth—no matter how painful it is. It's too late to back off now."

—Meribor to Picard
TNG / "The Inner Light"

"I know you have your doubts about me…about each other…about the ship. All I can say is that although we have only been together for a short time…I know that you are the finest crew in the fleet…and I would trust each of you with my life. So I'm asking you for a leap of faith—and to trust me."

—Picard to bridge crew
TNG / "All Good Things…"

"You're becoming more human all the time, Data…now you're learning how to lie."

—Borg queen to Data
First Contact

"…I have the bad habit of telling the truth…even when people don't want to hear it."

—Kira to Sisko
DS9 / "Emissary"

"Never trust ale from a god-fearing people…or a Starfleet commander that has one of your relatives in jail."

—Quark to Sisko
DS9 / "Emissary"

"It sounds like you're trying to talk yourself into something. Or out of something."
"Either way I have to betray someone."
"Only important thing is not to betray *yourself*."

—Odo and Kira
DS9 / "Past Prologue"

"Never trust anyone who places your prosperity above their own…."

—Zek to Quark
DS9 / "The Nagus"

"You gave me answers, all right. But they were all different. What I want to know is…out of all the stories you told me, which ones were true and which ones weren't?"

"My dear Doctor, they're all true."

"Even the lies?"

"Especially the lies."

—Bashir and Garak
DS9 / "The Wire"

"Truth is not always easy to recognize."

—Bareil to Kira
DS9 / "The Collaborator"

"…The point is, if you lie all the time, nobody's going to believe you even when you're telling the truth."

"Are you sure that's the point, Doctor?"

"Of course, what else could it be?"

"That you should never tell the same lie twice…."

—Bashir and Garak, on the boy who cried wolf
Source: Aesop, "The Shepherd Boy and the Wolf"
DS9 / "Improbable Cause"

"Well, the truth…is usually just an excuse for a lack of imagination."

—Garak to Odo
DS9 / "Improbable Cause"

"This is not a fight. It's the search for the truth."

"The truth must be won. I'll see you on the battlefield."

—Sisko and Ch'Pok, on an impending hearing
DS9 / "Rules of Engagement"

"Lying is a skill like any other. And if you want to maintain a level of excellence, you have to practice constantly."

—Garak to Worf
DS9 / "In Purgatory's Shadow"

"Right now I wouldn't believe your father if he said rain was wet."

—Kira to Ziyal on Dukat
DS9 / "By Inferno's Light"

"Well, it's just that lately, I've noticed everyone seems to…trust me. It's quite unnerving. I'm still trying to get used to it. Next thing I know, people are going to be inviting me to their homes for dinner."

"Well, if it makes you feel any better, I promise I will never have you over."

"I appreciate that, Chief."

—Garak and O'Brien
DS9 / "Empok Nor"

"You're more talented in the art of deception than you led me to believe."

"I was inspired by the presence of a master."

—Seska and the Doctor, on her deceptive history aboard *Voyager*
VGR / "Basics, Part II"

"I didn't tell the truth. I made a mistake—which happens to people—but if I'd admitted that mistake it would have been a lot better. But I lied about it. And it nearly ruined my life."

—Paris to Neelix
VGR / "Fair Trade"

15. Courtesy and Respect

"You keep interrupting, Mister Evans. That's considered wrong."
—Kirk to Charlie
TOS / "Charlie X"

"It's not nice...to laugh at people."
—Charlie to Kirk
TOS / "Charlie X"

"You sound bitter, Captain."
    "Not bitter enough to forget to thank you for your efforts."
—Spock and Kirk, on Spock finding no exculpatory evidence
TOS / "Court Martial"

"If you do not come with me, your engines will be destroyed
and you will remain in orbit here forever."
    "I must say that's a gracious invitation."
—Norman and Kirk
TOS / "I, Mudd"

"There is a word. Among us there is no corresponding meaning.
But it seems to mean something to you humans."
    "And what is that word?"
"Please."
—Norman and Kirk
TOS / "I, Mudd"

"I'm trying to thank you, you pointed-ear hobgoblin!"
"Oh, yes, you humans have that emotional need to express gratitude. 'You're welcome,' I believe, is the correct response."
—McCoy and Spock, on Spock saving McCoy's life
TOS / "Bread and Circuses"

"We have granted your crew the permission not to kneel in our presence, what else do you want?"
"Courtesy."
—Elaan and Kirk
TOS / "Elaan of Troyius"

"If you respect our customs and we see that respect, we will be friends...."
—Lutan to Picard
TNG / "Code of Honor"

"Good manners, Madam, are never a waste of time. Civility, gentlemen. Always civility."
—Cyrus Redblock to Beverly
TNG / "The Big Good-bye"

"You read me well enough to sense how I feel about you and what you do on this ship, but I just wanted to say the words. Thank you. Well done."
—Picard to Troi
TNG / "Loud as a Whisper"

"Respect is earned, not bestowed."
—Troi to Kyle Riker
TNG / "The Icarus Factor"

"Good tea. Nice house."
—Worf to his hostess, Rishon Uxbridge
TNG / "The Survivors"

"I have always tried to keep an open mind...not to judge someone else's culture by my own...."
—Riker to Picard
TNG / "Ethics"

"Long ago, a storm was heading toward the city of Quin'lat. The people sought protection within the walls all except one man who remained outside. I went to him and asked what he was doing. 'I am not afraid,' he said. 'I will not hide my face behind stone and mortar. I will stand before the wind and make it respect me.' I honored his choice and went inside. The next day the storm came…and the man was killed. The wind does not respect a fool."

—Kahless to Gowron
TNG / "Rightful Heir"

"I suppose you want the office."
        "Well, I thought I'd say hello first and then take the office…but we could do it in any order you like."

—Kira and Sisko
DS9 / "Emissary"

"Don't contradict your elders. It's impolite."

—Zek to Quark
DS9 / "The Nagus"

"A good host knows the needs of his guests."

—Tain to Bashir
DS9 / "The Wire"

"You can't buy respect, Brother."

—Rom to Quark
DS9 / "The House of Quark"

"Rudeness will get you nowhere—I don't need another waiter."

—Quark to Garak
DS9 / "For the Cause"

"I will apologize for this at a later time."

—Worf to Morn on preparing Morn to be tossed out of his chair
DS9 / "Looking for *par'Mach* in All the Wrong Places"

"Giving me a name tag that read, 'Elim Garak—Former Cardassian Oppressor' was hardly polite."

—Garak to Dax, on a conference about the Cardassian occupation of Bajor
DS9 / "Things Past"

"Bad manners are the fault of the parent, not the child."

—Dukat to Dax, on the Bajoran rebelliousness
DS9 / "Things Past"

"If you stand up to them, you'll earn their respect."

—Sisko to Nog, on the Klingons
DS9 / "Blaze of Glory"

"Dismissed. That's a Starfleet expression for 'get out....'"

—Janeway to Neelix
VGR / "The Cloud"

"I am curious. Have the Q always had an absence of manners? Or is it the result of some natural evolutionary process that comes with omnipotence?"

—Tuvok to Quinn
VGR / "Death Wish"

"The two hundred and ninety-ninth Rule of Acquisition: 'Whenever you exploit someone, it never hurts to thank them.' That way, it's easier to exploit them the next time."

—Neelix to Arridor, making up a new Rule of Acquisition
VGR / "False Profits"

"Have a pleasant day."

—Seven of Nine to the Doctor, trying out her etiquette lessons
VGR / "Prey"

16. Communication
and Diplomacy

"It is the custom of Earth people to try and avoid misunderstanding whenever possible."
—Kirk to Balok
TOS / "The Corbomite Maneuver"

"Maybe you're a soldier so often that you forget you're also trained to be a diplomat. Why not try a carrot instead of a stick?"
—McCoy to Kirk on dealing with the Companion
TOS / "Metamorphosis"

"We must acknowledge, once and for all, that the purpose of diplomacy is to prolong a crisis."
—Spock
TOS / "The Mark of Gideon"

"…The only tool diplomacy has is language. It is of the utmost importance that the meaning be crystal clear."
—Hodin and Spock
TOS / "The Mark of Gideon"

"It is difficult to answer if one does not understand the question."
—Sarek to Council President on a signal from an orbiting probe
The Voyage Home

"That's simply the way they talk here. Nobody pays any attention to you unless you swear every other word."

—Kirk to Spock, on Kirk's use of "colorful metaphors" while visiting twentieth-century Earth
The Voyage Home

"…Words are here—on top. What's under them, their meaning…is what's important."

—Troi interprets Riva's signing
TNG / "Loud as a Whisper"

"While they are learning how to communicate with Riva, they'll be learning how to communicate with each other."
    "…and that is the first and most important aspect of any relationship."

—Data and Troi, on the deaf negotiator, Riva, and the warring factions he's attempting to unite
TNG / "Loud as a Whisper"

"Is anybody out there?"
    "Yes."

—Sarjenka and Data. A child initiates first contact with a passing space traveler
TNG / "Pen Pals"

"There is a loneliness inherent in that whisper from the darkness."

—Picard to Data, on an attempt at communication by an alien child
TNG / "Pen Pals"

"Perhaps that is a part of our difficulty. Words are all we have been using. Humans seem to take much stronger notice of actions."

—Data to Ard'rian McKenzie
TNG / "The Ensigns of Command"

"Speak softly, Governor. Those who cannot hear an angry shout…may strain to hear a whisper."

—Riker/Odan to Governor Trion Leka
TNG / "The Host"

"In my experience, communication is a matter of patience, imagination. I would like to believe that these are qualities that we have in sufficient measure."

—Picard to Riker, on contact with the Children of Tama
TNG / "Darmok"

"A single word can lead to tragedy. One word misspoken, or misunderstood."

—Troi to Data
TNG / "Darmok"

"The Tamarian was willing to risk all of us—just for the hope of communication, connection. Now the door is open between our peoples. That commitment meant more to him than his own life."

—Picard to Riker on Dathon
TNG / "Darmok"

"One can begin to reshape the landscape with a single flower, Captain."

—Spock to Picard, on taking small steps to establish relations between Romulus and Vulcan
TNG / "Unification, Part II"

"Jean-Luc...sometimes I think the only reason I come here is to listen to these wonderful speeches of yours."

—Q to Picard
TNG / "True-Q"

"Would you like to talk about what's bothering you...or would you like to break some more furniture?"

—Troi to Worf
TNG / "Birthright"

"These are our stories. They tell us who we are."

—Worf to Toq, on Klingon mythology
TNG / "Birthright, Part II"

"...It is always good to understand one's adversary in any negotiation."

—Anthwara to Picard
TNG / "Journey's End"

"These people know that we are neither the enemy nor the devil. We don't always agree. We have some damn good fights in fact. But we always come away from them with a little more understanding and appreciation of each other."

—Sisko to Winn on the Bajorans and the Federation
DS9 / "In the Hands of the Prophets"

"You both go to such lengths to hide the true meaning of your words you end up saying nothing."

—Odo to Tain and Garak
DS9 / "Improbable Cause"

"My mother taught me if you try to combine talking and eating, you'll end up doing neither very well."

—O'Brien to Bashir
DS9 / "The Die Is Cast"

"But where you offer kindness, I offer mystery. Where you offer sympathy, I offer intrigue. Just give me a seat next to Odo's bed and I promise you I'll conjure up enough innuendoes, half-truths, and bald-faced lies about my so-called 'career' in the Obsidian Order to keep the constable distracted for days. If there's one thing Cardassians excel at, it's conversation."

—Garak to Sisko
DS9 / "Broken Link"

"What about freedom of the press?"
  "Please tell me you're not that naive."

—Weyoun and Jake
DS9 / "A Time to Stand"

"Stories can be whimsical…or frightening…or melancholy…or many other things. But noble stories…are the ones that can most affect our lives."

—Eudana to Kim
VGR / "Prime Factors"

"I may never put my hands on my hips again."
    "You had no way of knowing you were making one of the worst insults possible."

— Janeway and Neelix on Tak Tak body language
VGR / "Macrocosm"

"One voice…can be stronger than a thousand voices."

—Janeway to Seven of Nine
VGR / "The Gift"

17. Justice and Law

"Do you play God? Carry his head through the corridors in triumph? That won't bring back the dead, Jim."

"No. But they may rest easier."

—McCoy and Kirk, on proving Karidian is Kodos the Executioner
TOS / "The Conscience of the King"

"This is where the law is. Not in that homogenized, pasteurized, synthesized....Do you want to know the law? The ancient concepts in their own language? Learn the intent of the men who wrote them? From Moses to the tribunal of Alpha III? Books."

—Samuel T. Cogley to Kirk, on favoring books over computers
TOS / "Court Martial"

"I wouldn't want to slow the wheels of progress...but then on the other hand, I wouldn't want those wheels to run over my client in their unbridled haste."

—Cogley to Commodore Stone and Areel, on the reading of Kirk's long list of commendations
TOS / "Court Martial"

"Your words promise justice for all."

"We try, sir."

"Yes, well, I have learned to wait for *actions*."

—Bele and Kirk
TOS / "Let That Be Your Last Battlefield"

"Then what do you do, carry justice on your tongues? You will beg for it, but you won't fight or die for it."
—Lokai to Ensign Pavel A. Chekov, on Bele
TOS / "Let That Be Your Last Battlefield"

"Father, are we so sure of our methods that we never question what we do?"
—Droxine to Plasus
TOS / "The Cloud Minders"

"If we're going to be damned, let's be damned for what we really are."
—Picard to Riker, on Q's judgment of the human race
TNG / "Encounter at Farpoint"

"I say to any creature who may be listening, there can be *no* justice so long as laws are absolute. Even life itself is an exercise in exceptions."
—Picard to the Edo god
TNG / "Justice"

"When has justice ever been as simple as a rulebook?"
—Riker to the Edo god
TNG / "Justice"

"Beverly, the Prime Directive is not just a set of rules; it is a philosophy and a very correct one. History has proved again and again that whenever mankind interferes with a less developed civilization, no matter how well intentioned that interference may be, the results are invariably disastrous."
—Picard to Beverly
TNG/ "Symbiosis"

"You see the Prime Directive has many different functions. Not the least of which is to protect us. To prevent us from allowing our emotions to overwhelm our judgment."
—Picard to Pulaski
TNG / "Pen Pals"

"Of course you know of the Prime Directive, which tells us that we have no right to interfere in the natural evolution of alien worlds. Now I have sworn to uphold it, but nevertheless I have disregarded that directive on more than one occasion...because I thought it was the right thing to do."
—Picard to Berlinghoff Rasmussen
TNG / "A Matter of Time"

"But perhaps next time you are judged unfairly, it will not take so many bruises for you to protest."
—Worf to Sito Jaxa, on being tested
TNG / "Lower Decks"

"If you didn't want me on your ship you should have said so when I was assigned to it. It's not your place to punish me for what I did at the academy. I've worked hard here. My record is exemplary. If you're going to judge me, judge me for what I am *now*."
—Sito to Picard
TNG / "Lower Decks"

"Commander, laws change depending on who's making them...Cardassians one day, Federation the next...but *justice*...is justice...."
—Odo to Sisko
DS9 / "A Man Alone"

"Justice. Really? *Is* it justice you're after...or just some way to express your anger? Your fear. Look at yourselves...in an hour, you'll regret what you tried to do here. Do not condemn this man because he is different than you are...."
—Sisko to mob, on attacking Odo
DS9 / "A Man Alone"

"You already know if you punish him without reason, it won't mean anything. And you already know vengeance isn't enough."
—Dax to Kira, on Aamin Marritza, a suspected war criminal
DS9 / "Duet"

"Cardassian rules, Bajoran rules, Federation rules…they're all meaningless to you…because you have a personal code that's always mattered more…and I'm sorry to say you're in slim company.…"

—Odo to Kira
DS9 / "The Circle"

"Stupidity is no excuse."

—Zek to Quark, on the law
DS9 / "Rules of Acquisition"

"There's no room in Justice for loyalty or friendship or love.…Justice, as the humans like to say, is blind."

—Odo's log
DS9 / "Necessary Evil"

"It's an interesting system of justice you have, Captain. It does have its flaws, however. It emphasizes procedure over substance…form over fact."

—Ch'Pok to Sisko
DS9 / "Rules of Engagement"

"There is more to life than…the rule of law."

—Odo to Thrax
DS9 / "Things Past"

"I think you can't judge people by what they think or say…only by what they do."

—Kira to Ziyal
DS9 / "By Inferno's Light"

"…You function as judge, jury, and executioner. And I think that's too much power for anyone."

—Bashir to Sloan, on Section Thirty-one
DS9 / "Inquisition"

"How many times have we been in the position of refusing to interfere when some kind of disaster threatened an alien culture? It's all very well to say we do it on the basis of an enlightened principle...but how does it feel to the aliens? I'm sure many of them think the Prime Directive is a lousy idea."

—Janeway to Paris; the tables are turned, and a technogically superior race is refusing to help *Voyager*
DS9 / "Prime Factors"

"I thought Starfleet rules said that was an unacceptable risk...going back to save him."
    "It was. However, I recently realized that there are times...when it is desirable to—bend the rules."

—Kenneth Dalby and Tuvok, on Gerron
VGR / "Learning Curve"

"And you find nothing contradictory in a society that outlaws suicide but practices capital punishment?..."

—Tuvok to Q
VGR / "Death Wish"

"In a part of space where there are few rules, it's more important than ever that we hold fast to our own. In a region where shifting allegiances are commonplace, we have to have something stable to rely on. And we do—the principles and ideals of the Federation. As far as I'm concerned, those are the best allies we could have."

—Janeway to senior staff
VGR / "Alliances"

"Your brig...it's a puzzling concept—shutting someone away as punishment. Do you find that it rehabilitates the prisoner?"

—Nimira to Tuvok
VGR / "Random Thoughts"

"You know the rules, Tom. We can't pick and choose which laws we'll respect and which we won't...."

—Janeway to Paris
VGR / "Random Thoughts"

18. Peace and War

"First, study the enemy, seek weakness."
—Romulan commander to centurion
TOS / "Balance of Terror"

"Our gift to the homeland…another war."
    "If we are the strong, is this not the signal for war?"
"Must it always be so? How many comrades have we lost in this way?"
—Romulan commander and centurion
TOS/ "Balance of Terror"

"You're discussing tactics. Do you realize what this really comes down to? Millions and millions of lives hanging on what this vessel does next."
    "Or on what this vessel fails to do, Doctor."
—McCoy and Spock, on the ramifications of fighting the Romulans
TOS / "Balance of Terror"

"War is never imperative, Mister Spock."
—McCoy to Spock, on fighting the Romulans
TOS / "Balance of Terror"

"I regret that we meet in this way.…You and I are of a kind. In a different reality, I could've called you 'friend.'"
—Romulan commander to Kirk, on being political enemies
TOS/ "Balance of Terror"

"You've been beaten!"

"But I'm not defeated...."

—Trelane and Kirk, on a deadly game of tag
TOS / "The Squire of Gothos"

"Death...destruction, disease, horror. That's what war is all about, Anan. That's what makes it a thing to be avoided. You've made it neat and painless. So neat and painless you've had no reason to stop it."

—Kirk to Anan, on computer-fought war in a society where "casualties" report in for their deaths
TOS / "A Taste of Armageddon"

"There can be no peace. Don't you see, we've admitted it to ourselves. We're a killer species, it's instinctive. It's the same with you—your General Order Twenty-four!"

"All right, it's instinctive. But the instinct can be fought. We're human beings with the blood of a million savage years on our hands. But we can stop it. We can admit that we're killers but we're not going to kill today. That's all it takes—knowing that we're not going to kill...*today*. Contact Vendikar. I think you'll find that they're just as terrified, appalled, horrified as you are, that they'll do anything to avoid the alternative I've given you. Peace or utter destruction—it's up to you."

—Anan and Kirk
TOS / "A Taste of Armageddon"

"You are an excellent tactician, Captain. You let your second in command attack, while you sit and watch for weakness."

"You have a tendency to express ideas in military terms, Mister Khan. This is a social occasion."

"It has been said that social occasions are only warfare concealed. Many prefer it more honest, more open."

—Khan and Kirk
TOS / "Space Seed"

"Well, there it is. War. We didn't want it. But we've got it."
　　"Curious how often you humans manage to obtain that which you do not want."

—Kirk and Spock
TOS / "Errand of Mercy"

"Today we conquer. Though if someday we are defeated…well, war has its fortunes, good and bad."

—Kor to Spock
TOS / "Errand of Mercy"

"We have the right…"
　　"To wage war, Captain? To kill millions of innocent people? To destroy life on a planetary scale? Is that what you're defending?"

—Kirk and Ayelborne, on the impending conflict between the Federation and the Klingon Empire
TOS / "Errand of Mercy"

"I think that one day they're going to take all the money that they spend now on war and death…"
　　"And make them spend it on life.…"

—Edith and Kirk
TOS / "The City on the Edge of Forever"

"We cannot make peace with…with people we detest."
　　"Stop trying to kill each other, then worry about being friendly."

—Petri and Kirk, on relations between Troyians and Elasians
TOS / "Elaan of Troyius"

"Military secrets are the most fleeting of all."

—Spock to Romulan commander
TOS / "The *Enterprise* Incident"

"The best defense is a strong offense. And I intend to start offending right now."

—Kirk to Spock
TOS / "The Empath"

"We have always fought. We must. We are hunters, Captain, tracking and taking what we need. There are poor planets in the Klingon systems. We must push outward if we are to survive."
    "There's another way to survive. Mutual trust and help."

—Mara and Kirk
TOS / "Day of the Dove"

"Those who hate and fight must stop themselves, Doctor. Otherwise it is not stopped."

—Spock to McCoy
TOS / "Day of the Dove"

"Only a fool fights in a burning house."

—Kang to alien entity
TOS / "Day of the Dove"

"No one talks peace unless he's ready to back it up with war."
    "He talks peace if it is the only way to live."

—Colonel Green and Surak
TOS / "The Savage Curtain"

"Your Surak is a brave man."
    "Men of peace usually are, Captain."

—Spock and Kirk
TOS / "The Savage Curtain"

"There's no honorable way to kill, no gentle way to destroy; there is nothing good in war except its ending."

—Abraham Lincoln to Kirk
TOS / "The Savage Curtain"

"Ah, Kirk, my old friend, do you know the Klingon proverb that tells us revenge is a dish that is best served cold? It is very cold in space."

—Khan to Kirk
The Wrath of Khan

"Now, now, Captain, there's no need to mince words: in space all warriors are cold warriors."

—General Chang to Kirk
The Undiscovered Country

"I say *fight*, sir. There is nothing shameful in falling before a superior enemy."

"And nothing shameful in a strategic retreat, either."

—Worf and Picard
TNG / "The Last Outpost"

"Sometimes, Riker, the best way to fight is not to be there."

"Yes, sir. 'He will triumph who knows when to fight and when not to fight.'"

—Picard and Riker
Source: Sun Tzu, *The Art of War*
TNG / "The Last Outpost"

"Cowards take hostages—Klingons do not."

—Worf to Tasha
TNG / "Heart of Glory"

"The true test of the warrior is not without—it is within."

—Worf to Captain Korris
TNG / "Heart of Glory"

"Yet in all you say, where are the words... *duty*... *honor*... *loyalty*—without which a warrior is *nothing*."

—Worf to Korris
TNG/ "Heart of Glory"

"I would rather outthink them than outfight them."

—Picard to command staff, on the Romulans
TNG / "The Neutral Zone"

"The victors invariably write the history to their own advantage."

—Picard to Worf
TNG / "Contagion"

"The man I was is still inside me...but this conditioning has been imposed...woven together with my thoughts and my feelings and my responses. How do you separate the program from the man?"

—Roga Danar to Data, on being trained as a soldier, "programmed" to kill
TNG / "The Hunted"

"You are dangerous. They're only victims. You made them what they are. You asked them to defend your way of life…and then you discarded them."
—Picard to Nayrok, on the treatment of military prisoners who are their veterans of war
TNG / "The Hunted"

"The difference between generals and terrorists, Doctor, is only the difference between winners and losers. You win, you're called a general. You lose…."
—Finn to Beverly
TNG / "The High Ground"

"He could have killed you. He didn't. Maybe the end begins with one boy putting down his gun."
—Riker to Alexana Devos
TNG / "The High Ground"

"It's not you I hate, Cardassian. I hate what I became…because of you."
—O'Brien to Glinn Daro, on O'Brien being forced to kill in the war against the Cardassians
TNG / "The Wounded"

"I have been told…that patience is sometimes a more effective weapon than the sword."
—Worf to Picard
TNG / "Redemption"

"The trouble with wolves is that sometimes in the fight for dominance one of them ends up dead."
    "In that case the trick is…to be the wolf that's still standing at the end."
—Troi and Captain Edward Jellico, on comparing the Cardassians to wolves
TNG / "Chain of Command, Part I"

"People blame the military for the wars that we are asked to fight."
—Commander Toreth to Troi
TNG / "Face of the Enemy"

"In order to defeat your enemy, you must first understand them."
—Troi to Toreth
TNG / "Face of the Enemy"

"Size is not the most important thing....Skill...cunning...powers of observation are the most important weapons."
—K'mtar to Alexander
TNG / "Firstborn"

"When an old fighter like me dies...someone always steps forward to take his place...."
—Macias to Ro
TNG / "Preemptive Strike"

"I will *not* sacrifice the *Enterprise*. We've made too many compromises already, too many retreats! They invade our space and we fall back—they assimilate *entire worlds* and we fall back! Not again! The line must be drawn *here*—this far, no further! And I will make them *pay* for what they've done!"
—Picard to Lily, on the Borg
First Contact

"Danar, in war, both sides commit atrocities...."
—Sisko to Gul Danar
DS9 / "Past Prologue"

"When you cease to fear death, the rules of war change."
—Shel-La to Kira
DS9 / "Battle Lines"

"Nothing justifies genocide."
—Kira to Marritza
DS9 / "Duet"

"'So honor the valiant who die 'neath your sword...'"
   "'But pity the warrior who slays all his foes.'"
—Seyetik and Sisko quoting "The Fall of Kang" by the Klingon poet G'trok
DS9 / "Second Sight"

"The splendor of fighting and killing; a bloodbath in the cause of vengeance; who *wouldn't* want to come?"

—Kor to Dax on the upcoming attack on an enemy
DS9 / "Blood Oath"

"A sharp knife is nothing without a sharp eye."

—Koloth to Kor
DS9 / "Blood Oath"

"Oh, anyone can blow up a ship. Ha. But to look your enemy in the eye…knowing you'll remember his face for the rest of your life….Now that takes a stomach much stronger than you'll ever have."

—Dukat to Amaros
DS9 / "The Maquis, Part II"

"You're trying to be a hero…terrorists don't get to be heroes."

—Kira to Thomas Riker
DS9 / "Defiant"

"The Prophets teach us that while violence may keep an enemy at bay…only peace can make him a friend."

—Winn to Sisko on peace with Cardassia
DS9 / "Life Support"

"Kahless himself said, 'Destroying an empire to win a war is no victory.'"
"'And ending a battle to save an empire is no defeat.'"

—Worf and Gowron
DS9 / "The Way of the Warrior, Part II"

"The best way to survive a knife fight is to never get in one."

—Kira to Ziyal
DS9 / "Return to Grace"

"Fighting hit and run, always outgunned, living on hate and adrenaline. It's not much of a life, and it eats away at you so that every day a little bit of you dies."

—Kira to Dukat
DS9 / "Return to Grace"

"I could never make them understand violence is a precision instrument. It's a scalpel, not a club."
—Intendant to Sisko
DS9 / "Shattered Mirror"

"They'll never succeed as long as they value their lives more than victory."
—Omet'iklan to Weyoun, on the Federation personnel
DS9 / "To the Death"

"Some people say that you don't know what you're really made of until you've been in battle...."
    "Well, let me tell you Jake, there are many situations in life which test a person's character—thankfully, most of them don't involve death and destruction...."
—Jake and Bashir
DS9 / "Nor the Battle to the Strong"

"I've been on the station when it was under attack plenty of times...but somehow the danger never seemed as real as it does here. Maybe it's because I spent all day seeing first-hand what the Klingons are capable of...or maybe it's because for the first time in my life, my father's not here to protect me."
—Jake's journal
DS9 / "Nor the Battle to the Strong"

"They kill us....We kill them. It's nothing worth celebrating."
—Kira to Furel, on the Cardassians
DS9 / "Ties of Blood and Water"

"A man shouldn't allow his enemies to outlive him."
—Tain to Garak
DS9 / "In Purgatory's Shadow"

"If you can't have victory, sometimes you just have to settle for revenge."
—Michael Eddington to Sisko
DS9 / "Blaze of Glory"

"You don't wait for the enemy to come to you—you go to him."
—O'Brien to Nog
DS9 / "Empok Nor"

"We used to have a saying in the Resistance: if you're not fighting them, you're helping them."
—Kira to Odo
DS9 / "Rocks and Shoals"

"Do you really want to give up your life for 'the order of things'?"
    "It is not my life to give up, Captain. And it never was."
—Sisko and Remata'Klan, on the life of a Jem'Hadar soldier
DS9 / "Rocks and Shoals"

"I tell you, Worf, war is much more fun when you're winning. Defeat makes my wounds ache."
—Martok to Worf
DS9 / "Sons and Daughters"

"Because a true victory is to make your enemy see they were wrong to oppose you in the first place. To force them to acknowledge your greatness."
—Dukat to Weyoun
DS9 / "The Sacrifice of Angels"

"One ship against an entire fleet…that's a helluva plan B."
—Dax to Sisko
DS9 / "The Sacrifice of Angels"

"That's why you came to me, isn't it, Captain? Because you knew I could do those things that you weren't capable of doing? Well, it worked. And you'll get what you want—a war between the Romulans and the Dominion. And if your conscience is bothering you, you should soothe it with the knowledge that you may have just saved the entire Alpha Quadrant. And all it cost was the life of one Romulan senator, one criminal, and the self-respect of one Starfleet officer. I don't know about you, but I'd call that a bargain."
—Garak to Sisko
DS9 / "In the Pale Moonlight"

"I lied. I cheated. I bribed men to cover the crimes of other men. I am an accessory to murder. But the most damning thing of all...I think I can live with it. And if I had to do it all over again...I would. Garak was right about one thing—a guilty conscience is a small price to pay for the safety of the Alpha Quadrant."

—Sisko's log, on manipulating the Romulans into entering the war against the Dominion
DS9 / "In the Pale Moonlight"

"But this war is different. Maybe I'm different. I have this...growing sense of isolation....I see people, I talk to them, I laugh with them, but...some part of me is always saying, 'They may not be here tomorrow. Don't get too close....'"

—O'Brien to Lisa
DS9 / "The Sound of Her Voice"

"I'm simply a scientist. Yes, I developed the weapon. But it was the government, and the military leaders, who decided to use it. Not I."

"That must be a very convenient distinction for you. Does it help you sleep at night?"

—Jetrel and Neelix
VGR / "Jetrel"

"The strongest tactical move is always the one in which you will reap the highest gain at the lowest cost. 'Going out with phasers firing' may seem heroic, but in the long run it is merely foolish. Retreat is often the best possible option."

—Tuvok to Dalby
VGR / "Learning Curve"

"War can be an engine of change. War can transform a society for the better. Your own Civil War brought about an end to slavery and oppression."

—Q to Janeway
VGR / "The Q and the Grey"

"In any covert battle...logic is a potent weapon. You might try it sometime."

—Tuvok to Neelix
VGR / "The Killing Game, Part I"

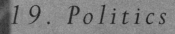

19. Politics

"He has friends. And friends of his kind mean power. And power is danger."

— Centurion to Romulan commander, on upsetting Decius
TOS / "Balance of Terror"

"Conquest is easy. Control is not."

—Kirk to the mirror Spock
TOS / "Mirror, Mirror"

"If change is inevitable, predictable, beneficial...doesn't logic *demand* that you be a part of it?"

—Kirk to the mirror Spock
TOS / "Mirror, Mirror"

"You're somewhat different than the way history paints you, Colonel Green."

"History tends to exaggerate."

—Kirk and Green
TOS / "The Savage Curtain"

"There's an old Vulcan proverb: only Nixon could go to China."

—Spock to Kirk
The Undiscovered Country

"What do you know of conspiracies, Captain?"

"Not nearly enough I suppose."

"That's the charming thing about them, isn't it? When a machination is real, *no one knows about it*. And when it's suspected, it's almost never real."

—Admiral Aaron and Picard
TNG / "Conspiracy"

"I have never subscribed to the theory that political power flows from the barrel of a gun...."

—Picard to Data
TNG / "The High Ground"

"You are innocent bystanders, and I cannot condone violence against those who are not our enemies."

—Keeve Falor to Picard
TNG / "Ensign Ro"

"How convenient that must be for you. To turn a deaf ear to those who suffer behind a line on a map."

—Keeve to Picard on Picard's justification of noninterference because Bajor is not part of the Federation
TNG / "Ensign Ro"

"We live in different universes, you and I. Yours is about diplomacy, politics, strategy. Mine is about blankets. If we were to exchange places for one night, you might better understand."

—Keeve to Picard
TNG / "Ensign Ro"

"Every member of the Federation entered as a unified world...and that unity said something about them...that they had resolved certain social and political differences and they were now ready to become part of a larger community."

—Picard to Beverly on the divided Kesprytt world
TNG / "Attached"

"You don't *grab* power. You accumulate it...quietly...without anyone noticing."

—Zek to Krax
DS9 / "The Nagus"

"If you want to change the government, Minister Jaro, you *vote* to change it. You don't sneak up from behind it with a dagger."
—Kira to Minister Jaro
DS9 / "The Circle"

"The Federation believes that it can solve every problem with a treaty. But out here, on the frontier, without the power of the Federation to back them up, a treaty is only a piece of paper."
—Cal Hudson to Sisko, on the Demilitarized Zone
DS9 / "The Maquis, Part II"

"On Earth there is no poverty, no crime, no war. You look out the window of Starfleet headquarters and you see…Paradise. Well, it's easy to be a saint in Paradise. But the Maquis do not live in Paradise. Out there in the Demilitarized Zone, all the problems haven't been solved yet. Out there, there are no saints…just people. Angry, scared, determined people who are going to do whatever it takes to survive. Whether it meets with Federation approval or not."
—Sisko to Kira
DS9 / "The Maquis, Part II"

"You know, I've been a soldier and I've been a politician…and I have to say, I'm beginning to think that being a soldier was easier."
—Shakaar to Odo
DS9 / "Crossfire"

"Who are we to swoop in, play god, and then continue on our way without the slightest consideration of the long-term effects of our actions?"
—Janeway to Torres, on affecting the balance of power in the Delta Quadrant
VGR / "Prototype"

"I was the greatest threat the Continuum had ever known. They feared me so much they had to lock me away for eternity. And when they did that, they were saying that the individual's rights will be protected only so long as they don't conflict with the state. Nothing is so dangerous to a society."
—Quinn to Janeway
VGR / "Death Wish"

20. Freedom

"There's a way out of any cage, and I'll find it."
—Pike to Talosians
TOS / "The Cage"

"It's wrong to create a whole race of humans to live as slaves."
—Number One to the Keeper
TOS / "The Cage"

"We had not believed this possible. The customs and history of your race show a unique hatred of captivity. Even when it's pleasant and benevolent, you prefer death."
—the Keeper to Pike
TOS / "The Cage"

"You said you wanted freedom. It's time you learned that freedom is never a gift. It has to be earned."
—Kirk to Marphon
TOS / "The Return of the Archons"

"Without freedom of choice, there is no creativity. Without creativity, there is no life."
—Kirk to Landru
TOS / "The Return of the Archons"

"Companion, try to understand…it is the nature of our species to be free. Just as it is your nature to stay here. We will…cease to exist in captivity."

—Kirk to Companion
TOS / "Metamorphosis"

"There's certain absolutes, Mister Spock, and one of them is the right of humanoids to a free and unchained environment. The right to have conditions which permit growth."

"Another is their right to choose a system which seems to work for them."

—McCoy and Spock
TOS / "The Apple"

"This was not written for chiefs. Hear me. Hear this. Among my people we carry many such words as this from many lands, many worlds. Many are equally good and are as well respected. But wherever we have gone no words have said this…thing of importance in quite this way. Look at these three words written larger than the rest with a special pride never written before or since. Tall words, proudly saying, 'We the people.…' That which you call '*E Plebnista*' was not written for the chiefs or kings or the warriors or the rich or the powerful but for *all* the people. Down the centuries, you have slurred the meaning of the words, 'We the People of the United States, in order to form a more perfect union, establish justice, insure domestic tranquillity, provide for the common defense, promote the general welfare and secure the blessings of liberty to ourselves and our posterity do ordain and establish this Constitution…' These words and the words that follow were not written only for the Yangs, but for the Kohms as well.…"

"For the Kohms?"

"They must apply to *everyone* or they mean nothing! Do you understand?"

—Kirk and Cloud William. "Yangs" and "Kohms", descendants of yankees and communists on an alternate Earth, rediscover the essence of a lost ideology.
Source: "The Preamble to the Constitution of the United States"
TOS / "The Omega Glory"

"We merely showed them the *meaning* of what they were fighting for. Liberty and freedom have to be more than just words."
—Kirk to Spock, on "interfering" with the Yangs
TOS / "The Omega Glory"

"A species that enslaves other beings is hardly superior, mentally or otherwise."
—Kirk to the Providers
TOS / "The Gamesters of Triskelion"

"*No* being is so important that he can usurp the rights of another."
—Picard to Data/Graves, on Data
TNG / "The Schizoid Man"

"Well, consider that in the history of many worlds there have always been disposable creatures. They do the dirty work. They do the work that no one else wants to do because it's too difficult or too hazardous. And an army of Datas…all disposable. You don't have to think about their welfare, you don't think about how they feel. Whole generations of disposable people."
—Guinan to Picard on determining if the android Data is a person or property
TNG / "The Measure of a Man"

"The decision you reach here today will determine how we will regard this creation of our genius. It will reveal the kind of a people *we* are. And what…he is destined to be. It will reach far beyond this courtroom and this one android. It could significantly redefine the boundaries of personal liberty and freedom. Expanding them for some, savagely curtailing them for others. Are you prepared to condemn him and all who come after him to servitude and slavery? Your honor, Starfleet was founded to seek out new life. Well, there it sits, waiting. You wanted a chance to make law. Well, here it is. Make it a good one."
—Picard to Phillipa, on determining if the android Data is person or property
TNG / "The Measure of a Man"

"It sits there looking at me, and I don't know what it is. This case has dealt with metaphysics, with questions best left to saints and philosophers. I'm neither competent nor qualified to answer those. But I've got to make a ruling, to try to speak to the future. Is Data a machine? Yes. Is he the property of Starfleet? No. We have all been dancing around the basic issue—does Data have a soul? I don't know that he has. I don't know that I have. But I have got to give him the freedom to explore that question himself. It is the ruling of this court that Lieutenant Commander Data has the freedom to choose."
—Phillipa
TNG / "The Measure of a Man"

"How much innocent blood has been spilled for the cause of freedom in the history of your Federation, Doctor? How many good and noble societies have bombed civilians in war? Have wiped out whole cities. And now that you enjoy the comfort that has come from their battles, their killing…you frown on my immorality…? I am willing to die for my freedom, Doctor. And, in the finest tradition of your own great civilization, I'm willing to kill for it too."
—Kyril Finn to Beverly
TNG / "The High Ground"

"Imprisonment *is* an injury, regardless of how you justify it."
—Picard to alien
TNG / "Allegiance"

"'With the first link, the chain is forged. The first speech censured, the first thought forbidden, the first freedom denied—chains us all, irrevocably.' Those words were uttered by Judge Aaron Satie—as wisdom and warning. The first time any man's freedom is trodden on…we are all damaged."
—Picard to Admiral Norah Satie
TNG / "The Drumhead"

"It has been my observation that one of the prices of giving people freedom of choice…is that sometimes they make the wrong choice."
—Odo to Kira
DS9 / "Shakaar"

"You have imprisoned us in the name of humanity…yet you will not grant us your most cherished human right. To choose our own fate. You are hypocritical…manipulative. We do not want to be what you are."
—Seven of Nine to Janeway
VGR / "The Gift"

"You lost the capacity to make a rational choice the moment you were assimilated. They took that from you. And until I'm convinced you've gotten it back…I'm making the choice for you. You're staying here."
"Then you are no different than the Borg."
—Janeway and Seven of Nine, on Janeway's unilateral decision to free Seven from the Borg
VGR / "The Gift"

"When are we *not* in prison? When are our lives free from the influence of those who have more power than us?"
—Leonardo hologram to Janeway
VGR / "Concerning Flight"

"Here I am free to do what I wish…free from judgment…free to *fail*. Without a sense of shame…without…without the taunts of the ignorant."
—Leonardo hologram to Janeway, on being away from his homeland and his own reputation
VGR / "Concerning Flight"

"I believe that you are punishing me because I do not think the way that you do…because I am not becoming more like you. You claim to respect my individuality…when in fact you are frightened by it."
—Seven of Nine to Janeway
VGR / "Prey"

21. *Leadership*

"Chris, you set standards for yourself no one could meet. You treat everyone on board like a human being, except yourself."

—Boyce to Pike
TOS / "The Cage"

"Command and compassion is a fool's mixture."

—Mitchell to Kirk
TOS / "Where No Man Has Gone Before"

"You'll find out that ships' captains are already married, girl, to their vessels. You'd find out the first time you came between him and the ship."

—Mudd to Eve
TOS / "Mudd's Women"

"You're the captain of this ship. You haven't the right to be vulnerable in the eyes of the crew. You can't afford the luxury of being anything less than perfect. If you do, they lose faith and you lose command."

—Spock to Kirk
TOS / "The Enemy Within"

"And what is it that makes one man an exceptional leader? We see here indications that it is his negative side which makes him strong. That his 'evil side,' if you will, properly controlled and disciplined, is vital to his strength. Your negative side, removed from you, the power of command begins to elude you."

—Spock to Kirk. After a transporter malfunction, Kirk is split into two, one good, one evil
TOS / "The Enemy Within"

"You've never voiced it, but you've always thought that logic was the best basis on which to build command."

—McCoy to Spock
TOS / "The Galileo Seven"

"Not one man in a million could do what you and I have done…command a starship. A hundred decisions a day—hundreds of lives staked on you making every one of them right."

—Stone to Kirk
TOS / "Court Martial"

"R.H.I.P., Captain. Rank hath its privileges."

—Commodore José Mendez to Kirk
TOS / "The Menagerie"

"You've got your problems. I've got mine. But he's got ours, plus his, plus four hundred and thirty other people."

—McCoy to Sulu on Kirk
TOS / "Shore Leave"

"A statement Lucifer made when he fell into the pit: 'It is better to rule in Hell than serve in Heaven.'"

—Kirk to Scott, paraphrasing Milton as a way of explaining Khan's choice of exile
Source: John Milton, "Paradise Lost"
TOS / "Space Seed"

"To blazes with regulations! You can't let him take command when you know he's wrong!"

—McCoy to Spock on Decker
TOS / "The Doomsday Machine"

"One man cannot summon the future."

"But one man can change the present."

—the mirror Spock and Kirk
TOS / "Mirror, Mirror"

"In every revolution, there's one man with a vision...."

—Kirk to the mirror Spock
TOS / "Mirror, Mirror"

"Mister Spock, a starship can function with a chief engineer, a chief medical officer, even a first officer under physical par. But it's disastrous to have a commanding officer whose condition is any less than perfection."

—Commodore Stocker to Spock
TOS / "The Deadly Years"

"Command requirements do not recognize personal privilege."

—Spock to McCoy
TOS / "Journey to Babel"

"Have I the right to jeopardize my crew, my ship, for a feeling I can't even put into words? No man achieves Starfleet command without relying on intuition, but have I made a rational decision? Am I letting the horrors of the past distort my judgment of the present?"

—Kirk's log
TOS / "Obsession"

"Intuition, however illogical, Mister Spock, is recognized as a command prerogative."

—Kirk to Spock
TOS / "Obsession"

"I think we're somewhat alike, Captain. Each of us cares less for his own safety than for the lives of his command. We feel pain when others suffer for our mistakes."

—Rojan to Kirk
TOS / "By Any Other Name"

"If I can accomplish my mission by turning tail and running, I'll gladly do that."

—Kirk to Elaan on why he did not attack the Klingon ship
TOS / "Elaan of Troyius"

"I can offer only one small piece of advice, for whatever it's worth: use every scrap of knowledge and logic you have to save the ship, but temper your judgment with intuitive insight. I believe you have those qualities, but if you can't find them in yourself, seek out McCoy. Ask his advice and if you find it sound, take it."

—Kirk to Spock, speaking from prerecorded orders
TOS / "The Tholian Web"

"Help him if you can, but remember he is the captain; his decisions must be followed without question. You might find that he is capable of human insight and human error. They are most difficult to defend. But you will find that he is deserving of the same loyalty and confidence each of you have given me."

—Kirk to McCoy on helping Spock in his command decisions in case of Kirk's death
TOS / "The Tholian Web"

"A no-win situation is a possibility every commander may face."

—Kirk to Saavik
The Wrath of Khan

"If I may be so bold, it was a mistake for you to accept promotion. Commanding a starship is your first, best destiny. Anything else is a waste of material."

—Spock to Kirk
The Wrath of Khan

"I see. A captain's rank means nothing to you."
  "Rather the reverse, sir. But a captain's *life* means a great deal more to me."

—Picard and Riker, on overriding a captain's authority to keep him out of harm's way
TNG / "Encounter at Farpoint"

"For a ship and crew to function well it always starts with the captain. You set the tone."
—Minuet to Picard
TNG / "11001001"

"Just remember it's *you* they draw strength from. They look to you for guidance…and for leadership. Help them. Show confidence in them."
—Troi to La Forge, on inspiring his nervous crew
TNG / "The Arsenal of Freedom"

"One of your strengths is your ability to evaluate the dynamics of a situation, and then take a definitive, preemptive step, take charge. Now you're frustrated because, you not only can't see the solution…you can't even define the problem."
—Riker to Picard
TNG / "Time Squared"

"As the first officer of the *Enterprise* you have a position of distinction, prestige, even glamour, of a sort. You are the second in command of Starfleet's flagship. But still, second in command. Your promotion will transfer you to a relatively insignificant ship in an obscure corner of the galaxy. But it will be your ship. And, being who you are, it will soon be vibrant with your authority, your style, your vision. You know, there really is no substitute for holding the reins."
—Picard to Riker
TNG / "The Icarus Factor"

"Leadership grows from self-confidence, which is also part of a Starfleet officer's education."
  "All of this is true, but there is an old horse trainer's adage about putting too much weight on a young back—we don't want him to break under pressure."
—Troi and Picard, on deciding how big an assignment to give Wesley
TNG / "Pen Pals"

"…I respect an officer who is prepared to admit ignorance and ask a question rather than one who, out of pride, will blunder blindly forward."
—Picard to Wesley
TNG / "Pen Pals"

"Wes, there's being thorough, and then there's wasting time. It's also the mark of a good officer to recognize the difference."
—Ensign Davies to Wesley
TNG / "Pen Pals"

"Every time I try to give an order, something inside of me says what makes my judgment so superior to these people?"

"Wes, responsibility and authority go hand in hand. Now I know you're responsible, now we're going to teach you a little bit of authority. One of the reasons you've been given command is so you can make a few right decisions which will lead to a pattern of success and help build self-confidence. If you don't trust your own judgment, you don't belong in the command chair."
—Wesley and Riker
TNG / "Pen Pals"

"But what if I'm wrong?"

"Then you're wrong. It's arrogant to think that you'll never make a mistake."
—Wesley and Riker, on command
TNG / "Pen Pals"

"In *your* position it's important to ask yourself one question: what would Picard do?"

"He'd listen to everyone's opinion and then make his own decision."
—Riker and Wesley, on command
TNG / "Pen Pals"

"How did you like command?"

"Comfortable chair."
—Riker and Worf
TNG / "The Emissary"

"His work record is exemplary, but as you know, a starship captain is not manufactured—he, or she, is born from inside—from the character of the individual."
—Sirna Kolrami to Picard, on Riker
TNG / "Peak Performance"

"The test is whether the crew will follow where Commander Riker leads. His joviality is the means by which he creates that loyalty. And I will match his command style with your statistics anytime."
—Picard to Kolrami, on Riker
TNG / "Peak Performance"

"Knowing your own limitations is one thing. Advertising them to a crew can damage your credibility as a leader."
    "Because you will lose their confidence?"
        "And because you may begin to believe in those limitations yourself."
—Picard, Data, and Beverly
TNG / "The Ensigns of Command"

"He wants the impossible."
    "That's the short definition of 'captain.'"
—Wesley and La Forge, on Picard
TNG / "The Ensigns of Command"

"Lieutenant, sometimes the moral obligations of command are less than clear. I have to weigh the good of the many against the needs of the individual...and try to balance them as realistically as possible. God knows I don't always succeed."
—Picard to Worf
TNG / "The Enemy"

"Listen to what Shakespeare is telling you about the man, Data...a king who had true feeling for his soldiers would wish to share their fears with them on the eve of battle."
—Picard to Data, on *Henry V*
TNG / "The Defector"

"I'm not good in groups....It's difficult to work in a group when you're omnipotent...."
—Q to Data
TNG / "Déjà Q"

"Gentlemen, I have the utmost confidence in your ability to perform the impossible."
—Picard to La Forge, Wesley, and Data
TNG / "Ménage à Troi"

"I always said I wanted my own command. And yet something's holding me back. Is it wrong for me to want to stay...?"

—Riker to Troi, on continuing to turn down offers to captain his own ship in order to stay on the *Enterprise*
TNG / "The Best of Both Worlds, Part I"

"When it comes to this ship, and this crew, you're damned right I play it safe."

—Riker to Lieutenant Commander Shelby
TNG / "The Best of Both Worlds, Part I"

"If you can't make the big decisions, Commander, I suggest you make room for someone who can."

—Shelby to Riker
TNG / "The Best of Both Worlds, Part I"

"I will have to say...this morning, I was the leader of the universe as I knew it....This afternoon, I am only a voice in a chorus. But I think it was a good day."

—Chancellor Avel Durken to Picard, on telling his family of first contact with an alien species—humanity
TNG / "First Contact"

"Starfleet captains are like children. They want everything right now and they want it their way...but the secret is to give them only what they need, not what they want."

—Scott to La Forge
TNG / "Relics"

"The first vessel that I served on as captain was called the *Stargazer*....It was an overworked, underpowered vessel always on the verge of flying apart at the seams. In every measurable sense, my *Enterprise* is far superior. But there are times when I would give almost anything to command the *Stargazer* again."

—Picard to Scott
TNG / "Relics"

"You see, I've always believed that becoming involved with someone under my command would compromise my objectivity."

—Picard to Troi
TNG / "Lessons"

"You know, when you're a doctor and you have patients, you're in control. But when you send somebody out on a mission, all you can do is sit and watch."
—Guinan to Beverly
TNG / "Suspicions"

"Do not forget that a leader need not answer questions of those he leads. It is enough that he says to do a thing and they will do it. If he says to run, they run. If he says to fight, they fight. If he says to die, they die."
—the clone of Kahless to Worf, on leading Klingons
TNG / "Rightful Heir"

"Real power comes from within the heart."
—Worf to Gowron
TNG / "Rightful Heir"

"Kahless left us—all of us—a powerful legacy...a way of thinking and acting that makes us Klingon. If his words hold wisdom and his philosophy is honorable...what does it matter if he returns? What is important is that we follow his teachings... perhaps the words are more important than the man."
—the clone of Kahless to Worf
TNG / "Rightful Heir"

"I mean you're acting like you know exactly which way to go...but you're only guessing. Do you do this all the time?"
—Beverly to Picard
TNG / "Attached"

"...There are times when it is necessary for a captain to give the appearance of confidence."
—Picard to Beverly
TNG / "Attached"

"I wanted someone who would stand up to me...someone who was more concerned with the safety of the ship and accomplishing the mission than with how it might look on his record. To me, that's one of the marks of a good officer."
—Picard to Admiral Erik Pressman, on Riker
TNG / "The Pegasus"

"Frankly, I've always felt it was more important for an officer to trust his captain's judgment. In a crisis, there's no time for explanations....Orders have to be obeyed without question or lives may be lost."

—Pressman to Picard
TNG / "The Pegasus"

"You did exactly what you had to do. You considered all your options. You tried every alternative…and then you made the hard choice."

—Riker to Troi, on passing the test for command by being willing to order a crew member into a deadly situation to save the ship
TNG / "Thine Own Self"

"Don't let them promote you…don't let them transfer you…don't let them do anything that takes you off the bridge of that ship....Because while you're there…you can *make a difference*."

—Kirk to Picard
Generations

"I always thought I'd get a shot at this chair one day."
    "Perhaps you still will....Somehow, I doubt that this will be the last ship to carry the name *Enterprise*."

—Riker and Picard, on the destroyed *Enterprise*-D
Generations

"The crew is accustomed to following my orders."
    "They're probably accustomed to your orders making sense."

—Picard and Lily, on ordering the crew to fight the Borg against overwhelming odds
First Contact

"You don't lose by saying no."
    "Maybe. But a great leader…like your father…is one who's willing to risk saying yes."

—Varis Sul and Benjamin Sisko, on compromise
DS9 / "The Storyteller"

"But if you pull a stunt like that again, I'll court-martial you…or I'll promote you. Either way, you'll be in a lot of trouble."

—Admiral Toddman to Sisko, on disobeying orders to rescue Odo and Garak
DS9 / "The Die Is Cast"

"He's their commander. They trusted him. He can't leave them."

—O'Brien to Bashir, on Goran'Agar and his dying men
DS9 / "Hippocratic Oath"

"Let them do what they're good at…and give them a little encouragement now and then."

—O'Brien to Worf, on command
DS9 / "Starship Down"

"You can give them a little slack, but you can't take your hands off the reins.…"

—O'Brien to Worf, on command
DS9 / "Starship Down"

"You made a…military decision to protect your ship and crew. But you're a Starfleet officer, Worf. We don't put civilians at risk—or even potentially at risk—to save ourselves. Sometimes that means we lose the battle…and sometimes our lives. But if you can't make that choice, then you can't wear that uniform."

—Sisko to Worf
DS9 / "Rules of Engagement"

"Part of being a captain is knowing when to smile, make the troops happy. Even when it's the last thing in the world you want to do. Because they're *your* troops, and you have to take care of them."

—Sisko to Worf
DS9 / "Rules of Engagement"

"I did what had to be done, what any First would do. I placed the good of the unit above my personal feelings."

—Omet'iklan to Sisko
DS9 / "To the Death"

"I told Muniz he was going to make it."

"That's what a captain's supposed to say."

—Sisko and Dax, on the loss of a crew member
DS9 / "The Ship"

"I may not be First, but I am the unit leader. You may discipline me, but only I discipline the men. That is the order of things."

—Remata'Klan to Keevan, protecting his men from rebuke
DS9 / "Rocks and Shoals"

"You mean if I had to take command, I would be called Captain, too?"

"Cadet, by the time you took command, there'd be nobody left to call you anything."

—Nog and O'Brien, on protocol
DS9 / "Behind the Lines"

"I'm not an impatient man. I'm not one to agonize over decisions once they're made. I got that from my father. He always says worry and doubt are the greatest enemies of a great chef. 'The soufflé will either rise or it won't. There's not a damn thing you can do about it, so you might as well just sit back and wait and see what happens.'"

—Sisko's log
DS9 / "In the Pale Moonlight"

"Who is she to be making these decisions for all of us?"

"She's the captain."

—Torres and Chakotay, on Janeway
VGR / "Caretaker"

"In command school, they taught us to always remember that maneuvering a starship is a very delicate process. But over the years, I've learned that sometimes…you just have to punch your way through."

—Janeway to Paris
VGR / "Parallax"

"One of the nice things about being captain is that you can keep some things to yourself."

—Janeway to Chakotay
VGR / "Parallax"

"Here, in the Delta Quadrant, we are virtually the entire family of man. We are more than a crew. And I must find a way to be more than a captain to these people. But it's not clear to me exactly how to begin. At the academy, we're taught that a captain is expected to maintain a certain distance. Until now, I've always been comfortable with that distance."
—Janeway's log
VGR / "The Cloud"

"Maybe more than ever now they need me to be larger than life. I only wish I *felt* larger than life."
—Janeway's log, on the needs of her crew
VGR / "The Cloud"

"Principles, principles…that's what it comes down to. Do I compromise my almighty principles…? But how do I *not* compromise them…if it involves the chance to get the crew more than halfway home? How do I tell them my principles are so important I would deny them that opportunity?"
—Janeway to Tuvok
VGR / "Prime Factors"

"In general, I believe it demonstrates faulty leadership to be guided by the emotions of a distraught crew. However, as captain, I must not ignore the sensibilities of those I command."
—Tuvok to bridge crew
VGR / "Resolutions"

"I dread the day when everyone on this ship agrees with me."
—Janeway to Seven of Nine, appreciating the challenge of working with individuals
VGR / "Random Thoughts"

"I realize that I've been hard on you at times. But it was never out of anger…or regret that I brought you on board. I'm your captain. That means I can't always be a friend."
—Janeway to Seven of Nine
VGR / "Hope and Fear"

22. Duty and Honor

"What's the mission of this vessel, Doctor? To seek out and contact alien life and an opportunity to demonstrate what our high-sounding words mean. Any questions?"
—Kirk to McCoy, on why he is beaming over to a hostile alien ship
TOS / "The Corbomite Maneuver"

"A crewman's right ends where the safety of the ship begins."
—Kirk to Spock, insisting that a "recalcitrant crewman" take shore leave
TOS / "Shore Leave"

"We're on a difficult mission, but it's not the first time. Our orders do not say 'stay alive' or 'retreat.' Our mission is to investigate."
—Kirk to crew
TOS / "The Immunity Syndrome"

"You sleep lightly, Captain."
    "Yes. Duty is a good teacher."
—Vanna and Kirk
TOS / "The Cloud Minders"

"Honor is *everything*."
—Lutan to Picard
TNG / "Code of Honor"

"A true protector cannot have two charges."
—Anya to Worf
TNG / "The Dauphin"

"You reminded us that there are obligations that go beyond duty."
—Picard to Data, on rescuing Sarjenka despite the Prime Directive of noninterference
TNG / "Pen Pals"

"There are times, sir, when men of good conscience cannot blindly follow orders. You acknowledge their sentience, but you ignore their personal liberties and freedom. Order a man to hand his child over to the state? Not while I am his captain."
—Picard to Haftel on Data and his creation, the android Lal
TNG / "The Offspring"

"The claim, 'I was only following orders,' has been used to justify too many tragedies in our history."
—Picard to Data
TNG / "Redemption, Part II"

"A Klingon's honor is more important to him than his life. A Klingon would gladly face the most horrible punishment rather than bring shame or disgrace to his family name. His word is his bond....Without it, he is nothing."
—Worf to Alexander
TNG / "New Ground"

"When I was a child, younger than you, I lost my parents, my family, my people....Everything I had was taken from me...except my sense of honor. It was the one thing I had that was truly Klingon...which no one could take away."
—Worf to Alexander
TNG / "New Ground"

"I feel as though I've been handed a weapon, sent into a room, and told to shoot a stranger. Well, I need some moral context to justify that action. And I don't have it. I'm not content simply to obey orders. I need to *know* that what I am doing is right."
—Picard to Keiran MacDuff. Suffering from memory loss, the captain refuses to follow orders to fight a war he knows nothing about
TNG / "Conundrum"

"My mother always said Klingons had a lot of dumb ideas about honor."
—Alexander to Troi
TNG / "Ethics"

"You did what you had to do.... You did what you thought was best....I just made sure that you listened to yourself...."
—Boothby to Picard, on Picard's acceptance of responsibility for a mistake he made as a cadet
TNG / "The First Duty"

"Duty. That's all that really matters to you, isn't it? Well, I refuse to be bound by an abstraction. The lives of the people of Boraal are far more important to me."
—Nikolai Rozhenko to Worf. Worf's willingness to follow the Prime Directive would have condemned the Boraalans to death
TNG / "Homeward"

"As much as I care about you, my first duty is to the ship. I cannot let any bridge officer serve who's not qualified."
—Riker to Troi, on her failing the test to become a bridge officer
TNG / "Thine Own Self"

"I know Admiral Nechayev gave you an order and she was given an order from the Federation Council...but it's still *wrong*."
—Wesley to Picard
TNG / "Journey's End"

"Your problem is that you really *do* have a sense of honor...and you really do care about things like trust and loyalty. Don't blame me for knowing you so well."
—Picard to Worf
TNG / "All Good Things..."

"I was like you once...so worried about duty and obligation I couldn't see past my own uniform. And what did it get me? An empty house."
—Kirk to Picard
Generations

"You robbed my son of his honor just to get my attention?"
    "You cannot take away what someone does not have."
—Martok and Worf
DS9 / "The Way of the Warrior, Part I"

"There is nothing honorable about killing those who cannot defend themselves."
—Worf to Ch'Pok
DS9 / "Rules of Engagement"

"It's the honorable thing to do."
    "You use that word, but you have no idea what it means."
—Garak and Worf
DS9 / "In Purgatory's Shadow"

"You fight because that is what you were designed to do. All that motivates him is some barbaric sense of honor."
    "And that is something *you* will never understand."
—Deyos and Ikat'ika, on Worf
DS9 / "By Inferno's Light"

"You don't understand because you've never put on one of these uniforms. You don't know anything about sacrifice or honor or duty or any of the things that make up a soldier's life. I'm part of something larger than myself. All you care about is *you*."
—Nog to Jake
DS9 / "Valiant"

"All this running around you do…your 'mission.' You're so *dedicated*, you know? Like you care about something more than just your own little life."
—Rain Robinson to Paris
VGR / "Future's End, Part II"

"You can't just walk away from your responsibilities because you made a mistake."

—Janeway to Neelix
VGR / "Fair Trade"

"I'm going to die—without a shred of honor. And for the first time in my life, that really bothers me."

—Torres to Paris
VGR / "Day of Honor"

23. *Humor*

"I was making a little joke, sir."
　　"Extremely little, Ensign."
—Chekov and Spock
TOS / "The Trouble with Tribbles"

"What do you call those?"
　　"I call them ears."
"Are you trying to be funny?"
　　"Never."
—Flavius and Spock
TOS / "Bread and Circuses"

"Humor...it is a difficult concept....It is not logical...."
—Saavik to Kirk
The Wrath of Khan

"And there was a rather peculiar limerick being delivered by
someone in the shuttlecraft bay. I'm not sure I understand
it....There was a young lady from Venus whose body was
shaped like a—"
—Data to Picard
TNG / "The Naked Now"

"I don't understand their humor either."
—Worf to Data on humans
TNG / "The Naked Now"

"I simply want to know what is funny. I want to involve myself in other people's laughter. I wish to 'join in.'"

—Data to the Comic
TNG / "The Outrageous Okona"

"I've noted that some people use humor as a shield....They talk much yet say little."

"Whereas others take a simpler approach—say *nothing*."

—Worf and K'Ehleyr
TNG / "The Emissary"

"Commander Riker's easygoing manner and sense of humor is fascinating to me. I believe it to be one reason he is so popular among the crew. It may also be partly responsible for his success in matters of love. There may be a correlation between humor and sex....The need for more research is clearly indicated."

—Data's log
TNG / "Data's Day"

"If you go into my quarters and examine the bulkhead next to the replicator, you'll notice there's a false panel. Behind that panel is a compartment containing an isolinear rod. If I'm not back within seventy-eight hours...I want you to take that rod and eat it."

"Eat it? You're joking."
"Yes, Doctor. I am."

—Garak and Bashir
DS9 / "Improbable Cause"

"Well, after six years in a place like this, you either learn to laugh...or you go insane. I prefer to laugh."

—Ee'Char to O'Brien, on incarceration
DS9 / "Hard Time"

"It's not easy being funny wearing these teeth."

—O'Brien to Worf, on his Klingon disguise
DS9 / "Apocalypse Rising"

"At the first sign of betrayal, I will kill him. But I promise to return the body intact."

"I assume that's a joke."

"We will see."

—Worf and Sisko, on Garak
DS9 / "In Purgatory's Shadow"

"You've got to laugh at a universe that allows such radical shifts in fortune, Benjamin."

—Dukat to Sisko
DS9 / "Waltz"

"I have a sense of humor. On the *Enterprise*, I was considered to be quite amusing."

"That must've been one dull ship."

"That is a joke. I get it. It is not funny, but I get it."

—Worf and Dax
DS9 / "Change of Heart"

"You keep working on that sense of humor, Commander Vulcan. You'll get it one of these days."

—Neelix to Tuvok
VGR / "Before and After"

"I understand the concept of humor. It may not be apparent...but I am often amused...by human behavior."

—Seven of Nine to Kim
VGR / "Revulsion"

24. Challenge and Risk

"Well, gentlemen, we all have to take a chance. Especially if one is all you have."

—Kirk to Scott and Spock
TOS / "Tomorow Is Yesterday"

"No wants. No needs. We weren't meant for that. None of us. Man stagnates if he has no ambition, no desire to be more than he is."

—Kirk to Spock, on paradise
TOS / "This Side of Paradise"

"Our species can only survive if we have obstacles to overcome. You take away all obstacles. Without them to strengthen us, we will weaken and die."

—Kirk to the Companion
TOS / "Metamorphosis"

"Risk is our business. That's what this starship is all about. That's why we're aboard her."

—Kirk to crew
TOS / "Return to Tomorrow"

"I changed the conditions of the test. I got a commendation for original thinking. I don't like to lose."

"Then—you never faced that situation—faced death...."

"I don't believe in the no-win scenario."

—Kirk and Saavik on beating the no-win *Kobayashi Maru* test at Starfleet Academy
The Wrath of Khan

"I need some challenge in my life. Some adventure...maybe even just a surprise or two."

"Well, you know what they say, Lieutenant. Be careful what you wish for: you may get it."

—Starfleet Lieutenant "Mr. Adventure" and Uhura
The Search for Spock

"Who's trying to break any records? I'm doing this because I enjoy it. Not to mention the most important reason for climbing a mountain..."

"And that is?"

"Because it's there."

—Kirk and Spock
The Final Frontier

"In life, one is always tested."

—Portal to Riker
TNG / "The Last Outpost"

"The only person you're truly competing against, Wesley, is yourself."

—Picard to Wesley
TNG / "Coming of Age"

"Wesley, you have to measure your successes and failures within. Not by anything that I or anyone else might think....But if it helps you to know this, I failed the first time. And you may not tell anyone!"

"You? You failed?"

"Yes. But not the second time."

—Picard and Wesley, on Wesley's failing the Starfleet Academy entrance exam
TNG / "Coming of Age"

"To feel the thrill of victory…there has to be the possibility of failure. Where's the victory in winning a battle you can't possibly lose?"

"Are you suggesting there is some value in losing?"

"Yes. That's the great teacher. We humans learn more often from a failure or a mistake than we do from an easy success."

—Pulaski and Data
TNG / "Elementary, Dear Data"

"Well, the game isn't big enough unless it scares you a little."

—Riker to Pulaski, on giving Wesley a big job
TNG / "Pen Pals"

"If there is nothing to lose—no sacrifice—then there is nothing to gain."

—Worf to Riker
TNG / "Peak Performance"

"What's the Zakdornian word for 'mismatch'?"

"*Challenge!* We do not whine about the inequities of life. And how you perform in a 'mismatch' is precisely what is of interest to Starfleet. After all—when one is in the superior position, one is *expected* to win."

—Riker and Kolrami
TNG / "Peak Performance"

"You will never come up against a greater adversary than your own potential, my young friend."

—Dr. Paul Stubbs to Wesley
TNG / "Evolution"

"Given the choice between slim and none, I'll take slim any day…."

—Riker to Picard
TNG / "Déjà Q"

"It is the struggle itself that is most important. We *must* strive to be more than we are, Lal. It does not matter that we will never reach our ultimate goal. The effort yields its own rewards."

—Data to Lal, on why he emulates humans
TNG / "The Offspring"

"The more difficult the task, the sweeter the victory."
—Riker to Troi
TNG / "Captain's Holiday"

"By refusing to help me, you left me with the same choice I had to begin with; to try or not to try...to take a risk or to play it safe. And your arguments have reminded me how precious the right to choose is...And because I've never been one to play it safe...I choose to try."
—Picard to Rasmussen
TNG / "A Matter of Time"

"If you want to get ahead, you have to take chances...stand out in a crowd...get noticed."
—Riker to Lieutenant Picard
TNG / "Tapestry"

"Beverly, the important thing during any confinement is to think positively and not give up hope....There is a way out of every box...a solution to every puzzle....It's just a matter of finding it."
—Picard to Beverly
TNG / "Attached"

"In a lot of ways it would have been easier to just walk away. But I didn't. I stuck with it. Doesn't that say something about my character, too...?"
—Sito to Picard, on staying at the academy after being disgraced
TNG / "Lower Decks"

"I chose instead to treat the problems I was having with my systems as...challenges to overcome, rather than obstacles to be avoided."
—Data to La Forge, on positive thinking
TNG / "Eye of the Beholder"

"There are also times when a people sacrificed too much...when a people must hold on to what we have...even against overwhelming opposition."
—Anthwara to Picard
TNG / "Journey's End"

"I take it the odds are against us, and the situation is grim?"

"You could say that."

"You know, if Spock were here, he'd say that I was an irrational, illogical human being for taking on a mission like that.... Sounds like fun."

—Kirk and Picard
Generations

"I envy you...the world you're going to."

"I envy *you*...taking these first steps into a new frontier."

—Lily and Picard on Picard returning to the twenty-fourth century while Lily gets to witness the beginning of Earth's new age
First Contact

"The Cardassians probably told you you didn't stand a chance either. Did you surrender?"

"No."

"Why do you expect me to act any different than you?"

—Mullibok and Kira, on standing your ground
DS9 / "Progress"

"I dreamt about exploring the stars as a child. And I wasn't going to allow any...'handicap,' not a chair, not a Cardassian station...to stop me from chasing that dream."

—Melora to Sisko. Native to coming from a planet with low gravity, Melora is confined to a wheelchair when she's away from home
DS9 / "Melora"

"Look, I don't know how you people live, but all of us corporeal, linear whatevers have certain things in common. And one of those things is...the need to improve ourselves. Our ambition to improve ourselves motivates everything we do. Without ambition, without...dare I say it...*greed*, people would lie around all day, doing nothing. They wouldn't work, they wouldn't bathe, they wouldn't even eat. They'd starve to death. Is that what you want?

—Quark to wormhole aliens, asking them to restore Zek to his greedy true self
DS9 / "Prophet Motive"

"There is something attractive about a lost cause."

—Sisko to Dax
DS9 / "Blaze of Glory"

"A vital mission, impossible odds, and a ruthless enemy. What more could we ask for?"

—Martok to Worf
DS9 / "Sons and Daughters"

"I don't care if the odds are against us. If we're going to lose, then we're going to go down fighting—so that when our descendants someday rise up against the Dominion, they'll know what they're made of."

—Sisko to Bashir
DS9 / "Statistical Probabilities"

"The only thing I can do. Stay here and finish the job I started. And if I fail…"
　　"'I have fought the good fight. I have finished the course. I have kept the faith.'"

—Benjamin Sisko and Joseph Sisko
Source: Paul the Apostle, Second Epistle to Timothy, Chapter 4, verse 7
DS9 / "Far Beyond the Stars"

"Why do you think I became an engineer? The challenge. What do you think's kept me kayaking down the same river week after week for the last seven years? The challenge. Why would I keep playing darts against somebody with a genetically engineered hand-eye coordination?"

—O'Brien to Bashir
DS9 / "Change of Heart"

"Most of the species we've encountered have overcome all kinds of adversity without a caretaker. It's the challenge of surviving on their own that helps them to evolve."

—Janeway to the Caretaker
VGR / "Caretaker"

"Some professors like students who challenge their assumptions, B'Elanna. And so do some captains."
—Janeway to Torres
VGR / "Parallax"

"Most of the challenges in life are the ones we create for ourselves."
—Old Man #2 to Janeway
VGR / "Sacred Ground"

"We're creating a society here—one that's based on tolerance, shared responsibility, and mutual respect that people like you and I were raised to believe in. We're not about to give it up just because it's difficult."
—Riley Frazier to Chakotay
VGR / "Unity"

"Everyone here has been so good to me….I don't want you to think I'm ungrateful….I've just been thinking that maybe— there's *more*. I don't know what that means…but I know I'm changing, and I know that there are things that I'm not satisfied with. I want—*complication* in my life."
—Kes to Janeway
VGR / "Darkling"

"All my life, I have wanted to fly. Perhaps my failure to do so has caused my heart to remain in flight…leaping from one thing to another…never satisfied, never complete."
—Leonardo hologram to Janeway
VGR / "Concerning Flight"

"We've come fifteen thousand light-years. We haven't been stopped by temporal anomalies, warp core breaches, or hostile aliens. And I am *damned* if I'm going to be stopped by a nebula."
—Janeway to Seven of Nine
VGR / "One"

25. Fear and Prejudice

"Those of you who have served for long on this vessel have encountered alien life-forms. You know the greatest danger facing us is ourselves, and irrational fear of the unknown. But there's no such thing as 'the unknown,' only things temporarily hidden, temporarily not understood."

—Kirk to crew
TOS / "The Corbomite Maneuver"

"Leave any bigotry in your quarters; there's no room for it on the bridge."

—Kirk to Lieutenant Stiles, on Stiles's implication that Spock is involved with the Romulans because he looks like them
TOS / "Balance of Terror"

"All I understand is that you apparently don't have the backbone to stand up and fight and protect the ones you love. I speak of courage, gentlemen. Does courage mean so little to you?"

—Kirk to Ayelborne, on the threat of a Klingon takeover of the planet
TOS / "Errand of Mercy"

"There's nothing disgusting about it. It's just another life-form, that's all. You get used to those things."

—McCoy to Cochrane, on the alien Companion's apparent love for Cochrane
TOS / "Metamorphosis"

"Zefram…we frighten you. We never frightened you before….Loneliness. This is loneliness. What a bitter thing. Oh, Zefram, it's so sad. How do you bear it, this loneliness?"
—Nancy/Companion to Cochrane
TOS / "Metamorphosis"

"Why do the Nazis hate Zeons?"
    "Why? Because without us to hate would be nothing to hold them together."
—Spock and Isak
TOS / "Patterns of Force"

"If we adopt the ways of the Nazis, we're as bad as the Nazis."
—Isak to Abrom insisting on helping Kirk and Spock, even though they are strangers
TOS / "Patterns of Force"

"It's been my experience that the prejudices people feel about each other disappear when they get to know each other."
—Kirk to Elaan
TOS / "Elaan of Troyius"

"The fear in each one of them is the beast which will consume him."
—Gorgan to children, on the *Enterprise* crew
TOS / "And the Children Shall Lead"

"Yes, I think that most of us are attracted by beauty and repelled by ugliness. One of the last of our prejudices."
—Kirk to Marvick
TOS / "Is There in Truth No Beauty?"

"Sooner or later, no matter how beautiful their minds are, you're going to yearn for someone who looks like yourself. Someone who isn't…ugly."
    "Ugly. What is ugly? Who is to say whether Kollos is too ugly to bear? Or too beautiful to bear?"
—Kirk and Miranda
TOS / "Is There in Truth No Beauty?"

"Alexander, where I come from, size, shape, or color makes no difference."

—Kirk to Alexander
TOS / "Plato's Stepchildren"

"How can I make your flesh know how it feels to see all those who are like you, and only because they are like you, despised, slaughtered and, even worse, denied the simplest bit of decency that is a living being's right?"

—Lokai to Chekov and Sulu
TOS / "Let That Be Your Last Battlefield"

"It is obvious to the most simple-minded that Lokai is of an inferior breed."
        "The obvious visual evidence, Commissioner, is that he is of
        the same 'breed' as yourself."
"Are you blind, Commander Spock? Well, look at me. Look at me."
            "You're black on one side and white on the other."
"I am black on the right side."
        "I fail to see the significant difference...."
"Lokai is *white* on the right side. All of his people are white on the right side."

—Bele, Spock, and Kirk
TOS / "Let That Be Your Last Battlefield"

"Your planet is dead! There's nobody alive on Cheron because of hate! The cause you fought about no longer exists. Give yourselves time to breathe. Give up your hate. You're welcome to live with us. Listen to me—you both must end up dead if you don't stop hating."

—Kirk to Bele and Lokai
TOS / "Let That Be Your Last Battlefield"

"All that matters to them is their hate."
        "Do you suppose that's all they ever had, sir?"
            "No. But that's all they have left."

—Spock, Uhura, and Kirk on Bele and Lokai's racial hatred
TOS / "Let That Be Your Last Battlefield"

"…In our century, we've learned not to fear words."
—Uhura to Lincoln
TOS / "The Savage Curtain"

"I don't know about you, but my compassion for someone is not limited to my estimate of their intelligence."
—Dr. Gillian Taylor to Bob Briggs
The Voyage Home

"You don't trust me, do you? I don't blame you. If there is to be a 'brave new world,' our generation is going to have the hardest time living in it."
—Gorkon to Kirk, on a potential truce with the Klingons
Source: William Shakespeare, *The Tempest*, Act 5, scene 1
The Undiscovered Country

"I was used to hating Klingons….It never even occurred to me to take Gorkon at his word."
—Kirk to McCoy
The Undiscovered Country

"People can be very frightened of change."
—Kirk to Azetbur
The Undiscovered Country

"Fear is the true enemy, the only enemy."
—Riker to Portal
TNG / "The Last Outpost"

"Only fools have no fear."
—Worf to Wesley
TNG / "Coming of Age"

"There's an unfortunate tendency in most cultures to fear what they don't understand."
—Picard to Worf
TNG / "Contagion"

"Judging a being by its physical appearance is the last major human prejudice, Wesley."
—Data to Wesley
TNG / "Manhunt"

"Differences sometimes scare people. I have learned that some of them use humor to hide their fear."
—Data to Lal
TNG / "The Offspring"

"Shall we continue accusing one another until hostility leads to violence? Shall we allow our suspicions to destroy us?"
—Picard to Kova Tholl
TNG / "Allegiance"

"If I had felt that nobody wanted to be around me, I'd probably be late and nervous, too."
—Guinan to La Forge, on Barclay's behavior
TNG / "Hollow Pursuits"

"I think…when one has been angry for a very long time…one gets used to it. Then it becomes comfortable like…like old leather. And finally, it becomes so familiar that one can't ever remember feeling any other way."
—Picard to O'Brien
TNG / "The Wounded"

"To admit that you're afraid…gives you strength."
—Troi to Worf
TNG / "Night Terrors"

"The road from legitimate suspicion to rampant paranoia is very much shorter than we think."
—Picard to Worf
TNG / "The Drumhead"

"Have we become so fearful? Have we become so cowardly that we must extinguish a man because he carries the blood of a current enemy?"
—Picard to Admiral Satie
TNG / "The Drumhead"

"We think we've come so far…the torture of heretics, the burning of witches is all ancient history…then…before you can blink an eye…suddenly it threatens to start all over again."
—Picard to Worf
TNG / "The Drumhead"

"But she—or someone like her—will always be with us...waiting for the right climate in which to flourish...spreading fear in the name of righteousness. Vigilance, Mister Worf. That is the price we have to continually pay."

—Picard to Worf, on Admiral Satie
TNG / "The Drumhead"

"I sense you have a closed mind, Captain. Closed minds have kept these two worlds apart for centuries."

—Spock to Picard, wanting to establish peaceful relations between Romulus and Vulcan
TNG / "Unification, Part II"

"Sometimes what we imagine can be just as scary as something real."

—Troi to Clara Sutter
TNG / "Imaginary Friend"

"Because it's been given a name by a member of my crew doesn't mean it's not a Borg. Because it's young doesn't mean that it's innocent."

—Picard to Guinan, on using Hugh to destroy the rest of the Borg collective
TNG / "I, Borg"

"It would seem that we are not *completely* dissimilar after all...in our hopes or in our fears...."

—Romulan captain to Picard, on discovering a common heritage
TNG / "The Chase"

"You probably can't imagine what it is like to be so lost and frightened that you will listen to any voice which promises change."

—Hugh to Riker, on Lore's influence upon the fragmented Borg collective
TNG / "Descent, Part II"

"Sometimes it takes courage to try, Data....And courage can be an emotion, too."

—Picard to Data, encouraging Data to continue to use his emotion chip
Generations

"You know the old saying...'a man who's always lookin' over his shoulder is waiting for trouble to find him.'"

—O'Brien to Sisko, on Tosk's nervousness
DS9 / "Captive Pursuit"

"I have no tolerance for the abuse of any life-form."

—Sisko to the Hunter, on using Tosk as prey
DS9 / "Captive Pursuit"

"You have no idea what it's like to be a coward. To see these horrors and do nothing."

—Marritza to Kira, on being unable to prevent atrocities during the Cardassian occupation of Bajor
DS9 / "Duet"

"Why?"
    "He's a Cardassian. That's reason enough."
"No. It's not."

—Kainon and Kira, on killing Marritza
DS9 / "Duet"

"Oh, we're all very good conjuring up enough fear to justify whatever we want to do."

—Bareil to Sisko
DS9 / "In the Hands of the Prophets"

"'Gentle' was bred out of these Cardassians a long time ago."
    "You know, that was a very ugly thing you just said."

—O'Brien and Keiko
DS9 / "Cardassians"

"You can't judge a whole race of people. You can't hate all Cardassians or all Klingons or all humans....I've met some Cardassians I didn't like. And I've met some I did. Like you."

—O'Brien to Rugal
DS9 / "Cardassians"

"Just because we don't understand a life-form doesn't mean we can destroy it."

—Odo to Kira
DS9 / "Playing God"

"You Federation types are all alike. You talk about tolerance and understanding...but you only practice it towards people who remind you of yourselves. Because you disapprove of Ferengi values, you scorn us...distrust us...insult us every chance you get."
—Quark to Sisko
DS9 / "The Jem'Hadar"

"It's amazing how some people will judge you based on nothing more than your job...."
—Mardah to Sisko
DS9 / "The Abandoned"

"Like I used to say...always burn your bridges behind you.... You never know who might be trying to follow."
—Tain to Garak
DS9 / "Improbable Cause"

"Stop being so naive, Julian, and look at them for what they are. They're *killers*. That's all they know how to do. That's all they *want* to do."
—O'Brien to Bashir, on the Jem'Hadar
DS9 / "Hippocratic Oath"

"Worried? I'm scared to death. But I'll be damned if I'm going to let them change the way I live my life."
—Joseph Sisko to Odo, on the idea of shape-shifters on Earth
DS9 / "Paradise Lost"

"Paranoid is what they call people who *imagine* threats against their life. I *have* threats against my life."
—Garak to Quark
DS9 / "For the Cause"

"The idea of a Ferengi courting a great lady is offensive."
    "You know it's attitudes like that that keep you people from getting invited to all the really good parties."
—Worf and Quark
DS9 / "Looking for *par'Mach* in All the Wrong Places"

"But the truth is, I was just as scared in the hospital as I'd been when we went for the generator....So scared that all I could think about was doing whatever it took to stay alive....Once that meant running away, and once it meant picking up a phaser....The battle of Ajilon Prime will probably be remembered as a pointless skirmish, but I'll always remember it as something more—as the place I learned that the line between courage and cowardice is a lot thinner than most people believe...."

—Jake's journal
DS9 / "Nor the Battle to the Strong"

"It takes courage to look inside yourself...and even more courage to write it for other people to see."

—Sisko to Jake
DS9 / "Nor the Battle to the Strong"

"It takes a lot of courage to admit you're wrong."

—Kira to Winn
DS9 / "Rapture"

"There is no greater enemy than one's own fears."

—Martok to Worf
DS9 / "By Inferno's Light"

"You are either very brave or very stupid, Ferengi."
    "Probably a little of both."
"Indeed, courage comes in all sizes."

—Martok and Nog, on confronting the Klingons
DS9 / "Blaze of Glory"

"Sirella is...a woman of strong convictions. She believes that by bringing aliens into our families we risk losing our identity as Klingons."
    "That is a prejudiced, xenophobic view."
"We are *Klingons*, Worf. We don't embrace other cultures. We conquer them. If someone wishes to join us, they must honor *our* traditions and prove themselves worthy of wearing a crest of a Great House."

—Martok and Worf
DS9 / "You Are Cordially Invited…"

"If the world's not ready for a woman writer—imagine what would happen if it learned about a Negro with a typewriter—run for the hills! It's the end of civilization!"

—Herbert Rossoff to Pabst, New York City, circa 1950
DS9 / "Far Beyond the Stars"

"Look, Benny, I'm a magazine editor—I am not a crusader. I'm not here to change the world. I'm here to put out a magazine. That's my job. That means I have to answer to the publisher, the national distributors, the wholesalers—and none of them are going to want to put this story on the newsstand. For all we know, it could cause a race riot."

"Congratulations, Douglas. That's the most imbecilic attempt to rationalize personal cowardice I've ever heard."

—Pabst and Rossoff, on the idea of an African-American science fiction hero
DS9 / "Far Beyond the Stars"

"Well, there's nothing wrong with being a little nervous—as long as it doesn't get in the way."

"Of what?"

"Of enjoying yourself."

—Odo and Kira
DS9 / "His Way"

"So because he's a hologram, he doesn't have to be treated with respect…or any consideration at all?"

—Kes to Janeway, on the Doctor
VGR / "Eye of the Needle"

"Mister Neelix…just because a man changes his drink order doesn't mean he's possessed by an alien."

—the Doctor to Neelix, on paranoia
VGR / "Cathexis"

"Sometimes fear can be a good thing. Keeps you from taking unnecessary chances. Courage doesn't mean that you don't *have* fear. It means you've learned to *overcome* it."

—Paris to Human Torres
VGR / "Faces"

"We often fear what we don't understand. Our best defense is knowledge."

—Tuvok to Tressa
VGR / "Innocence"

"The ability to recognize danger...to fight it or run away from it...that's what fear gives us. But when fear holds you hostage...how do you make it let go...?"

—Janeway to Tuvok
VGR / "The Thaw"

"Fear can provide pleasure. To seek fear is to seek the boundaries of one's sensory experience...."

—the Doctor to Janeway
VGR / "The Thaw"

"I've known fear. It's a very healthy thing most of the time. You warn us of danger...remind us of our limits...protect us from carelessness....I've learned to trust fear...."

—Janeway to Clown
VGR / "The Thaw"

"Fear is the most honest of all emotions, Captain."

—Clown to Janeway
VGR / "The Thaw"

"You know as well as I do that fear only exists for one purpose—to be conquered."

—Janeway to Clown
VGR / "The Thaw"

"Ever since I entered the academy, I've had to endure the egocentric nature of humanity. You believe that everyone in the galaxy should be like you...that we should all share your sense of humor and your human values."

—Tuvok to Valtane
VGR / "Flashback"

"I know from the history of my own planet that change is difficult. New ideas are often greeted with skepticism...even fear. But sometimes, those ideas are accepted...and when they are, progress is made...eyes are opened."

—Chakotay to Minister Odala
VGR / "Distant Origin"

"...I won't allow fear to undermine this crew's sense of purpose...even if that fear is justified."

—Janeway's log
VGR / "Scorpion, Part I"

"We just need the courage to see this through to the end...."
　"There are other kinds of courage...like the courage to accept that there are some situations beyond your control. Not every problem has an immediate solution."

—Janeway and Chakotay
VGR / "Scorpion, Part I"

"You know, sometimes people say terrible things about their enemies to make them seem worse than they really are. There might be some young Kradin soldier out there who's more afraid of you than you are of him."

—Chakotay to Rafin
VGR / "Nemesis"

"I wish it were as easy to stop hating...as it was to start...."

—Chakotay to Janeway
VGR / "Nemesis"

"Sometimes fear should be respected."

—Janeway to Seven of Nine
VGR / "The Omega Directive"

"I just don't like closed places. I never have. I don't know why."
　"Perhaps...you dislike being alone."

—Paris and Seven of Nine
VGR / "One"

26. *Logic and Emotion*

"Well, it'll take more than logic to get us out of this."
　　"Perhaps, Doctor...but I know of no better way to begin."
—McCoy and Spock
TOS / "The Galileo Seven"

"I examined the problem from all angles and it was plainly
hopeless. Logic informed me that under the circumstances the
only possible action would have to be one of desperation. A
logical decision, logically arrived at."
　　"You mean, you reasoned that it was time for an emotional
　　outburst."
—Spock and Kirk
TOS / "The Galileo Seven"

"Unlike you, we humans are full of unpredictable emotions that
logic cannot solve."
—Kirk to the android Ruk
TOS / "What Are Little Girls Made Of?"

"A feeling is not much to go on."
　　"Sometimes a feeling, Mister Spock, is all we humans have
　　to go on."
—Spock and Kirk
TOS / "A Taste of Armageddon"

"Our logic is to be illogical. That is our advantage."

—Kirk to Norman
TOS / "I, Mudd"

"Well, we found a whole world of minds that work just like yours: logical, unemotional, completely pragmatic. And we poor irrational humans whipped them in a fair fight. Now you'll find yourself back among us illogical humans again."
"Which I find eminently satisfactory, Doctor. For nowhere am I so desperately needed as among a shipload of illogical humans."

—McCoy and Spock on leaving the android planet
TOS / "I, Mudd"

"Doctor, if I were able to show emotion, your new infatuation with that term would begin to annoy me."
"What term? 'Logic'? Medical men are trained in logic, Mister Spock."
"Really, Doctor? I had no idea you were trained. Watching you, I assumed it was trial and error."

—Spock and McCoy
TOS / "Bread and Circuses"

"There is no logic in Thelev's attack upon the captain. There is no logic in Gav's murder."
"Perhaps you should forget logic and devote yourself to motivations of passion or gain. *Those* are reasons for murder."

—Spock and Shras
TOS / "Journey to Babel"

"One does not thank logic, Amanda."
"Logic! Logic! I'm sick to death of logic. Do you want to know how I feel about your logic?"
"Emotional, isn't she?"
"She has always been that way."
"Indeed? Why did you marry her?"
"At the time it seemed the logical thing to do."

—Sarek, Amanda, and Spock
TOS / "Journey to Babel"

"Shall I tell you what human companionship means to me? A struggle. A defense against the emotions of others. At times, the emotions burst in on me—hatred, desire, envy, pity. Pity is the worst of all. No, I agree with the Vulcans, violent emotion is a kind of insanity."

—Miranda to Kirk
TOS / "Is There in Truth No Beauty?"

"Well, personally, I find it *fascinating* that with all their scientific knowledge and advances, that it was good old-fashioned *human emotion* that they valued the most."

—McCoy to Kirk on the Vians and teasing Spock
TOS / "The Empath"

"The release of emotions, Mister Spock, is what keeps us healthy. Emotionally healthy, that is."

"That may be, Doctor. However, I have noted that the healthy release of emotion is frequently very *unhealthy* for those closest to you."

—McCoy and Spock
TOS / "Plato's Stepchildren"

"Logic and knowledge are not enough."

—Spock to Kirk
The Motion Picture

"What V'ger needs in order to evolve…is a human quality. Our capacity to leap beyond logic."

—Kirk to Spock
The Motion Picture

"You're about to remind me that logic alone dictates your actions?"

"I would not remind you of that which you know so well."

—Kirk and Spock
The Wrath of Khan

"In any case, were I to invoke logic, logic clearly dictates that the needs of the many outweigh the needs of the few."

"Or the one."

—Spock and Kirk
The Wrath of Khan

"To hunt a species to extinction is not logical."

—Spock to Gillian
The Voyage Home

"We must help Chekov."

"Is that the logical thing to do, Spock...?"

"No, but it is the human thing to do."

—Kirk and Spock, on trying to rescue Chekov
The Voyage Home

"Logic is the beginning of wisdom, Valeris, not the end."

—Spock to Valeris
The Undiscovered Country

"Even logic must give way to physics."

—Spock to Valeris
The Undiscovered Country

"...All these feelings that get in the way of human judgment...that confuse the hell out of us...that make us second-guess ourselves. Well, we need them. We need them to help us fill in the missing pieces...because we almost never have all the facts."

—La Forge to Data
TNG / "The Defector"

"I always had a different vision than my father...the ability to see *beyond* pure logic. He considered it...weak. But I have discovered it to be a source of extraordinary strength."

—Spock to Picard
TNG / "Unification, Part II"

"Data, feelings aren't positive and negative, they simply exist. It's what we do with those feelings that becomes good or bad. For example, feeling angry about an injustice could lead someone to take a positive action to correct it."

—Troi to Data
TNG / "Descent, Part I"

"...Extremists often have a logic all their own."

—Tallera to Picard
TNG / "Gambit, Part II"

"Part of having feelings is learning to integrate them into your life, Data...learning to live with them, no matter what the circumstance."

—Picard to Data
Generations

"Don't deny the violence inside of you, Kira. Only when you accept it, can you move beyond it."

—Opaka to Kira
DS9 / "Battle Lines"

"Let this be a lesson to you, Doctor...perhaps the most valuable one I can ever teach you....Sentiment is the greatest weakness of all."

—Garak to Bashir
DS9 / "In Purgatory's Shadow"

"You can use logic to justify almost anything. That's its power—and its flaw."

—Janeway to Tuvok
VGR / "Prime Factors"

"Every culture has its 'demons'...they embody the darkest emotions of its people. Giving them physical form in heroic literature is a way of exploring those feelings."

—Chakotay to Tuvok
VGR / "Heroes and Demons"

"When every logical course of action is exhausted, the only option that remains is *in*action."
—Tuvok to Chakotay
VGR / "Twisted"

"The logical course isn't always the right course."
—Chakotay to Tuvok
VGR / "Tattoo"

"You're right. It *is* disturbing…never knowing when that impulse may come…or whether or not you can control it when it does.…You live on the edge of every moment…and yet in its own way…violence is *attractive* too…maybe because *it doesn't require logic*.…Perhaps that's why it's so liberating.…"
—Suder to Tuvok
VGR / "Meld"

"If you can't control the violence…the violence controls you. Be prepared to yield your entire being to it…to sacrifice your place in civilized life…for you will no longer be a part of it…and there's no return."
—Suder to Tuvok
VGR / "Meld"

"You have no feelings for me, but you have feelings *against* me. For three years you've ridiculed me, and made it obvious to everyone that you have no respect for me. And I've tolerated it. You know why? You know why? Because you *are* smarter than I am, Tuvok…and more logical and stronger and superior in almost every way. And I admire you. But you don't have any instincts, you don't have any gut feelings…and you don't really understand people. But non-Vulcans have feelings and they have to listen to them. And I've got to listen to mine.…"
—Neelix to Tuvok
VGR / "Rise"

"Your 'instincts' were correct. However, one day, your intuition will fail...and you will finally understand that logic is primary above all else. 'Instinct' is simply another term for serendipity."
—Tuvok to Neelix
VGR / "Rise"

"Free of passion? One might as well be free of humanity."
—Lord Byron hologram to Gandhi hologram
VGR / "Darkling"

"...All I'm saying, is that there is room in every good story for a little bit of passion."
—Torres to Paris on the holoprogram he is attempting to write
VGR / "Worse Case Scenario"

27. *Business*

"What's to trust? Business is business."
—Oxmyx to Spock
TOS / "A Piece of the Action"

"At the negotiating table it can be fatal to have a heart...."
—Devinoni Ral to Troi
TNG / "The Price"

"The point of negotiating is to take advantage. I don't know what the other side is offering, and they don't know what I'm offering. So we dance around each other until somebody wins. I never cry foul when I lose."
—Devinoni to Troi
TNG / "The Price"

"Everyone wants a piece of the new frontier...."
    "And I'm sure you've already tried to sell it to a few of them...."
—Quark and Odo
DS9 / "A Man Alone"

"I'll never understand this obsession with accumulating material wealth. You spend your entire life plotting and scheming to acquire more and more possessions, until your living areas are bursting with useless junk. Then you die, your relatives sell everything and start the cycle all over again."

—Odo to Quark
DS9 / "Q-Less"

"Commander, I'm a host. A host is an ambassador of goodwill. The more goodwill that I can generate, the longer they'll stay...the greater my profits."

—Quark to Sisko, on the Wadi
DS9 / "Move Along Home"

"One man's priceless is another man's worthless."

—Quark to Falow
DS9 / "Move Along Home"

"'Once you have their money...you never give it back.'"

—Rom to Quark, the First Rule of Acquisition
DS9 / "The Nagus"

"'Never allow family to stand in the way of opportunity.'"

—Zek to Quark, the Sixth Rule of Acquisition
DS9 / "The Nagus"

"And remember, when in doubt...be ruthless."

—Zek to Quark
DS9 / "The Nagus"

"Never underestimate the importance of a first impression."

—Quark to Krax
DS9 / "The Nagus"

"There's no profit in kindness."

—Odo to Quark, questioning Quark's motives
DS9 / "Vortex"

"Maybe this isn't a problem. Maybe it's an opportunity."

—Nog to Varis, on her difficulties with a neighboring group of people
DS9 / "The Storyteller"

"The Ninth Rule of Acquisition clearly states that 'opportunity plus instinct equals profit.'"

—Nog to Varis
DS9 / "The Storyteller"

"Keep your ears open."
    "Are you kidding? That's the Seventh Rule of Acquisition."

—Odo and Quark
DS9 / "In the Hands of the Prophets"

"Every once in a while, declare peace. It confuses the hell out of your enemies."

—Quark to Rom, the Seventy-sixth Rule of Acquisition
DS9 / "The Homecoming"

"Never make fun of a Ferengi's mother. Rule of Acquisition Number Thirty-one."

—Quark to Bashir
DS9 / "The Siege"

"There's nothing quite so depressing as a winning streak that won't stop streaking."

—Quark to Bashir
DS9 / "Cardassians"

"A deal is a deal. Rule of Acquisition Number Sixteen."

—Quark to Ashrok
DS9 / "Melora"

"I think I agree with the Fifty-ninth Rule of Acquisition, 'Free advice is seldom cheap.'"

—Quark to Pel
DS9 / "Rules of Acquisition"

"True, but the Twenty-second Rule says, 'A wise man can hear profit in the wind.'"

—Pel to Quark
DS9 / "Rules of Acquisition"

"'It never hurts to suck up to the boss.'"

—Quark and Pel, the Thirty-third Rule of Acquisition
DS9 / "Rules of Acquisition"

"Just remember one thing; 'The bigger the smile, the sharper the knife.'"

—Pel to Quark, the Forty-eighth Rule of Acquisition
DS9 / "Rules of Acquisition"

"Why're you being so nice to me?"
    "For twenty percent of your profits. Why else?"

—Quark and Pel
DS9 / "Rules of Acquisition"

"'Never place friendship above profit.'"

—Quark to Pel, the Twenty-first Rule of Acquisition
DS9 / "Rules of Acquisition"

"'The riskier the road, the greater the profit.'"

—Pel to Quark, the Sixty-second Rule of Acquisition
DS9 / "Rules of Acquisition"

"'Wives serve, brothers inherit.' Rule of Acquisition Number One Hundred and Thirty-nine, if I'm not mistaken."

—Odo to Rom
DS9 / "Necessary Evil"

"The Forty-seventh Rule of Acquisition says, 'Don't trust a man wearing a better suit than your own.'"

—Quark to Martus
DS9 / "Rivals"

"'Dignity and an empty sack is worth the sack.' Rule of Acquisition number a Hundred and Nine."

—Quark to Martus
DS9 / "Rivals"

"At times like this I'm reminded of the Fifty-seventh Rule of Acquisition: 'Good customers are as rare as latinum—treasure them.'"

—Quark to Kira, on the presumed loss of O'Brien and Bashir
DS9 / "Armageddon Game"

"It's always good business to know about new customers before they walk in your door."

—Quark to O'Brien
DS9 / "Whispers"

"Rule of Acquisition One-twelve. 'Never have sex with the boss's sister.'"

—Quark to Arjin
DS9 / "Playing God"

"Before I became a tailor, I lived by a simple motto: 'Never let sentiment get in the way of your work.' A bit of a cliché, but true nonetheless."

—Garak to Quark
DS9 / "Profit and Loss"

"Rule of Acquisition Number Two-fourteen: 'Never begin a business negotiation on an empty stomach.'"

—Quark to Sakonna
DS9 / "The Maquis, Part I"

"Now the Third Rule clearly states, 'Never spend more for an acquisition than you have to.'"

—Quark to Sakonna
DS9 / "The Maquis, Part II"

"But I happen to be a firm believer in Rule of Acquisition Number Two Hundred and Eighty-five.... 'No good deed ever goes unpunished.'"

—Quark to Kira
DS9 / "The Collaborator"

"As a wise man once wrote… 'Nature decays, but latinum lasts forever.'"

—Quark to Sisko, the One Hundred Second Rule of Acquisition
DS9 / "The Jem'Hadar"

"Rule of Acquisition Two-eighty-six: 'When Morn leaves, it's all over.'"
    "There is no such rule."
"There should be."

—Quark and Rom
DS9 / "The House of Quark"

"I should've gone into insurance…better hours…more money…less scruples…."

—Quark
DS9 / "The House of Quark"

"But no, I had to follow the Seventy-fifth Rule of Acquisition: 'Home is where the heart is…but the stars are made of latinum.'"

—Quark to Odo
DS9 / "Civil Defense"

"'Treat people in your debt like family…exploit them.'"

—Sisko to Quark, the One Hundred Eleventh Rule of Acquisition
DS9 / "Past Tense, Part I"

"'You can't free a fish from water.'"

—Quark to Sisko, the Two Hundred Seventeenth Rule of Acquisition
DS9 / "Past Tense, Part I"

"And 'A Ferengi without profit…'"
    "'…is no Ferengi at all.'"

—Sisko and Nog, the Eighteenth Rule of Acquisition
DS9 / "Heart of Stone"

"'Peace is good for business....'"

—Dax to Quark, the Thirty-fifth Rule of Acquisition
DS9 / "Destiny"

"'War is good for business....'"

—Quark to Dax, the Thirty-fourth Rule of Acquisition
DS9 / "Destiny"

"The Tenth Rule of Acquisition is 'Greed is Eternal.'"

—Quark to Rom
DS9 / "Prophet Motive"

"Relax, Brother. Nog isn't going to destroy the Ferengi way of life. He just wants a job with better hours."

—Rom to Quark, on Nog joining Starfleet
DS9 / "Family Business"

"Hard work, bribes, sucking up to the boss. Just like any job."

—Brunt to Rom, on how he got his job with the FCA
DS9 / "Family Business"

"You're taking this too personally. Okay, I cheated you. I cheat everyone. It's *business*. You see what you can get away with, and you've got to figure the other guy's doing the same to you."

—Quark to Hanok
DS9 / "Starship Down"

"If there's no risk, there's no thrill. Your way is just...barter. If you want to win big, you gotta be willing to play the odds, it's like...gambling."

—Quark to Hanok, on business
DS9 / "Starship Down"

"New customers are like razor-toothed gree-worms. They can be succulent, but sometimes they bite back."

—Rom to Quark, the Two Hundred Third Rule of Acquisition
DS9 / "Little Green Men"

"You don't understand. Ferengi workers don't want to stop the exploitation. We want to find a way to become the exploiters."

—Rom to Bashir
DS9 / "The Bar Association"

"Remember Rule of Acquisition Two-Sixty-Three: 'Never allow doubt to tarnish your lust for latinum.'"

—Rom to Grimp
DS9 / "The Bar Association"

"Your brother can quote Rules of Acquisition, too. I believe his favorite is Two-eleven: 'Employees are the rungs on the Ladder of Success. Don't hesitate to step on them.'"

—Grimp to Rom
DS9 / "The Bar Association"

"Rule of Acquisition Seventeen: 'A contract is a contract is a contract. But only between Ferengi.'"

—Rom to Quark
DS9 / "Body Parts"

"That's who I am.…That's what I do. I'm a businessman. And more than that, I'm a *Ferengi* businessman. Do you know what that means? It means that I'm not exploiting and cheating people at random. I'm doing it according to a specific set of rules. The Rules of Acquisition. And I won't disregard them when I find them inconvenient."

—Quark to Rom
DS9 / "Body Parts"

"They're just rules.…They're written in a book, not carved in stone. And even if they were in stone, so what? A bunch of us just made them up."

—Grand Nagus Gint to Quark, on the Rules of Acquisition
DS9 / "Body Parts"

"Rule of Acquisition Two Hundred and Thirty-nine: Never be afraid to mislabel a product."

—Gint to Quark
DS9 / "Body Parts"

"The Jem'Hadar don't eat, don't drink, and they don't have sex. And if that wasn't bad enough, the Founders don't eat, and don't drink, and they don't have sex either. Which between you and me, makes my financial future less than promising."

"It might not be so bad. For all we know the Vorta could be gluttonous, alcoholic sex maniacs."

—Quark and Ziyal
DS9 / "By Inferno's Light"

"My dear Quark, not every deal is about making money. Sometimes you have to look at the big picture…and at times gaining a friend is more important than making profit."

—Hagath to Quark
DS9 / "Business as Usual"

"'Sometimes the only thing more dangerous than a question is an answer.'"

—Zek to Quark, the Two Hundred Eighth Rule of Acquisition
DS9 / "Ferengi Love Songs"

"'Females and finances don't mix.' Rule of Acquisition Ninety-four."

—Rom to Leeta
DS9 / "Ferengi Love Songs"

"'Latinum lasts longer than lust.' Rule of Acquisition Two-twenty-nine."

"Maybe, but lust can be a lot more fun."

—Rom and O'Brien
DS9 / "Ferengi Love Songs"

"Just don't forget the One Hundred Ninetieth Rule of Acquisition."

"'Hear all; trust nothing.' Good advice, Sir."

—Sisko and Nog
DS9 / "Call to Arms"

"I tried. I tried my best to run my establishment under this occupation. But you know what? It's no fun. I don't like Cardassians—they're mean and arrogant. And I can't *stand* the Jem'Hadar. They're creepy. They just stand there like statues, staring at you. That's it. I don't want to spend the rest of my life doing business with these people. I want the Federation back. I want to sell root beer again!"

—Quark to Kira
DS9 / "Behind the Lines"

"Poisoning the customers is bad for business."

—Quark to Damar
DS9 / "Favor the Bold"

"It always comes down to profit with you people, doesn't it?"

"We're Ferengi."

—Gaila and Quark
DS9 / "The Magnificent Ferengi"

"Thank you for restoring my faith in the Ninety-eighth Rule of Acquisition: 'Every man has his price.'"

—Quark to Sisko, on being bribed
DS9 / "In the Pale Moonlight"

"No one involved in an 'extralegal' activity thinks of himself as nefarious."

—Quark to Jake, on how Quark conducts business
DS9 / "The Sound of Her Voice"

"It never fails to impress me....No matter how vast the differences may be between cultures...people always have something that somebody else wants. And *trade* is born."

—Janeway to Tuvok
VGR / "Concerning Flight"

28. Technology

"What a mess."

"Picturesque descriptions will not mend broken circuits, Mister Scott."

—Scott and Spock
TOS / "The Galileo Seven"

"I signed aboard this ship to practice medicine, not to have my atoms scattered back and forth across space by this gadget."

"You're an old-fashioned boy, McCoy."

—McCoy and Kirk, preparing to transport
TOS / "Space Seed"

"Captain, you're asking me to work with equipment which is hardly very far ahead of stone knives and bearskins."

—Spock to Kirk, on lacking adequate technology on twentieth-century Earth
TOS / "The City on the Edge of Forever"

"We're all sorry for the other guy when he loses his job to a machine, but when it comes to *your* job…that's different. And it always will be different."

—McCoy to Kirk
TOS / "The Ultimate Computer"

"Granted, it can work a thousand, a million times faster than the human brain, but it can't make a value judgment, it hasn't intuition, it can't *think*."
—Kirk to Dr. Richard Daystrom, on the M-5 computer
TOS / "The Ultimate Computer"

"Machine over man, Spock? It was impressive. Might even be practical."

"Practical, Captain? Perhaps, but not desirable. Computers make excellent and efficient servants, but I have no wish to serve under them. Captain, a starship also runs on loyalty to one man and nothing may replace it or him."
—Kirk and Spock, on the M-5 computer
TOS / "The Ultimate Computer"

"Compassion. That's the one thing no machine ever had. Maybe it's the one thing that keeps men ahead of them. Care to debate that, Spock?"

"No, Doctor. I simply maintain that computers are more efficient than human beings. Not better."
—McCoy and Spock
TOS / "The Ultimate Computer"

"She's supposed to have transwarp drive...."

"Aye. And if my grandmother had wheels, she'd be a wagon."
—Sulu and Scott on the new *Excelsior*-class starship
The Search for Spock

"All systems automated and ready. A chimpanzee and two trainees could run her."

"Thank you, Mr. Scott, I'll try not to take that personally."
—Scott and Kirk, on the *Enterprise*
The Search for Spock

"The more they overthink the plumbing, the easier it is to stop up the drain."
—Scott to Kirk, on the new *Excelsior*-class ship
The Search for Spock

"Computer. Computer. Ah—Hello? Computer...?"
     "Just use the keyboard...."
"Keyboard...how quaint."

—Scott and Dr. Nichols
The Voyage Home

"How many times do I have to tell you? The right tool for the right job...."

—Scott to crew member
The Final Frontier

"People can be selfish, irrational, stubborn, malicious—you name it. But computers don't have those failings."

—Ard'rian to Data
TNG / "The Ensigns of Command"

"You know, Number One, you missed something not playing with model ships. They were the source of imaginary voyages, each holding a treasure of adventures. Manning the earliest spacecraft. Flying an aeroplane with only one propeller to keep you in the sky. Can you imagine that? Now, the machines are flying us."

—Picard to Riker
TNG / "Booby Trap"

"You know, I've always thought that technology could solve almost any problem. It enhances the quality of our lives...lets us travel across the galaxy...even gave me my vision. But sometimes you just have to turn it all off...."

—La Forge to the Leah Brahms Hologram
TNG / "Booby Trap"

"A good engineer is always a wee bit conservative...at least on paper."

—Scott to La Forge
TNG / "Relics"

"She brought me closer to humanity than I ever thought possible. And for a time, I was tempted by her offer."

"How long a time?"

"Zero point six-eight seconds, sir. For an android, that is nearly an eternity."

—Data and Picard, on the Borg queen
First Contact

"This is no computer. This is my archenemy."

—O'Brien to Sisko, on the station's recalcitrant computer
DS9 / "The Forsaken"

"You have got to make use of what you have. If you need a hammer and you don't have one, use a pipe."

—Kira to Dukat
DS9 / "Return to Grace"

"When a bomb starts talking about itself in the third person, I get worried."

—Paris to Torres, on the Dreadnought computer
VGR / "Dreadnought"

"My products benefit the entire world. Without me there would be no laptops...no Internet...no barcode readers. What's good for Chronowerx is good for *everybody*."

—Starling to Janeway, on stealing technological knowledge from the future
VGR / "Future's End, Part II"

"The secondary gyrodyne relays in the propulsion field inter-matrix have depolarized."

"In English!"

"I'm just reading what it says here!"

—Emergency Medical Hologram II and the Doctor
VGR / "Message in a Bottle"

29. Medicine

"Sometimes a man'll tell his bartender things he'll never tell his doctor."

—Boyce to Pike, on the doctor making the captain a martini
TOS / "The Cage"

"Now you're beginning to talk like a doctor, bartender."
    "You take your choice. We both get the same two kinds of customers, the living and the dying."

—Pike and Boyce
TOS / "The Cage"

"What am I, a doctor or a moon-shuttle conductor?"

—McCoy to Kirk, on ignoring the alert lights flashing in order to finish giving Kirk a physical exam
TOS / "The Corbomite Maneuver"

"The machine is capable of almost anything, but I'll still put my trust in a healthy set of tonsils."

—McCoy to Professor Crater, on medical technology vs. medical practice
TOS / "The Man Trap"

"In the long history of medicine, no doctor has ever caught the first few minutes of a play."

—McCoy, to himself
TOS / "The Conscience of the King"

"Blast medicine anyway! We've learned to tie into every human organ in the body except one: the brain. And the brain is what life is all about. Now that man can think any thought that we can, and love, hope, dream as much as we can. But he can't reach out and no one can reach in!"

—McCoy to Kirk, on the paralyzed Pike
TOS / "The Menagerie"

"Pure speculation, just an educated guess—I'd say that man is alive."

—McCoy to Kirk, on meeting Elias Sandoval, who they'd expected to be deceased
TOS / "This Side of Paradise"

"I'm a doctor, not a bricklayer."

—McCoy to Kirk
TOS / "The Devil in the Dark"

"By golly, Jim, I'm beginning to think I can cure a rainy day!"

—McCoy to Kirk, on saving the Horta's life
TOS / "The Devil in the Dark"

"I'm a surgeon, not a psychiatrist."

—McCoy to Edith
TOS / "The City on the Edge of Forever"

"Look, I'm a doctor, not an escalator."

—McCoy to Eleen, on needing help to get her up the mountain
TOS / "Friday's Child"

"I'm a doctor, not an engineer."

—McCoy to Scott
TOS / "Mirror, Mirror"

"'Give us some more blood, Chekov.' 'The needle won't hurt, Chekov.' 'Take off your shirt, Chekov.' 'Roll over, Chekov.' 'Breathe deeply, Chekov.' 'Blood sample, Chekov.' 'Marrow sample, Chekov.' 'Skin sample, Chekov.' If...if I live long enough, I'm going to run out of samples."
    "You'll live."
"Oh, yes, I'll live. But I won't enjoy it."

—Chekov and Sulu
TOS / "The Deadly Years"

"I'm not a magician, Spock, just an old country doctor."

—McCoy to Spock
TOS / "The Deadly Years"

"Now this isn't going to hurt a bit."
    "That's what you said the last time."
"Did it hurt?"
    "Yes."

—McCoy and Chekov
TOS / "The Deadly Years"

"It might eventually cure the common cold. But lengthen lives?
Poppycock. I can do more for you if you just eat right and exercise regularly."

—McCoy to Kirk, on the doctor's studies of the immunological results of biological warfare
TOS / "The Omega Glory"

"I'm a doctor, not a coal miner."

—McCoy to Spock
TOS / "The Empath"

"Jim! You've got to let me go in there! Don't leave him in the
hands of twentieth-century medicine."

—McCoy to Kirk, on saving Chekov
The Voyage Home

"Damnit, do you want an acute case on your hands? This
woman has immediate postprandial upper abdominal distension! Out of the way....Get out of the way."
    "What did you say she's got?"
"Cramps."

—McCoy and Kirk on getting past the policemen
The Voyage Home

"How's the patient, Doctor?"
    "He's gonna make it!"
"He? You came in with a she...."
    "One little mistake..."

—policeman and Kirk
The Voyage Home

"Where are the calluses we doctors are supposed to grow over our feelings?"

"Perhaps the good ones never get them."

—Beverly and Picard
TNG / "Code of Honor"

"It's hard to be philosophical when faced with suffering."

—Beverly to Picard, on the philosophy of the Prime Directive
TNG / "Symbiosis"

"It's no secret that I don't like people much, and I like doctors even less!"

"That's funny, I thought most doctors *were* people."

"Then you were wrong. Ask any patient."

—Graves and Troi
TNG / "The Schizoid Man"

"It's a time-honored way to practice medicine—with your head and your heart and your hands."

—Pulaski to Doctor
TNG / "Contagion"

"I like to help. When they hurt, I hurt."

"Doctor Pulaski's greatest medical skill is her empathy."

—Pulaski and Troi
TNG / "The Icarus Factor"

"Your bedside manner is admirable, Doctor. I'm sure your patients recover quickly just to get away from you."

—Q to Beverly
TNG / "Déjà Q"

"The first tenet of good medicine is never make the patient any worse."

—Beverly to Picard
TNG / "Ethics"

"You scare me, Doctor. You risk your patients' lives and justify it in the name of research. Genuine research takes time…sometimes a lifetime of painstaking, detailed work in order to get any results. Not for you—you take shortcuts…right through living tissue. You put your 'research' *ahead* of your patients' lives and as far as I'm concerned, that's a violation of our most sacred trust. I'm sure your work will be hailed as a stunning breakthrough. Enjoy your laurels, Doctor. I'm not sure I could."
—Beverly to Dr. Russell
TNG / "Ethics"

"I'm a doctor…not a doorstop."
—the *Enterprise*-E EMH to Beverly
First Contact

"I just seem to have a…talent, I suppose, a vision…that sees past the obvious, 'round the mundane, right to the target. Fate has granted me a gift, Major, a gift to be a healer."
     "I feel privileged to be in your presence."
—Bashir and Kira
DS9 / "The Passenger"

"We've conquered seventeen illnesses with the most powerful resource man has. His ingenuity."
—Alixus to Sisko
DS9 / "Paradise"

"I'm a doctor, not a botanist."
—Bashir to Dax on her sick plant
DS9 / "The Wire"

"I'm a doctor. You're my patient. That's all I need to know."
—Bashir to Garak
DS9 / "The Wire"

"Listen to me. I don't care about your negotiations, and I don't care about your treaty. All I care about is my patient, and at the moment, he needs more treatment and less politics."
—Bashir to Winn, on Bareil
DS9 / "Life Support"

"I wouldn't be much of a doctor if I gave up on a patient, would I?"

—Bashir to Ekoria, on Kukalaka
DS9 / "The Quickening"

"Some people don't like to be around the sick. It reminds them of their own mortality."

"It doesn't bother you?"

"Sometimes…but I prefer to confront mortality rather than hide from it. When you make someone well, it's like you're chasing Death off, making him wait for another day."

—Bashir and Ekoria
DS9 / "The Quickening"

"Bashir…how good could he be? He doesn't even charge."

—Quark to Rom, on getting a second medical opinion
DS9 / "Body Parts"

"I'm a doctor, not an historian."

—Bashir to O'Brien
DS9 / "Trials and Tribble-ations"

"But if you think about it, medicine isn't that different from engineering….It's all about keeping things running—fixing broken parts."

—Nog to Rom
DS9 / "The Magnificent Ferengi"

"So it begins. The trivia of medicine is my domain now. Every runny nose, stubbed toe, pimple on a cheek becomes my responsibility."

—the Doctor to Kes, on being the ship's permanent replacement doctor
VGR / "Parallax"

"I'm a doctor, Mister Neelix, not a decorator."

—the Doctor to Neelix
VGR / "Phage"

"I am a doctor, not a bartender."

—the Doctor to Sandrine
VGR / "Twisted"

"You see these hands? These are surgeon's hands, created by the most sophisticated computer imaging technology available. They do not play games and they do *not* mop floors."

—the Doctor to Sandrine. The hologram bar owner is convinced the Doctor is her new hired help
VGR / "Twisted"

"I am a *doctor*, not a voyeur."

—the Doctor to Janeway
VGR / "Parturition"

"I'm sorry. It's in my program. I see something wrong, I must attempt to diagnose it."
    "There are some things you can't cure."

—the Doctor and Kes, on Neelix's jealousy at Paris's attentions
VGR / "Parturition"

"Choose the word that would best describe your pain. 'Burning,' 'throbbing,' 'piercing,' 'pinching,' 'biting,' 'stinging,' 'shooting...'"

—the Doctor to Ensign Samantha Wildman
VGR / "Tattoo"

"You've never been sick or in pain....I just wish once in your life you could know what it's like...how it makes you feel vulnerable and a little afraid...then you'd understand."

—Kes to the Doctor
VGR / "Tattoo"

"You can't leave me like this. I need help. Now. Get me somebody who can treat the computer and make me feel better. Immediately."

—the Doctor to Janeway
VGR / "Tattoo"

"I'm a doctor, not a performer."

—the Doctor to Neelix
VGR / "Investigations"

"I'm a doctor, not a counterinsurgent."

—the Doctor, on saving the ship from the Kazon
VGR / "Basics, Part II"

"If a crew member came down with a debilitating illness, you'd do everything in your power to make them well again. I think we owe you nothing less."

—Janeway to the Doctor
VGR / "The Swarm"

"The Doctor has taken it upon himself to become a person who grows, and learns, and feels. It's made him a *better* physician."

—Kes to Lewis Zimmerman hologram
VGR / "The Swarm"

"A paranoid response indicative of bipolar personality disorder. If my history is accurate, Southern California in the late twentieth century had no shortage of psychotherapists, competent and otherwise. I suggest you find one."

—the Doctor to Starling
VGR / "Future's End, Part II"

"I'm a doctor, not a database."

—the Doctor to Starling
VGR / "Future's End, Part II"

"'I swear this oath by Apollo Physician, by Asclepius, by Health, and by all the gods and goddesses.…In whatsoever place that I enter, I will enter to help the sick and heal the injured.…And I will do no harm.'"

—the Doctor
Source: Hippocrates, "The Physician's Oath"
VGR / "Darkling"

"Welcome to sickbay. Take a number."

—the Doctor to Nyrian
VGR / "Displaced"

"I'm a doctor, not a commando."

—EMH-2 to the Doctor
VGR / "Message in a Bottle"

"We don't use scalpels or leeches anymore. I suggest you let me handle the medical side of things."

—EMH-2 to the Doctor
VGR / "Message in a Bottle"

Run along. I'll reattach any severed limbs, just don't misplace them."

—the Doctor to Neelix
VGR / "The Killing Game, Part II"

30. Dramatis Personae

"Captain Kirk is one of a kind, Charlie."
—McCoy to Charlie
TOS / "Charlie X"

"I am a logical man, Doctor."
—Spock to McCoy
TOS / "The Galileo Seven"

"All of my old friends look like doctors. All of his look like you."
—McCoy to Areel on Kirk
TOS / "Court Martial"

"It is impossible for Captain Kirk to act out of panic or malice. It is not his nature."
—Spock to Areel
TOS / "Court Martial"

"Doctor, you are a sensualist."
   "You bet your pointed ears I am."
—Spock and McCoy on an upcoming meal
TOS / "Arena"

"I have a responsibility to this ship, to that man on the bridge. I am what I am, Leila. And if there are self-made purgatories, then we all have to live in them. Mine can be no worse than someone else's."

—Spock to Leila
TOS / "This Side of Paradise"

"Interesting. Where would you estimate we belong, Miss Keeler?"
"You? At his side, as if you've always been there and always will."

—Edith and Spock, on Spock and Kirk being out of place in early twentieth-century Earth
TOS / "The City on the Edge of Forever"

"Mister Spock is the best first officer in the fleet."

—McCoy to Kirk
TOS / "Operation—Annihilate!"

"You're a man of integrity in both universes, Mister Spock."

—Kirk to the mirror Spock. In the mirror universe, the captain is impressed with his first officer's counterpart
TOS / "Mirror, Mirror"

"Another technical journal, Scotty?"
"Aye."
"Don't you ever relax?"
"I *am* relaxing."

—Kirk and Scott
TOS / "The Trouble with Tribbles"

"There is one Earthman who doesn't remind me of a Regulan bloodworm. That's Kirk. A Regulan bloodworm is soft and shapeless. But Kirk isn't soft. Kirk may be a swaggering, over-bearing, tin-plated dictator with delusions of godhood...but he's not soft."

—Korax
TOS / "The Trouble with Tribbles"

"Everybody's entitled to an opinion."
   "That's right. And if I think that Kirk is a Denebian slime
   devil, well, that's my opinion, too."
—Scott and Korax
TOS / "The Trouble with Tribbles"

"My world, Proconsul, is my vessel, my oath, my crew."
—Kirk to Merrick
TOS / "Bread and Circuses"

"This getting used to space travel, that takes some doing and
not everybody takes to it."
   "Did you?"
"Well, me, that's different. I was practically born to it."
—Scott and Mira
TOS / "The Lights of Zetar"

"They regard themselves as aliens in their own worlds, a condi-
tion with which I am somewhat familiar."
—Spock to Kirk, on Dr. Severin's followers
TOS / "The Way to Eden"

"I am proud of what I am. I believe in what I do. Can you say
that?"
—Chekov to Irina Galliulin
TOS / "The Way to Eden"

"A very old and lonely man…and a young and lonely man. We
put on a pretty poor show, didn't we?"
—Kirk to Spock, on the pain of meeting Flint and losing Rayna
TOS / "Requiem for Methuselah"

"The captain knows that I have fought at his side before and will
do so now if need be. However, I, too, am a Vulcan bred to
peace."
—Spock to Surak
TOS / "The Savage Curtain"

"Spock…You haven't changed a bit. You're just as warm and sociable as ever."

"Nor have you, Doctor, as your continued predilection for irrelevancy demonstrates."

—McCoy and Spock
The Motion Picture

"This is not about age! And you know it! It's about you flying a goddamn computer console when you wanna be out there, hopping galaxies."

—McCoy to Kirk, on Kirk taking a desk job
The Wrath of Khan

"Remember that overgrown Boy Scout you used to hang around with? That's exactly the kind of man that would…"

"Listen, kiddo, Jim Kirk was many things, but he was never a Boy Scout…."

—David and Dr. Carol Marcus
The Wrath of Khan

"There's a man out there I haven't seen in fifteen years who's trying to kill me. You show me a son that'd be happy to help him. My son. My life that could have been and wasn't. And what am I feeling? Old—worn out."

—Kirk to Carol
The Wrath of Khan

"Lieutenant, you are looking at the only Starfleet cadet who ever beat the no-win scenario."

—McCoy to Saavik, on Kirk and the *Kobayashi Maru*
The Wrath of Khan

"How much refit time till we can take her out again?"

"Eight weeks, sir. But you don't have eight weeks, so I'll do it for ya in two."

"Mr. Scott, have you always multiplied your repair estimates by a factor of four?"

"Certainly, sir. How else can I keep my reputation as a miracle worker?"

—Kirk and Scott
The Search for Spock

"Don't tell me: you're from outer space."

"No, I'm from Iowa. I only work in outer space."

"Oh, well, I was close. I mean, I knew outer space was gonna come into this sooner or later."

—Gillian and Kirk
The Voyage Home

"James T. Kirk. It is the judgment of this council that you be reduced in rank to captain...and that as a consequence of your new rank, you be given the duties for which you have repeatedly demonstrated unswerving ability: the command of a starship."

—Council president to Kirk, Kirk's "punishment" for disobeying orders
The Voyage Home

"It's a mystery to me what draws us together. All that time in space—getting on each other's nerves. And what do we do when shore leave comes along? We spend it together. Other people have families."

"Other people, Bones. Not us."

—McCoy and Kirk
The Final Frontier

"I've always known I'll die alone."

—Kirk to Spock
The Final Frontier

"I thought I was going to die."

"Not possible. You were never alone."

—Kirk and Spock
The Final Frontier

"I lost a brother once. I was lucky. I got him back."

"I thought you said men like us don't have families."

"I was wrong."

—Kirk and McCoy on the death and return of Spock *and* realizing his friends are his family
The Final Frontier

"This officer's record shows him to be an insubordinate, unprincipled career-minded opportunist, with a history of violating the chain of command whenever it suited him."

—Chang to court, on Kirk
The Undiscovered Country

"On occasion I have disobeyed orders."

—Kirk to Chang
The Undiscovered Country

"My God, that's a big ship."
 "Not so big as her captain, I think."

—McCoy and Scott, on *Excelsior* and Sulu
The Undiscovered Country

"I was never that young."
 "No...you were younger."

—Chekov and Kirk, on the youthful crew of the *Enterprise*-B
Generations

"I am superior, sir, in many ways. But I would gladly give it up to be human."
 "Nice to meet you, Pinocchio."

—Data and Riker
TNG / "Encounter at Farpoint"

"We are more alike than unlike, my dear Captain. I have pores. Humans have pores. I have fingerprints. Humans have fingerprints. My chemical nutrients are like your blood. If you prick me, do I not leak?"

—Data to Picard
Source: William Shakespeare, *The Merchant of Venice*, Act 3, scene 1
TNG / "The Naked Now"

"More than anything in the world...anything...you want to be a starship captain."

—Troi to Riker
TNG / "Haven"

"And such musical genius as I saw in one of your ship's libraries. One called Mozart, who as a small child wrote astonishing symphonies…a genius who made music not only to be heard but *seen* and *felt* beyond the understanding, the ability, of others? Wesley is such a person. Not with *music* but with the equally lovely intricacies of time, energy, propulsion…and the instruments of this vessel which allow all that to be played."

—the Traveler to Picard
TNG / "Where No One Has Gone Before"

"I am the culmination of one man's dream. This is not ego or vanity, but when Doctor Soong created me he added to the substance of the universe. If by your experiments I am destroyed, something unique, something wonderful will be lost. I cannot permit that, I must protect his dream."

—Data to Maddox
TNG / "The Measure of a Man"

"You're a wise man, my friend."
    "Not yet sir, but with your help I am learning."

—Riker and Data
TNG / "The Measure of a Man"

"Lieutenant Worf. I like him. To be more accurate, I understand him. A warrior. Proud, fearless, living only for combat. Exactly the type that will get us all killed if we're not careful."

—Jarok to Riker
TNG / "The Defector"

"You could learn a lot from this one."
    "Sure, the robot who teaches the course in humanities."

—Guinan and Q, on Data
TNG / "Déjà Q"

"I am Klingon…if you doubt it, a demonstration can be arranged."

—Worf to Kurn
TNG / "Sins of the Father"

"'He was a man. Take him for all in all. I shall not look upon his like again.'"
—Picard on Data, who is presumed dead
Source: William Shakespeare, *Hamlet*, Act 1, scene 2
TNG / "The Most Toys"

"The captain says Shelby reminds him of the way that I used to be. And he's right. She comes in here, full of drive and ambition, impatient, taking risks....I look at her and I wonder what happened to those things in me? I *liked* those things about me. I've lost something."
—Riker to Troi
TNG / "The Best of Both Worlds, Part I"

"I am not a hero."
    "Of course you are, admit it....You've never settled for less than that...and you never will."
—Jean-Luc Picard and Robert Picard
TNG / "Family"

"Sir...in the past three years...I've lived more than most people do in a lifetime....I think I'm very lucky. No matter what happens. How many people get to serve with Jean-Luc Picard? Sir, you don't know this....No one knows this, because I never told anyone....All of the things that I've worked for...school, my science projects, getting into the academy...I've done it all because I want you to be proud of me."
—Wesley to Picard
TNG / "Final Mission"

"Wesley, you remember....I was...always proud of you...."
—Picard to Wesley
TNG / "Final Mission"

"There are still many human emotions I do not fully comprehend...anger, hatred, revenge....But I am not mystified by the desire to be loved...or the need for friendship...these are things I *do* understand."
—Data's log
TNG / "Data's Day"

"You are simply the most impossible person to buy a gift for."
—Q to Picard
TNG / "QPid"

"Not 'just Beverly'…it's Beverly's smile, it's her kindness, her beauty within and without…so much more than 'just Beverly.…'"
—Ambassador Odan to Beverly
TNG / "The Host"

"I was rescued from Khitomer by humans…raised and…loved by human parents. I spent most of my life around humans…fought beside them. But I was born Klingon. My heart is of that world. I *do* hear the cry of the warrior.…I belong with my people."
—Worf to Picard
TNG / "Redemption"

"Being the only Klingon ever to serve in Starfleet…gave you a singular distinction. But I felt that what was unique about you was your…humanity. Compassion… generosity… fairness… You took the best qualities of humanity and made them part of you. The result…was a man who I was proud to call one of my officers."
—Picard to Worf
TNG / "Redemption"

"My name is Guinan. I tend bar. And I listen."
—Guinan to Ro
TNG / "Ensign Ro"

"Guinan is very selective about whom she calls a friend."
—Picard to Ro
TNG / "Ensign Ro"

"That's an interesting challenge. And I rarely refuse an interesting challenge."
—Ro to Picard, on staying aboard the *Enterprise*
TNG / "Ensign Ro"

"I was involved with… 'cowboy diplomacy,' as you describe it, long before you were born."
—Spock to Picard
TNG / "Unification, Part II"

"In your own way, you are as stubborn as another captain of the *Enterprise* I once knew."
"Then I am in good company, sir."
—Spock and Picard
TNG / "Unification, Part II"

"I was driving starships while your great grandfather was still in diapers. I'd think you'd be a little grateful for some help."
—Scott to La Forge
TNG / "Relics"

"Oh, I may be captain by rank, but…I never wanted to be anything else but an engineer."
—Scott to La Forge
TNG / "Relics"

"Enjoy these times, Geordi. You're the chief engineer of a starship…and it's a time of your life that'll never come again.…When it's gone…it's gone."
—Scott to La Forge
TNG / "Relics"

"And a fine ship…a credit to her name. But I've always found that a ship is only as good as the engineer who takes care of her…and from what I can see…the *Enterprise* is in good hands."
—Scott to La Forge
TNG / "Relics"

"I've never settled for anything in my life. I know what I want—I know what I've *got*. And you'd be lucky to do so well, Lieutenant."
—Will Riker to Thomas Riker
TNG / "Second Chances"

"Mister Data, you're a clever man—in any time period."
—Picard to Data
TNG / "All Good Things…"

"If there's one thing I've learned over the years—it's never to underestimate a Klingon."
—Picard to Worf
Generations

"You are an imperfect being…created by an imperfect being. Finding your weakness is only a matter of time."
—Borg queen to Data
First Contact

"As a matter of fact I think…you're the bravest man I've ever known."
—Picard to Worf
First Contact

"You will find the temple. Not for Bajor. Not for the Federation. But for your own *pagh*. It is, quite simply, Commander, the journey you have always been destined to take."
—Opaka to Sisko, on the Celestial Temple of the Prophets
DS9 / "Emissary"

"All my life, I've been forced to pass myself off as one of you…always wondering who I really am. Well, the answers to a lot of my questions may be somewhere on the other side of that wormhole. You coming?"
—Odo to Kira. The shape-shifter looks for answers on his origins
DS9 / "Emissary"

"I can't believe you're defending him, Quark. You're his worst enemy."
      "Guess that's the closest thing he has in this world to a friend."
—Zayra and Quark, on Odo
DS9 / "A Man Alone"

"Pretense. There's a special talent to it. It's as hard for me as creating one of your noses."

"Maybe that's why I've learned to respect your opinion, Constable. Never any...pretense."

—Odo and Kira
DS9 / "Past Prologue"

"You hit me....Picard never hit me."

"I'm not Picard."

"Indeed not. You're much easier to provoke. How fortunate for me."

—Q and Sisko
DS9 / "Q-Less"

"*Enterprise*? Oh yes. Weren't you one of the little people?"

—Q to O'Brien, on their last meeting
DS9 / "Q-Less"

"What kind of fool *are* you?"

"My own special variety."

—Ty Kajada and Odo
DS9 / "The Passenger"

"I don't enjoy fighting. Yes, I've fought my entire life...but for a good cause, for our freedom, our independence...and it was brutal and ugly and...but that's over for me now...that's not who I am. I don't want you to think that I'm...this...violent person...without a soul...without a conscience....That's not who I am."

—Kira to Opaka
DS9 / "Battle Lines"

"My way of trying to fit in. I found I could be entertaining. Odo be a chair. I'm a chair. Odo, be a razorcat. I'm a razorcat. Life of the party. I hate parties."

—Odo to Lwaxana, on using his shape-shifting abilities in early attempts to be social
DS9 / "The Forsaken"

"Odo, I am not a killer."

"No, but most of your friends are."

"True. And I would gladly sell one of them to you if I could."

—Quark and Odo
DS9 / "In the Hands of the Prophets"

"You're up to something."

"Why would you say that?"

"Because you're always up to something."

—Odo to Quark
DS9 / "The Homecoming"

"Patience is a lost virtue to most. To me, an ally."

—Odo's log
DS9 / "Necessary Evil"

"That's why all of you always come to me with problems. I'm the outsider. I'm on no one's side. All I'm interested in is justice."

—Odo to Kira
DS9 / "Necessary Evil"

"I'm a *science officer*. It's my job to have a better idea."

—Dax to Kira
DS9 / "Paradise"

"Don't mistake a new face for a new soul, Kang."

—Dax to Kang
DS9 / "Blood Oath"

"Doctor, did anyone ever tell you that you are an infuriating pest?"

"Chief O'Brien. All the time. And I don't pay any attention to him either."

—Garak and Bashir
DS9 / "The Wire"

"I can see that Garak hasn't changed a bit. Never tell the truth when a lie will do. That man has a rare gift for obfuscation."

—Tain to Bashir
DS9 / "The Wire"

"I've been in service to the Federation…Starfleet…all my adult life. No one has ever questioned my loyalty. No one…in my entire life has ever had cause to ask: 'Miles O'Brien, are you a criminal?' I took an oath to defend the Federation and what it stands for. I don't steal from them. I don't lie to them. I'm no angel, but I try to live every day as the best human being I know how to be. I need my little girl to wake up in the morning and look up at me and see a man she can respect."

—O'Brien to Odo, on being accused of crimes against Cardassia
DS9 / "Tribunal"

"He thought that just *making* the decisions would never satisfy you. *You* had to implement them…see the results…face the consequences. Curzon always thought you were the kind of man who had to be in the thick of things…not behind some desk at Headquarters."

—Dax to Sisko, on an admiral's pips being the wrong goal
DS9 / "The Search, Part I"

"Quark…I've met a lot of Ferengis in my time…and the truth is…though some of them may have been more wealthy…I've never met one more devious."

—Odo to Quark
DS9 / "Civil Defense"

"I hope I don't offend your beliefs, but I don't see myself as an icon…religious or otherwise. I'm a Starfleet officer, and I have a mission to accomplish. If I call it off, it has to be for some concrete reason, something solid, something…*Starfleet*."

—Sisko to Kira, on being the Emissary
DS9 / "Destiny"

"But the thing is, for the longest time, whenever anyone would use my name, the first thing I would think of was what it meant: 'Nothing.' What better way to describe me? I had no family, no friends, no place where I belonged. I thought it was the most appropriate name anyone could give me. And then I met you...and the others. Sisko, Dax, even Quark. And now, when I hear one of you call me 'Odo,' I no longer think of myself as 'Nothing.' I think of myself as...me."

—Odo to Kira, on the origin/translation of his name
DS9 / "Heart of Stone"

"I may not have an instinct for business, but I have my father's hands and my uncle's tenacity. I know I've got something to offer; I just need the chance to prove it."

—Nog to Sisko on what he can bring to Starfleet
DS9 / "Heart of Stone"

"The Kira I know has far too much regard for our friendship to lie to me, even for the best of reasons."

—Odo to the female shape-shifter
DS9 / "Heart of Stone"

"I've lived seven lifetimes...and I have never had a friend quite like you."

—Dax to Sisko
DS9 / "Rejoined"

"It's been my observation that you always act from a sense of justice...or at least what you consider justice. There's no feeling behind what you do, no emotion beyond a certain distaste for loose ends and disorder. You don't know what it means to care about someone, do you? People are just interesting creatures...to be studied and analyzed."

—Garak to Odo
DS9 / "Improbable Cause"

"I tried to deny it....I tried to forget...but I can't....They're my people...and I want to be with them...in the Great Link."

—Odo to Garak
DS9 / "The Die Is Cast"

"Do you know what the sad part is, Odo...? I'm a very good tailor."
—Garak to Odo, on being an ex-spy exiled to his tailor shop
DS9 / "The Die Is Cast"

"But I've been a security officer most of my humanoid existence. And in all that time, I've never found it necessary to fire a weapon or take a life. I don't intend to start now."
—Odo to Eddington
DS9 / "The Adversary"

"It is not what I owe them that matters. It is what I owe myself. Worf, son of Mogh, does not break his word."
—Worf to Gowron, on siding with the Federation in a conflict with the Klingons
DS9 / "The Way of the Warrior, Part II"

"But wearing that uniform must remind you of what you have lost."
    "Sometimes. But it also reminds me of what I've gained. And who I am. Oh, I can throw away the uniform, resign my commission, run all the way to the Nyberrite Alliance, but it really wouldn't matter. A Starfleet officer. That's what I am, and that's what I'll always be."
—Worf and Sisko. Having lost his wife in a battle against the Borg, Sisko knows his career gives him a focus
DS9 / "The Way of the Warrior, Part II"

"But I have a lot to learn about command."
    "Well, you couldn't ask for a better teacher."
—Worf and O'Brien. As Worf moves from security into command, O'Brien knows Sisko will be a great role model
DS9 / "The Way of the Warrior, Part II"

"Let's just say DS9 has more...shades of gray. And Quark definitely is a shade of gray. He has his own set of rules, and follows them diligently. Once you understand them, you understand Quark."
—Sisko to Worf
DS9 / "Hippocratic Oath"

"It's funny…a year ago if you'd done something like this, I would've thought you were just trying to be a hero."

"And now?"

"Now that I know you better…I realize it was just a really stupid thing to do."

—Dax and Bashir, on trying to rescue her
DS9 / "Starship Down"

"I've always been smart, brother. I've just lacked self-confidence."

—Rom to Quark
DS9 / "Little Green Men"

"You humanoids are all alike…you have no sense of order. And Dax is the most…*humanoid* person I know."

—Odo to Quark, on Dax rearranging Odo's quarters as a joke
DS9 / "Homefront"

"Everything I know I learned from Quark."

—Odo to Sisko, on breaking into classified files
DS9 / "Paradise Lost"

"I have never understood you, Worf. But I do know this…in your own way…you are an honorable man."

—Kurn to Worf
DS9 / "Sons of Mogh"

"What you were trying to do was make yourself feel important. Making me feel dumb made you feel smart. But I'm *not* dumb…and you're not half as smart as you think you are."

—Rom to Quark
DS9 / "The Bar Association"

"Isn't that what an artist wants, to be remembered? Isn't that why you write?"

—Onaya to Jake
DS9 / "The Muse"

"I've spent most of my life bringing people to justice. Now that it's my turn, how can I run away?"

—Odo to Sisko, on being charged by his people for the murder of a changeling
DS9 / "Broken Link"

"You know, for a Klingon who was raised by humans, wears a Starfleet uniform, and drinks prune juice, you're pretty attached to 'tradition.' But that's okay. I like a man riddled with contradictions."

—Dax to Worf
DS9 / "Looking for *par'Mach* in All the Wrong Places"

"Seventeen separate temporal violations. The biggest file on record."
	"The man was a menace."

—Lucsly and Dulmer on Kirk
DS9 / "Trials and Tribble-ations"

"He's so much more handsome in person…and those eyes…."
	"Kirk had quite the reputation as a ladies' man."
"Not him. Spock."

—Dax and Sisko
DS9 / "Trials and Tribble-ations"

"All I know is that I've spent lifetimes defending the Federation, and I deserve a vacation every now and then."

—Dax to Worf
DS9 / "Let He Who Is Without Sin"

"Because he has the courage of a berserker cat and he has the heart of a poet."

—Dax to Bashir on what she sees in Worf
DS9 / "Let He Who Is Without Sin"

"You're a paragon of Klingon honor and discipline, but when it comes to the Klingon passion for life, the exuberance, the enjoyment of the moment, you are constantly holding yourself back."

—Dax to Worf
DS9 / "Let He Who Is Without Sin"

"But you have to realize, there're some things in life you *can't* control. And one of them is me."

—Dax to Worf
DS9 / "Let He Who Is Without Sin"

"What was it the moderator said? That 'You may have worked for the Cardassians, but your only master was Justice.'"

—Dax to Odo
DS9 / "Things Past"

"You know, Odo, I used to think all your problems stemmed from the fact that you were a changeling, isolated from your own kind, forced to live among strangers who didn't understand you. You couldn't eat, you couldn't drink, you couldn't sleep, you couldn't make love. Was it any wonder you had such a bad disposition? But...you're not a changeling anymore. You're one of us. Life is yours for the taking. All you have to do is reach out and grab it. But do you? No. Because solid or Changeling, you're still a miserable self-hating misanthrope. That's who you are and that's who you'll always be."

—Quark to Odo
DS9 / "The Ascent"

"Think of it, Julian. If this works, you'll be able to irritate hundreds of people you've never even met."

—O'Brien to Bashir, on being the template for the new Longterm Medical Holographic Program
DS9 / "Doctor Bashir, I Presume?"

"Well, the truth is...he's an extraordinary person. A real sense of honor and integrity...great sense of humor...warm, caring—you're sure he's not going to read this?"

—O'Brien to Zimmerman, being interviewed about Bashir
DS9 / "Doctor Bashir, I Presume?"

"Don't you think about anyone but yourself?"
    "Of course I do, I just think about myself first."

—Ishka and Quark
DS9 / "Ferengi Love Songs"

"Maybe it's true...maybe you're not a soldier anymore."
    "You're right. I'm an engineer."

—Garak and O'Brien, on being just as dangerous
DS9 / "Empok Nor"

"You're not genetically engineered, you're a Vulcan."

"If I'm a Vulcan, then how do you explain my boyish smile?"

"Not so boyish anymore, Doctor."

—Garak and Bashir, on Bashir's sudden infatuation with statistics
DS9 / "A Time to Stand"

"I don't plan to say good-bye. I plan to build a house on Bajor."

"And what if Starfleet assigns you to a different sector?"

"I will go wherever they send me. But when I go home...it will be to Bajor."

—Sisko and Ross
DS9 / "Favor the Bold"

"So you're the commander of Deep Space 9. And the Emissary to the Prophets. Decorated combat officer, widower, father, mentor....And oh yes, the man who started the war with the Dominion. Somehow I thought you'd be taller."

—Vreenak to Sisko
DS9 / "In the Pale Moonlight"

"You're not exactly the most lovable person in the galaxy. You're not even the most lovable person in this sector. Or on this station. Or even in this room."

—Quark to Odo
DS9 / "His Way"

"I do enjoy my work. But I'm afraid I've used it as an excuse to avoid the rest of my life."

—Odo to Kira
DS9 / "His Way"

"That's my Odo—always ready to turn victory into defeat."

—Vic to Odo
DS9 / "His Way"

"I'm sure nothing gives you more pleasure than stifling my creativity."

"Only you would consider barstools to be a form of artistic expression."

—Quark and Odo
DS9 / "The Sound of Her Voice"

"Nice guys. But absolutely clueless."

—Vic, on Bashir and Quark
DS9 / "Tears of the Prophets"

"When I first met you, you told me that my relationship with Jadzia Dax wouldn't be any different than the one I had with Curzon Dax. Things didn't work out that way. I had a helluva lot of fun with both of you. But Curzon was my mentor. You...you were my friend. And I am going to miss you."

—Sisko to Dax, mourning over her death
DS9 / "Tears of the Prophets"

"Mister Kim...at ease before you sprain something."

—Janeway to Harry Kim
VGR / "Caretaker"

"Whatever you need is what I have to offer. You need a guide— I'm your guide. You need supplies—I know where to procure them—I have friends among races you don't even know exist. You need a cook—you haven't lived until you've tasted my *angla'bosque*. It will be my job to anticipate your needs before you know you have them. And I anticipate your first need will be me."

—Neelix to Janeway, on wanting to join the crew
VGR / "Caretaker"

"I have no intention of being your token Maquis officer."

—Chakotay to Janeway
VGR / "Parallax"

"I am not *just* a doctor. I've been designed with information from two thousand medical reference sources and the experience of forty-seven individual medical officers. I am the embodiment of modern medicine. How much *dirt* do you need…?"

—the Doctor to Kes, on being overqualified to fill her request for soil samples
VGR / "Parallax"

"Sometimes I think B'Elanna goes out of her way to find solutions that ignore Starfleet procedures."

—Janeway to Chakotay
VGR / "Phage"

"Captain Janeway has made me realize that I must function as more than an emergency medical replacement. I must think of myself as a member of the crew."

—the Doctor to Kes
VGR / "Eye of the Needle"

"On the contrary, the demands on a Vulcan's character are extraordinarily difficult. Do not mistake composure for ease."

—Tuvok to Chakotay
VGR / "State of Flux"

"I can describe every detail of every piece of equipment in this sickbay, from biobed to neurostimulator. But I've never even seen a sky, or a forest…let alone Vikings and monsters. I can't afford to fail. But I don't know what to expect in that holodeck."

—the Doctor to Kes, on the hologram's upcoming mission to the holodeck
VGR / "Heroes and Demons"

"That's the way you respond to every situation, isn't it? If it doesn't work, hit it. If it's in your way, knock it down."

—Human Torres to Klingon Torres
VGR / "Faces"

"I came to admire a lot of things about her…her strength…her bravery. I guess I just have to accept the fact…that I'll spend the rest of my life fighting with her."

—Human Torres to Chakotay, on her Klingon side
VGR / "Faces"

"These are *Keela* flowers. Beautiful...and remarkably strong. The stem is flexible...impossible to break. But occasionally...on the same plant...there's a bloom whose stem is not so flexible...ah, here's one. And when the stem is brittle...it breaks."

"You're saying that the Maquis crew is rigid and inflexible. That they will never adjust to Starfleet rules."

"No, Mister Vulcan. I'm saying that *you* are rigid and inflexible. But maybe if you learned to bend a little...you might have better luck with your class."

—Neelix and Tuvok
VGR / "Learning Curve"

"Just because you're made of projected light and energy...doesn't mean you're any less real than someone made of flesh and blood. It doesn't matter what you're made of...what matters is who you are. You're our friend. And we want you back."

—Chakotay to the Doctor
VGR / "Projections"

"My name was a gift. From my tribe. I cherish it. Every day of my life. Just as I cherish the Federation uniform."

—Chakotay to Kar
VGR / "Initiations"

"It's typical of Kes that she would befriend someone like you...someone who really needs a friend."

—Neelix to Paris
VGR / "Parturition"

"If you ever doubt yourself, just look into her eyes, see the way she looks at you. You'll never doubt yourself again."

—Paris to Neelix on Kes
VGR / "Parturition"

"I overlooked his bravery because I was focusing on his brashness. I ignored his courage because I saw it as arrogance. And I resented his friendliness because I mistook it for licentiousness. So while this man was giving us his best, every minute of every day, I was busy judging him."

—Neelix to crew, on Paris, who is leaving the ship
VGR / "Investigations"

"I am programmed to be heroic when the need arises."
—the Doctor to Kim
VGR / "Deadlock"

"I can tell you a story, an ancient legend among my people. It's about an angry warrior who lived his life in conflict with the rest of his tribe. A man who couldn't find peace, even with the help of his spirit guide. For years he struggled with his discontent. The only satisfaction he ever got came when he was in battle. This made him a hero among his tribe, but the warrior still longed for peace within himself. One day, he and his war party were captured by a neighboring tribe led by a woman warrior. She called on him to join her because her tribe was too small and weak to defend itself from all its enemies. The woman warrior was brave, and beautiful. And very wise. The angry warrior swore to himself that he would stay by her side, doing whatever he could to make her burden lighter. From that point on, her needs would come first. And in that way, the warrior began to know the true meaning of peace."
     "Is that really an ancient legend?"
"No. But that made it easier to say."
—Chakotay and Janeway
VGR / "Resolutions"

"Captain Janeway. Now that's a subject I want to discuss. Tell me: What are some of her favorite things? Chocolate truffles, stuffed animals, erotic art...?"
—Q to Neelix
VGR / "The Q and the Grey"

"You're afraid that your big, scary Klingon side might have been showing. Well, I saw it up close...and you know, it wasn't so terrible. In fact, I wouldn't mind seeing it again someday."
—Paris to Torres
VGR / "Blood Fever"

"She saw something in me that I didn't see. She saw a worthwhile person where I saw a lost and hostile misfit. And because she had faith in me, I began to have faith in myself. And when she died...the first thing I thought was that I couldn't do this without her. That I needed her too badly...her strength and her compassion. But then I realized that the gift that she gave me...and gave a lot of us here...was the knowledge that we are better, and stronger, than we think."

—Torres to crew, on Janeway
VGR / "Coda"

"My poor little bird...you always made it hard for yourself. If there was a rocky path and a smooth one, you chose the rocky one every time."

—Admiral Janeway to Kathryn Janeway
VGR / "Coda"

"Helping others, Chakotay, that's part of who you are."

—Janeway to Chakotay
VGR / "Unity"

"Seven of Nine, Tertiary Adjunct of Unimatrix Zero One. But you may call me...Seven of Nine."

—Seven of Nine to Janeway, on her designation
VGR / "Scorpion, Part II"

"Do you have a better idea?"
   "We are Borg."

—Janeway and Seven of Nine
VGR / "Scorpion, Part II"

"I've got an Ocampan who wants to be something more and a Borg who's afraid of becoming something less. Here's to Vulcan stability."

—Janeway to Tuvok
VGR / "The Gift"

"You can alter our physiology...but you cannot change our nature. We *will* betray you. We are Borg."

—Seven of Nine to Janeway
VGR / "The Gift"

"When I was first activated, I was regarded as little more than a talking tricorder. I had to ask for the privileges I deserved…the right to be included in crew briefings…the ability to turn my program on and off….It's taken some time, but I believe I've earned the respect of the crew as an equal."
—the Doctor to Dejaren
VGR / "Revulsion"

"I never realized you thought of me as 'reckless,' Tuvok."
    "A poor choice of words. It was clearly an understatement."
—Janeway and Tuvok
VGR / "Scientific Method"

"That little girl needs you, Neelix. Monsters in the replicator…who else on this ship can handle that?"
—Chakotay to Neelix, on Wildman's daughter and Neelix's value to *Voyager*
VGR / "Mortal Coil"

"Beady eyes…terrible bedside manner…I recognize you!"
—EMH-2 to the Doctor
VGR / "Message in a Bottle"

"I was saving *Voyager* from annihilation when you were only a gleam in your programmer's eye."
—the Doctor to EMH-2
VGR / "Message in a Bottle"

"Since when is not wanting to spend time with the Doctor a capital offense? You'd have to throw the whole crew in the brig for that one."
—Paris to Chakotay
VGR / "Vis-à-Vis"

"Why is everybody trying to shoot me today?"
—Paris to Daelen
VGR / "Vis-à-Vis"

"B'Elanna Torres…intelligent, beautiful, and with a chip on her shoulder the size of the Horsehead Nebula. She also had a kind of…vulnerability that made her…quite endearing."
—the Doctor to Quarren
VGR / "Living Witness"

"And the Doctor? Well…he served as our surgical chancellor for many years…until he decided to leave. He took a small craft…and set a course for the Alpha Quadrant…attempting to trace the path of *Voyager*. He said he had…'A longing for home.'"

—Tabris to museum visitors
VGR / "Living Witness"

"I know your bond with Seven is unique, different from every-one else's…. From the beginning you've seen things in her that no one else could. But maybe you could help me understand some of those things."

"I don't know if I can. It's just instinct. There's something inside me that says she can be redeemed. In spite of her insolent attitude, I honestly believe she *wants* to do well by us."

—Chakotay and Janeway
VGR / "One"

"I am no longer Borg…but the prospect of becoming human is…unsettling. I don't know where I belong."

"You belong with us."

—Seven of Nine and Janeway
VGR / "Hope and Fear"

31. For the Fans

"Check the circuit."

—Spock to José Tyler, first words spoken in *The Original Series*
TOS / "The Cage"

"Engage."

—Pike to Number One; first time order given
TOS / "The Cage"

"'My love has wings;
 slender feathered things;
 with grace in upswept curve
 and tapered tip...'
'Nightingale Woman,' written by Tarbolde on the Canopus
planet back in 1996."

—Mitchell to Dehner. A poem actually written by Gene Roddenberry
TOS / "Where No Man Has Gone Before"

"Energize."

—Kirk to Scott, first time order given
TOS / "Where No Man Has Gone Before"

"Space, the final frontier. These are the voyages of the *Starship Enterprise*. Its five-year mission: to explore strange new worlds, to seek out new life and new civilizations, to boldly go where no man has gone before."

—Kirk, first time opening narration used
TOS / "The Corbomite Maneuver"

"Hailing frequencies still open, sir."

—Uhura to Kirk; first time phrase used
TOS / "The Corbomite Maneuver"

"Fascinating."

—Spock on Balok's ship; first time comment used
TOS / "The Corbomite Maneuver"

"Being split in two halves is no theory with me, Doctor. I have a human half, you see, as well as an alien half, submerged, constantly at war with each other. Personal experience, Doctor. I survive it because my intelligence wins out over both, makes them live together. *(to Kirk)* Your intelligence would enable you to survive as well."

—Spock to McCoy and Kirk on recombining the two sides of Kirk split by a transporter malfunction
TOS / "The Enemy Within"

"He's dead, Jim."

—McCoy to Kirk, first time phrase used
TOS / "The Enemy Within"

"May the Great Bird of the Galaxy bless your planet!"

—Sulu to Rand, on-air use of Gene Roddenberry's nickname
TOS / "The Man Trap"

"And now, crew, your captain will render an ancient Irish favorite… 'I'll take you home again, Kathleeeeennn….'"

—Kevin Thomas Riley to crew, regaling them with song
TOS / "The Naked Time"

"I can't change the laws of physics."
—Scott to Kirk
TOS / "The Naked Time"

"You will be absorbed. Your individuality will merge into the unity of good. And in your submergence into the common being of the Body, you will find contentment, fulfillment. You will experience the absolute good."
—Landru. Before the Borg, there was Landru
TOS / "The Return of the Archons"

"I love you. I can love you."
—Spock to Leila. After being affected by the spores, Spock is free to express his feelings
TOS / "This Side of Paradise"

"I have little to say about it, Captain. Except that…for the first time in my life…I was happy."
—Spock to Kirk, on his experiences on Omicron Ceti III
TOS / "This Side of Paradise"

"A question. Since before your sun burned hot in space and before your race was born, I have awaited a question."
—The Guardian of Forever to Kirk
TOS / "The City on the Edge of Forever"

"You were saying you'll have no trouble explaining it.…"
    "My friend is obviously…Chinese. I see you've noticed the ears. They're actually easy to explain.…"
"Perhaps the unfortunate accident I had as a child.…"
    "The unfortunate accident he had as a child.…He caught his head in a mechanical…rice-picker. But fortunately there was an American…missionary living close by who was actually a…skilled plastic surgeon in civilian life.…"
—Spock and Kirk, trying to explain Spock's appearance to a human policeman in the year 1930
TOS / "The City on the Edge of Forever"

"You deliberately stopped me, Jim. I could've saved her. Do you know what you just did?"

"He knows, Doctor. He knows."

—McCoy and Spock on Kirk preventing McCoy from saving Edith in order to protect the timeline
TOS / "The City on the Edge of Forever"

"Let's get the hell out of here."

—Kirk to landing party
TOS / "The City on the Edge of Forever"

"We shield it with ritual and customs shrouded in antiquity. You humans have no conception. It strips our minds from us. It brings a madness which rips away our veneer of civilization. It is the *Pon farr*, the time of mating."

—Spock and Kirk, first mention of *Pon farr*
TOS / "Amok Time"

"Live long, T'Pau, and prosper."

—Spock to T'Pau; first time said
TOS / "Amok Time"

"Discard the warp drive nacelles if you have to and crack out of there with the main section but get that ship out of there!"

—Kirk to Scott, first implication that the *Enterprise* can be split into two sections as later seen with the *Enterprise*-D
TOS / "The Apple"

"I'm not sure, but I think we've been insulted."

"I'm sure."

—Kirk and McCoy, on Spock's inference that he found their savage mirror universe counterparts a refreshing change of pace
TOS / "Mirror, Mirror"

"I love you. However, I hate you."

"But I'm identical in every way with Alice 27."

"Yes, of course, that is exactly why I hate you. Because you are identical."

—Spock and Alice 210, confusing the android
TOS / "I, Mudd"

"Logic is a little tweeting bird chirping in a meadow. Logic is a wreath of pretty flowers which smell *bad*. Are you sure your circuits are registering correctly? Your ears are green."

—Spock to Norman, confusing the android
TOS / "I, Mudd"

"Does everybody know about this wheat but me?"
    "Oh, not everyone, Captain. It's a Russian invention."

—Chekov and Kirk, on the quadrotriticale
TOS / "The Trouble with Tribbles"

"Do you know what you get if you feed a tribble too much?"
    "A fat tribble?"
"No. You get a whole bunch of hungry little tribbles."

—McCoy and Kirk
TOS / "The Trouble with Tribbles"

"We like the *Enterprise*. We really do. That sagging old rust bucket is designed like a garbage scow, half the quadrant knows it—that's why they're learning to speak Klingonese!"
    "...Laddie, don't you think you should rephrase that?"
"You're right. I should. I didn't mean to say that the *Enterprise* should be *hauling* garbage....I meant to say that it should be hauled away *as* garbage!"

—Korax and Scott
TOS / "The Trouble with Tribbles"

"I heard you."
    "He simply could not believe his ears."

—Kirk and Spock on Nilz Baris's accusation that Cyrano is a Klingon agent
TOS / "The Trouble with Tribbles"

"And as captain I want two things done: first, find Cyrano Jones. And second, close that door."

—Kirk to Baris on being tribbled on
TOS / "The Trouble with Tribbles"

"Before they went into warp I transferred the whole kit and kaboodle into their engine room where they'll be no tribble at all."

—Scott to Kirk on the wherabouts of the tribbles
TOS / "The Trouble with Tribbles"

"Then the Prime Directive is in full force, Captain?"
   "No identification of self or mission. No interference with
   the social development of said planet."
      "No references to space or the fact that there *are* other
      worlds or more advanced civilizations."
—Spock, Kirk, and McCoy. The first real definition of the Prime Directive
TOS / "Bread and Circuses"

"A teddy bear…"
   "Not precisely, Doctor. On Vulcan the 'teddy bears' are
   alive and they have six-inch fangs."
—McCoy and Spock on Spock's childhood pet
TOS / "Journey to Babel"

"Captain, you are an excellent starship commander, but as a taxi
driver…you leave much to be desired."
—Spock to Kirk
TOS / "A Piece of the Action"

"My bairns. My poor bairns."
—Scott, on the abuse of his engines
TOS / "The Paradise Syndrome"

"Hail, hail, fire and snow,
Call the angel, we will go
Far away, for to see
Friendly Angel come to me."
—children summoning Gorgan
TOS / "And the Children Shall Lead"

"Take him where?"
   "In search of his brain, Doctor."
—McCoy and Kirk on Spock
TOS / "Spock's Brain"

"I know nothing about a brain."
—Luma to Kirk
TOS / "Spock's Brain"

"We just want to talk to somebody about Spock's brain, that's all."

—McCoy to Kara
TOS / "Spock's Brain"

"Brain and brain! What is brain?"

—Kara to Kirk
TOS / "Spock's Brain"

"Herbert. Herbert. Herbert. Herbert. Herbert."

—Severin's followers to Kirk
TOS / "The Way to Eden"

"We…reach, Mister Spock."

—Kirk to Spock
TOS / "The Way to Eden"

"They gave her back to me, Scotty."

—Kirk to Scott, on the *Enterprise*
The Motion Picture

"Heading, sir?"
    "Out there. Thataway."

—Chief DiFalco and Kirk
The Motion Picture

"The Human Adventure Is Just Beginning…"

—text superimposed at the end of
The Motion Picture

"Galloping around the cosmos is a game for the young, Doctor."

—Kirk to McCoy
The Wrath of Khan

"You are my superior officer. You are also my friend. I have been and always shall be yours."

—Spock to Kirk
The Wrath of Khan

"Suppose they went nowhere?"
    "Then this'll be your big chance to get away from it all."

—McCoy and Kirk, on following the transporter coordinates of the Marcuses
The Wrath of Khan

"He tasks me! He tasks me! And I shall have him. I'll chase him round the moons of Nibia and round the Antares maelstrom and round perdition's flames before I give him up."

—Khan to Joachim, paraphrasing Melville
Source: Herman Melville, *Moby Dick*
The Wrath of Khan

"Can I cook or can't I?"

—Carol to Kirk, on the results of the Genesis terraforming device
The Wrath of Khan

"Scotty, I need warp speed in three minutes or we're all dead!"

—Kirk to Scott
The Wrath of Khan

"No…you can't get away.…From hell's heart I stab at thee.…For hate's sake…I spit my last breath at thee!"

—Khan to Kirk
Source: Herman Melville, *Moby Dick*
The Wrath of Khan

"Don't grieve, Admiral—it is logical: the needs of the many outweigh—"
    "…the needs of the few…"
"Or the one."

—Spock and Kirk
The Wrath of Khan

"I never took the *Kobayashi Maru* test—until now. What do you think of my solution?"
    "Spock…!"
"I have been—and always shall be—your friend.…Live long and prosper."
    "No…!"

—Spock and Kirk, on the death of Spock
The Wrath of Khan

"Space, the final frontier…These are the continuing voyages of the *Starship Enterprise.*…Her ongoing mission: to explore strange new worlds…to seek out new life-forms and new civilizations…to boldly go where no man has gone before.…"

—Spock, the movie variation of the original opening narration
The Wrath of Khan

"*Qapla'*…"

—Valkris to Commander Kruge; first time Klingon phrase used (trans: Success)
The Search for Spock

"Don't call me Tiny."

—Sulu to Guard
The Search for Spock

"I'm not going to do anything about it, but you're going to sit in the closet."
    "The closet?! What, have you lost all your sense of reality?"
"This isn't reality. This is fantasy."

—Uhura and Starfleet Lieutenant "Mr. Adventure"
The Search for Spock

"It seems, Admiral, that I've got all his marbles."

—McCoy to Kirk, on Spock
The Search for Spock

"You! Help us or die!"
    "I do not deserve to live!"
"Fine, I'll kill you later! Let's get out of here."

—Kirk and Maltz
The Search for Spock

"Wait! You said you would kill me!"
    "I lied."

—Maltz and Kirk
The Search for Spock

"I don't know if you've got the whole picture or not, but he's not exactly working on all thrusters."

—McCoy to Kirk on Spock
The Voyage Home

"May fortune favor the foolish."

—Kirk to crew
The Voyage Home

"You really have gone where no man's gone before. Can't you tell me what it felt like?"

—McCoy to Spock, on death
The Voyage Home

"Judging by the pollution content of the atmosphere, I believe we have arrived at the latter half of the twentieth century."

—Spock to Kirk
The Voyage Home

"Are you sure it isn't time for a colorful metaphor?"

—Spock to Kirk
The Voyage Home

"Back in the sixties he was part of the Free Speech Movement at Berkeley. I think he did a little too much LDS."

—Kirk to Gillian, on Spock
The Voyage Home

"You're not exactly catching us at our best."
"That much is certain."

—Kirk and Spock, to Gillian
The Voyage Home

"Sure you won't change your mind?"
"Is there something wrong with the one I have?"

—Gillian and Spock
The Voyage Home

"Admiral, there be whales here!"

Scott to Kirk
The Voyage Home

"One damn minute, Admiral."

—Spock to Kirk, still trying to use those "colorful metaphors"
The Voyage Home

"My friends...we've come home."

—Kirk to crew, on the *Enterprise*-A
The Voyage Home

"All right, Mr. Sulu—let's see what she's got!"

—Kirk to Sulu, on the *Enterprise*-A
The Voyage Home

"Life is not a dream."
    "Go to sleep, Spock."

—Spock and Kirk, analyzing "Row, Row, Row Your Boat"
The Final Frontier

"I am well versed in the classics, Doctor."
    "Then how come you don't know 'Row, Row, Row Your
    Boat?'"

—Spock and McCoy
The Final Frontier

"I miss my old chair."

—Kirk to McCoy
The Final Frontier

"What are you standing around for? Do you not know a jail-
break when you see one?"

—Scott to Kirk, Spock, and McCoy
The Final Frontier

"I know this ship like the back of my hand."

—Scott to Kirk, the pride before the fall
The Final Frontier

"Excuse me. I'd just like to ask a question. What does God need
with a starship?"

—Kirk to Being
The Final Frontier

"Please, Captain, not in front of the Klingons."

—Spock to Kirk, on being hugged
The Final Frontier

"What is it with you, anyway?"

—McCoy to Kirk, on the captain's way with women as Martia succumbs to his charms
The Undiscovered Country

"I can't believe I kissed you."
        "Must've been your lifelong ambition!"

—Kirk and "Kirk"/Martia, on the shape-shifter Martia taking on Kirk's form
The Undiscovered Country

"Once again we've saved civilization as we know it."
        "The good news is: they're not gonna prosecute."

—Kirk and McCoy
The Undiscovered Country

"Nice to see you in action one more time, Captain Kirk."

—Captain Sulu to Kirk
The Undiscovered Country

"If I were human, I believe my response would be…'Go to Hell.' If I were human."

—Spock to Kirk, on being ordered to return to spacedock to be decommissioned
The Undiscovered Country

"Course heading, Captain?"
        "Second star to the right…and straight on till morning."

—Chekov and Kirk
Source: J.M. Barrie, *Peter Pan*
The Undiscovered Country

"Captain's log. Stardate 9529.1. This is the final cruise of the *Starship Enterprise* under my command. This ship and her history will shortly become the care of another crew. To them and their posterity will we commit our future. They will continue the voyages we have begun and journey to all the undiscovered countries, boldly going where no man…where no *one* has gone before.…"

—Kirk's log
The Undiscovered Country

"You left spacedock without a tractor beam?"
   "It won't be installed until Tuesday."

—Kirk and Captain John Harriman
Generations

"Space. The final frontier. These are the voyages of the *Starship Enterprise*. Its continuing mission, to explore strange new worlds, to seek out new life and new civilizations, to boldly go where no one has gone before...."

—Captain Jean-Luc Picard, first time new mission statement used
TNG / "Encounter at Farpoint"

"Permission to clean up the bridge?"

—Worf to Picard on Q
TNG / "Encounter at Farpoint"

"Let's see what this *Galaxy*-class starship can do."

—Picard to Worf
TNG / "Encounter at Farpoint"

"Engage!"

—Picard to conn, first time Picard gives order
TNG / "Encounter at Farpoint"

"Make it so."

—Picard to Data, first use of order, to assume standard parking orbit
TNG / "Encounter at Farpoint"

"Let's see what's out there."

—Picard to Riker
TNG / "Encounter at Farpoint"

"And what I want now is gentleness. And joy. And love. From *you*, Data. You *are* fully functional, aren't you?"

—Tasha to Data
TNG / "The Naked Now"

"Shut up, Wesley."

—Picard to Wesley
TNG / "Datalore"

"Shut up, Wesley?"

—Beverly to Picard
TNG / "Datalore"

"Shut up, Wesley!"

—Beverly to Wesley
TNG / "Datalore"

"So just tell me to 'shut up, Wesley,' and I will."

—Wesley to Beverly
TNG / "Datalore"

"Tell me about your ship, Riker—it's the *Enterprise*, isn't it?"
      "No…The name of my ship is the *Lollipop*."
"I have no knowledge of that ship."
      "It's just been commissioned. It's a good ship."

—false Captain Rice and Riker. Riker isn't fooled by the fake image of his friend
TNG / "The Arsenal of Freedom"

"So you will understand when I say, 'Death is that state in which one exists only in the memory of others…which is why it is not an end.' No good-byes. Just good memories. Hailing frequencies closed, sir."

—Tasha to Picard, her final farewell, recorded before her death
TNG / "Skin of Evil"

"Say good-bye, Data."
      "'Good-bye Data.'"

—Wesley and Data, paraphrasing George Burns and Gracie Allen
TNG / "The Outrageous Okona"

"Take my Worf, please."

—Data to bridge crew, paraphasing Henny Youngman
TNG / "The Outrageous Okona"

"Okay, the game is five-card stud, nothing wild. Ante up."

—Riker to Chief O'Brien, La Forge, Pulaski, and Data. First game of poker on the *Enterprise*-D
TNG / "The Measure of a Man"

"Tea. Earl Grey. Hot."

—Picard to replicator, first time Picard orders his favorite beverage
TNG / "Contagion"

"Fate protects fools, little children, and ships named *Enterprise*."

—Riker to bridge crew
TNG / "Contagion"

"You can't outrun them. You can't destroy them. If you damage them, the essence of what they are remains—they regenerate and keep coming....Eventually you will weaken—your reserves will be gone....They are relentless."

—Q to Picard, on the Borg
TNG / "Q Who?"

"You wanted to frighten us—we're frightened. You wanted to show us that we are inadequate—for the moment I grant that. You wanted me to say I need you. I need you."

—Picard to Q
TNG / "Q Who?"

"That was a difficult admission. Another man would've been humiliated to say those words. Another man would've rather died than ask for help."

—Q to Picard
TNG / "Q Who?"

"Send in the clones."

—Danilo to Picard, awaiting the new members of his society
TNG / "Up the Long Ladder"

"Jeremy, on the starship *Enterprise*, no one is alone. No one."

—Picard to Jeremy
TNG / "The Bonding"

"Please don't feel compelled now to tell me the story of the boy who cried *Worf*."

—Q to Worf
TNG / "Déjà Q"

"A warrior's drink."

—Worf to Guinan, on his first taste of prune juice
TNG / "Yesterday's *Enterprise*"

"Let's make sure history never forgets the name *Enterprise*."

—Picard to crew
TNG / "Yesterday's *Enterprise*"

"It is a good day to die, Duras…and the day is not yet over."

—Worf to Duras, first time phrase is used
TNG / "Sins of the Father"

"May I speak frankly, sir?"
    "By all means."
"You're in my way."

—Shelby and Riker
TNG / "The Best of Both Worlds, Part I"

"Strength is irrelevant. Resistance is futile. We wish to improve ourselves. We will add your biological and technological distinctiveness to our own. Your culture will adapt to service ours."

—Borg to Picard, first time speech is given
TNG / "The Best of Both Worlds, Part I"

"He wants to do something nice for me."
    "I'll alert the crew."

—Picard and Riker, on Q
TNG / "QPid"

"Sir, I protest. I am not a merry man."

—Worf to Picard
TNG / "QPid"

"I'll have you know I'm the greatest swordsman in all of Nottingham."
    "Very impressive. But there's something you should know."
"And what would that be?"
    "I'm not from Nottingham."

—Sir Guy of Gisbourne and Picard
TNG / "QPid"

"Shaka, when the walls fell..."

—Dathon to first officer, on failure to communicate
TNG / "Darmok"

"Darmok and Jalad at Tanagra."

—Dathon to Picard, inviting Picard to meet with him
TNG / "Darmok"

"But...you are Borg."
    "No. I am—Hugh."

—Picard and Hugh
TNG / "I, Borg"

"If you remember what we were, and how we lived...then we'll have found life again."

—Eline to Picard, on experiencing a lifetime in her society in a matter of moments
TNG / "The Inner Light"

"NCC-One-Seven-Oh-One. No bloody A, B, C, or D."

—Scott to computer, on requesting a holodeck program recreating his old ship
TNG / "Relics"

"You know, I served aboard eleven ships...freighters, cruisers, starships...but this is the only one I think of...the only one I miss."

—Scott to Picard, on the original *Enterprise*
TNG / "Relics"

"There comes a time when a man finds that he can't fall in love again....He knows that it's time to stop. I don't belong on your ship....I belong on this one. This was my home. This is where I had a purpose."

—Scott to Picard, on Scott's love for the original *Enterprise*
TNG / "Relics"

"*There are four lights!*"

—Picard to Madred refusing to break under torture
TNG / "Chain of Command, Part II"

"What I didn't put in the report...was that at the very end, he gave me a choice...between a life of comfort...or more torture...all I had to do was to say that I could see five lights when in fact there were only four."

"You didn't say it...."

"No...no, but I was going to. I would have told him anything...anything at all. But more than that, I *believed* that I could see five lights."

—Picard and Troi
TNG / "Chain of Command, Part II"

"Welcome to the afterlife, Jean-Luc. You're dead."

—Q to Picard
TNG / "Tapestry"

"I told you. You're dead. This is the afterlife. And I'm God."

—Q to Picard
TNG / "Tapestry"

"No. I am *not* dead. Because I refuse to believe that the afterlife is run by you. The universe is not so badly designed."

—Picard to Q
TNG / "Tapestry"

"I got angry."

—Data to Riker
TNG / "Descent, Part I"

"Congratulations. You just destroyed the *Enterprise*."

—Riker to Troi, on her failing the engineering test to become a bridge officer
TNG / "Thine Own Self"

"You cannot tarnish a rusted blade."

—Worf to Lursa and B'Etor, on their reputations
TNG / "Firstborn"

"It's time to put an end to your trek through the stars...make room for other, more worthy species."

—Q to Picard
TNG / "All Good Things..."

"Good-bye, Jean-Luc. I'm going to miss you. You had such potential. But then again…all good things must come to an end."
—Q to Picard
TNG / "All Good Things…"

"'The anomaly…my ship…my crew.' I suppose you're worried about your fish too. Well, if it puts your mind at ease, you've saved humanity once again."
—Q to Picard
TNG / "All Good Things…"

"You just don't get it, do you, Jean-Luc? The trial never ends."
—Q to Picard
TNG / "All Good Things…"

"See you out there."
—Q to Picard
TNG / "All Good Things…"

"Five-card stud, nothing wild. And the sky's the limit."
—Picard to Troi, Data, Beverly, Riker, Worf, and La Forge, on finally joining the poker game, ending the show
TNG / "All Good Things…"

"I would be happy to, sir. I just love scanning for life-forms. Life-forms…you tiny little life-forms…you precious little life-forms…where are you…?"
—Data to Riker; Data is somewhat overwhelmed by his new emotion chip
Generations

"You say history considers me dead. Who am I to argue with history?"
—Kirk to Picard
Generations

"I don't need to be lectured by you. I was out saving the galaxy when your grandfather was in diapers. Besides which, I think the galaxy owes me one."
—Kirk to Picard
Generations

"Who am I to argue with the captain of the *Enterprise*?"
—Kirk to Picard
Generations

"Good luck, Captain."
    "Call me Jim."
—Picard and Kirk
Generations

"It was...fun."
—Kirk to Picard, on life
Generations

"I'm going to miss this ship. She went before her time."
—Riker to Picard, on the destroyed *Enterprise*-D
Generations

"Tough little ship."
    "'*Little*?'"
—Riker and Worf, on the *Defiant*
First Contact

"You *do* remember how to fire phasers?"
—Riker to Worf
First Contact

"Would you three like to be alone?"
—Troi to Data and Picard, on touching the *Phoenix*
First Contact

"Timeline...this is no time to argue about time...we don't have the time."
—Troi to Riker
First Contact

"It's a primitive culture, I'm just trying to blend in...."
    "You're blended, all right."
—Troi and Riker
First Contact

"Your efforts to break the encryption codes will not be successful. Nor will your attempts to assimilate me into your collective."

"Brave words. I've heard them before from thousands of species across thousands of worlds...since long before you were created. But now...they are all Borg."

—Data and the Borg queen
First Contact

"Let me just make sure that I understand you correctly... 'Commander.' A group of cybernetic creatures from the future have traveled back through time to enslave the human race...and you're here to stop them."

"That's right."

"Hot damn, you're heroic."

—Cochrane and Riker
First Contact

"And you people...you're all astronauts on some kind of...star trek?"

—Cochrane to Riker
First Contact

"Assimilate *this*."

—Worf to Borg
First Contact

"If you were any other man...I would *kill* you where you stand."

—Worf to Picard, on the accusation of cowardice
First Contact

"You broke your little ships."

—Lily to Picard, on the *Enterprise* models
First Contact

"And he piled upon the whale's white hump the sum of all the rage and hate felt by his whole race...if his chest had been a cannon, he would've shot his heart upon it."

—Picard to Lily, paraphrasing Herman Melville, *Moby Dick*
First Contact

"Resistance…is futile."

—Data to Borg queen
First Contact

"It's good to see you, too…'Old Man.'"

—Sisko to Dax, first time nickname used
DS9 / "Emissary"

"Earth. Oh, don't get me wrong…a thousand years ago it had character. Crusades. Spanish Inquisition. Watergate….Now it's just mind-numbingly dull."

—Q to Vash
DS9 / "Q-Less"

"That's one of the great things about this station. You never know what's going to happen next…or who you're going to meet."

—Sisko to Fenna
DS9 / "Second Sight"

"Have you lost your mind?"
    "No. I didn't lose it. I just changed it."

—the mirror Sisko and Intendant, on helping Kira and Bashir escape
DS9 / "Crossover"

"I've brought back a little surprise for the Dominion."

—Sisko to Kira on the *Defiant*
DS9 / "The Search, Part I"

"To become a thing is to know a thing. To assume its form…is to begin to understand its existence."

—female shape-shifter to Odo
DS9 / "The Search, Part II"

"No Changeling has ever harmed another."

—female shape-shifter to Odo
DS9 / "The Search, Part II"

"Isn't there some petty thief you could harass?"
    "Just you."

—Quark and Odo
DS9 / "Meridian"

322 | QUOTABLE STAR TREK

"Looks like you've got your evening all planned. Hope you've got room for…the unexpected."

—Tom Riker to Kira
DS9 / "Defiant"

"I mean this whole thing is ridiculous. How could I be interested in Bareil? We both know it's always been you."

—Dax to Sisko, while under the influence of a Betazoid "love bug"
DS9 / "Fascination"

"I guess I'm just in the zone today."

—O'Brien to Sisko on his bull's-eye at darts
DS9 / "Shakaar"

"He said, 'You're too late. We're everywhere.'"

—Odo to Sisko, the last words of the changeling killed by Odo
DS9 / "The Adversary"

"Just what this station needs…another Klingon."

—Quark on Worf's arrival
DS9 / "The Way of the Warrior, Part I"

"I know her. She used to be my wife."

—Dax to Kira, on Lenara
DS9 / "Rejoined"

"Did you take care of that idiot in Roswell who told the press we captured a flying saucer?"
    "We convinced him to issue a retraction. Turns out it was just a weather balloon."

—General Denning and Captain Wainwright, on Quark's ship landing on twentieth-century Earth
DS9 / "Little Green Men"

"So if they don't have universal translators, then why are they banging their heads?"

—Rom to Quark, on the strange behavior of the humans
DS9 / "Little Green Men"

"A vast alliance of planets. You get the craziest ideas."
—Professor Carlson to Nurse Garland, on a twentieth-century dream of the future
DS9 / "Little Green Men"

"Where's the core memory interface?"
    "Oh…it's right behind the spatula."
—Eddington and Rom, on some minor modifications of the holosuite controls
DS9 / "Our Man Bashir"

"Kiss the girl, get the key. They never taught me that in the Obsidian Order."
—Garak to Bashir, in Bashir's secret agent holosuite program
DS9 / "Our Man Bashir"

"Interesting. You saved the day by destroying the world."
    "I bet they didn't teach you that in the Obsidian Order."
—Garak and Bashir, on Bashir's secret agent holosuite program
DS9 / "Our Man Bashir"

"Why is it when you smile, I want to leave the room?"
    "I suppose it's because of my overwhelming charm."
—Kira and Dukat
DS9 / "Return to Grace"

"Have you any idea how bored I used to get sitting in the transporter room waiting for something to break down? Here, I've half a dozen new problems every day. This station needs me."
—O'Brien to Worf, on life on the *Enterprise* vs. Deep Space 9
DS9 / "The Bar Association"

"So let me get this straight…no sleep, no food, no women. No wonder you're so angry. After thirty or forty years of that, I'd be angry, too."
—Dax to Virak'kara, on life as a Jem'Hadar
DS9 / "To the Death"

"So what you're telling me is that…Major Kira is going to have my baby."
—O'Brien to Bashir, on the need to transfer his unborn child from his wife to a surrogate mother
DS9 / "Body Parts"

"Maybe I wasn't clear. I'm not dying."
"Maybe I wasn't clear. I don't care. I want my merchandise.
I have a thousand ideas of how to defile your remains....
Want to hear my favorites?"

—Quark and Brunt on contracting for the desiccated remains of Quark
DS9 / "Body Parts"

"So you're not contending it was a predestination paradox?"
"A time loop. That you were *meant* to go back into the
past."
"No."
"Good."
"We hate those."

—Lucsly, Dulmer, and Sisko
DS9 / "Trials and Tribble-ations"

"Another glorious chapter of Klingon history. Tell me, do they
still sing songs of the Great Tribble Hunt?"

—Odo to Worf
DS9 / "Trials and Tribble-ations"

"We do not discuss it with outsiders."

—Worf to Bashir on twenty-third-century Klingons' appearance
DS9 / "Trials and Tribble-ations"

"He put a bomb in a tribble?"

—Sisko to Dax, on Darvin's revenge against Kirk
DS9 / "Trials and Tribble-ations"

"Benjamin Sisko, sir. I've been on temporary assignment here.
Before I leave, I just want to say…it's been an honor serving
with you, sir."

—Sisko to Kirk
DS9 / "Trials and Tribble-ations"

"Don't you get it? I'm not trying to rescue you. I'm taking you
along as emergency rations. If you die, I'm going to eat you."

—Quark to Odo
DS9 / "The Ascent"

"Constable—why are you talking to your beverage?"
"It's not a beverage, it's a changeling."
—Worf and Odo, on the changeling baby
DS9 / "The Begotten"

"You and I on the same side. It never seemed quite right, did it?"
—Dukat to Kira, on Dukat's decision to join Cardassia with the Dominion against the Federation
DS9 / "By Inferno's Light"

"My people have a saying, 'Never turn your back on a Breen.'"
—female Romulan to Bashir
DS9 / "By Inferno's Light"

"Please state the nature of the medical emergency."
"Oh, *that's* original."
—Bashir hologram and an EMH
DS9 / "'Doctor Bashir, I Presume?'"

"My *Marauder Mo* action figures. I thought you'd thrown these out...."
"All these years, I've been keeping them in storage for you. I figured you'd want to take them back to Deep Space 9 with you."
"I sure do. Do you have any idea how much these are worth?"
"Not as much as if you'd kept them in the original packaging...which is what I told you at the time."
—Quark and Ishka
DS9 / "Ferengi Love Songs"

"Is it true you can kill someone just by looking at them?"
"Only when I am angry."
—Gabriel and Worf, on being the infamous Son of Mogh
DS9 / "Children of Time"

"I love you, Nerys. I've always loved you."
—older Odo to Kira
DS9 / "Children of Time"

"And I might've idly suggested that there wasn't a chance in hell that any of us would get out of here alive."

"And that's when Morn hit you with the barstool and ran out onto the Promenade screaming, 'We're all doomed.'"
"Some people just don't react well to stress."

—Quark and Odo, on the Dominion threat
DS9 / "Blaze of Glory"

"It's a shame. And the worst part of it is…this isn't a coil spanner. It's a flux coupler."

—Garak to Amaro, on the tool Amaro had been searching for, with which a drug-affected Garak killed him
DS9 / "Empok Nor"

"A message. From Sisko."
    "I don't understand."
"He's letting me know…he'll be back."

—Dukat and Weyoun, on finding Sisko's baseball left behind
DS9 / "Call to Arms"

"Our men need to see that we're still allies. Smile. Dukat."
    "I'm smiling."

—Weyoun and Dukat
DS9 / "Behind the Lines"

"I wish I could make you understand, but you can't. You're not a changeling."
    "You're right. I'm a solid."

—Odo and Kira, on the Great Link
DS9 / "Behind the Lines"

"How about next time we switch roles? That way, I can rescue you."

—Dax to Worf
DS9 / "Favor the Bold"

"There's nothing more romantic than a wedding on DS9 in Springtime."

"When the neutrinos are in bloom."

—Bashir and O'Brien, on Dax and Worf's upcoming nuptials
DS9 / "You Are Cordially Invited…"

"I'm going to kill Worf. I'm going to kill Worf. That's what I'm going to do. I can see it clearly now. I'm going to kill him…."

"Kill Worf."

"Kill Worf."

—Bashir and O'Brien, on Bashir's "vision" after suffering through Klingon prenuptial rituals
DS9 / "You Are Cordially Invited…"

"A child. A moron. A failure. And a psychopath. Quite a little team you've put together…"

—Brunt to Quark
DS9 / "The Magnificent Ferengi"

"I can see it now—the lonely little girl, befriended by empathetic aliens who teach her how to smile. It's enough to make you go out and buy a television set."

—Herbert to Julius Eaton, on Julius's latest story
DS9 / "Far Beyond the Stars"

"She's got a worm in her belly? Oh, that's disgusting. That's interesting, but that's disgusting."

—Darlene Kursky on the Dax character in Benny's story, in-joke as actress is playing both roles
DS9 / "Far Beyond the Stars"

"You are the dreamer. And the dream."

—Preacher to Benny
DS9 / "Far Beyond the Stars"

"…Maybe, just maybe, Benny isn't the dream—we are. Maybe we're nothing more than figments of his imagination. For all we know, at this very moment, somewhere, far beyond all those distant stars…Benny Russell is dreaming of us."

—Benjamin Sisko to Joseph Sisko
DS9 / "Far Beyond the Stars"

"Our baby…would've been so beautiful."

—Dax to Worf, Jadzia's last words
DS9 / "Tears of the Prophets"

"He's not sure he's coming back."
  "What makes you say that?"
"His baseball. He took it with him."

—Kira and Odo, on Sisko
DS9 / "Tears of the Prophets"

"Please state the nature of the medical emergency."

—the Doctor to Kim, first use of phrase
VGR / "Caretaker"

"We're alone in an uncharted part of the galaxy. We've already made some friends here…and some enemies. We have no idea of the dangers we're going to face. But one thing is clear—both crews are going to have to work together if we're to survive. That's why Commander Chakotay and I have agreed that this should be *one* crew…a Starfleet crew. And as the only Starfleet vessel 'assigned' to the Delta Quadrant, we'll continue to follow our directive to seek out new worlds and explore space. But our primary goal is clear. Even at maximum speeds, it would take seventy-five years to reach the Federation.…But I'm not willing to settle for that. There's another entity like the Caretaker out there somewhere who has the ability to get us there a lot faster. We'll be looking for her. And we'll be looking for wormholes, spatial rifts, or new technologies to help us. Somewhere, along this journey—we'll find a way back."

—Janeway to crew
VGR / "Caretaker"

"There's coffee in that nebula."

—Janeway to Chakotay, on a new energy source for the ship's replicators
VGR / "The Cloud"

"This ship is the match of any vessel within a hundred light-years. And what do they do with it? 'Well let's see if we can't find some space anomaly today that might rip it apart....'"
—Neelix to Kes
VGR / "The Cloud"

"There's one more request...something of a personal nature....I would like...a name."
—the Doctor to Kes
VGR / "Eye of the Needle"

"Captain...I think I should tell you I've never actually landed a starship before."
"That's all right, Lieutenant. Neither have I."
—Paris and Janeway
VGR / "The 37's"

"I traveled the road many times. Sat on the porch...played the games...been the dog...everything....I was even the scarecrow for awhile...."
—Quinn to Janeway, on life in the Q Continuum
VGR / "Death Wish"

"Oh, we've all done the scarecrow, big deal."
—Q to Quinn
VGR / "Death Wish"

"Mister Kim...we're Starfleet officers. 'Weird' is part of the job."
—Janeway to Kim
VGR / "Deadlock"

"Space must've seemed a whole lot bigger back then. It's not surprising they had to bend the rules a little. They were a little slower to invoke the Prime Directive...and a little quicker to pull their phasers. Of course, the whole bunch of them would be booted out of Starfleet today. But I have to admit...I would've loved to ride shotgun at least once with a group of officers like that."
—Janeway to Kim, on the twenty-third century
VGR / "Flashback"

"I do not experience feelings of nostalgia. But there are times when I think back to those days...of meeting Kirk, Spock, and the others...and I am pleased that I was part of it."

"In a funny way...I feel like I was a part of it, too."

"Then perhaps you can be nostalgic for both of us."

—Tuvok and Janeway
VGR / "Flashback"

"What will we need to pass as locals in this era?"

"Simple. Nice clothes, fast car...and lots of money."

—Janeway and Paris, on the late twentieth century
VGR / "Future's End, Part I"

"Let's recap: UFO in orbit...laser pistols...people vanishing...I've seen every episode of *Mission: Impossible*—you're *not* secret agents."

—Rain to Paris
VGR / "Future's End, Part II"

"Tuvok...has anyone ever told you...you're a real freakasaurus?"

—Paris to Tuvok
VGR / "Future's End, Part II"

"I know that you're probably asking yourself: 'Why would a brilliant, handsome, dashingly omnipotent being like Q want to mate with a scrawny little bipedal specimen like me?'"

"Let me guess: no one else in the universe will have you."

—Q and Janeway
VGR / "The Q and the Grey"

"Oh, I see! This is one of those silly human rituals—you're playing hard to get."

"As far as you're concerned, Q, I'm *impossible* to get."

—Q and Janeway
VGR / "The Q and the Grey"

"I was wondering, Kathy: what could anyone possibly see in this big oaf anyway? Is it the tattoo? Because *mine's* bigger."
"Not big enough."
—Q and Janeway on Chakotay
VGR / "The Q and the Grey"

"Ah, there you are. I have several brilliant ideas for upcoming chapters of your holo-novel, as well as a list of revisions and dialogue changes that I believe will improve the earlier install-ments."
"I don't believe this."
"No thanks are necessary. In addition, I'm prepared to offer my expertise in the creation of holographic *mise-en-scene*..."
—the Doctor and Paris
VGR / "Worse Case Scenario"

"Welcome to the worst day of my life."
—Torres to Paris
VGR / "Day of Honor"

"I'm glad the last thing I'll see is you."
—Paris to Torres, trapped in space and running out of oxygen
VGR / "Day of Honor"

"I'm willing to explore my humanity. Take off your clothes."
—Seven of Nine to Kim
VGR / "Revulsion"

"Having fun?"
"No."
—Janeway and Seven of Nine, on socializing
VGR / "Mortal Coil"

"Traditionally, one crawls in head first."
—the Doctor to EMH-2, on entering a Jefferies tube
VGR / "Message in a Bottle"

"You hit the wrong ship!"

    "It wasn't my fault!"

"Well, then whose fault was it, the torpedo's?"

—the Doctor and EMH-2
VGR / "Message in a Bottle"

"Sixty thousand light-years...seems a little closer today."

—Janeway to Chakotay, on receiving a message from Starfleet
VGR / "Message in a Bottle"

"Sounds to me like you're starting to embrace your humanity...."

    "No. But as I said...nothing is impossible."

—Janeway and Seven of Nine
VGR / "Hope and Fear"

32. Personal Favorites

"'It was a dark and stormy night....' That's not a promising beginning."
"It may get better."
—Picard and Troi, on reading the novel *Hotel Royale* by Todd Matthews
Source: Edward Bulwer-Lytton, *Paul Clifford*
TNG / "The Royale"

"I've got my own system. Books, young man, books. Thousands of them. If time wasn't so important I'd show you something—my library. Thousands of books..."
—Cogley to Kirk
TOS / "Court Martial"

"There's an old, old saying on Earth, Mister Sulu. 'Fool me once, shame on you. Fool me twice, shame on *me*.'"
—Scott to Sulu
TOS / "Friday's Child"

"Ah, yes, the holding, the touching. Vaal has forbidden this."
"Well, there goes Paradise."
—Akuta and McCoy, on love
TOS / "The Apple"

"I mean, I know this world needs help. That's why some of my generation are kind of crazy and rebels, you know? We wonder if we're going to be alive when we're thirty."

—Roberta Lincoln to Gary Seven
TOS / "Assignment: Earth"

"And I'll love you, Miramanee...always."
  "Each kiss is as the first...."

—Kirk and Miramanee, as she dies
TOS / "The Paradise Syndrome"

"I suppose it has thorns."
  "I never met a rose that didn't."

—Miranda and Kirk, on his parting gift to her
TOS / "Is There in Truth No Beauty?"

"Indeed, Doctor, the young lady did show a marked preference for your company."
  "Well, now nobody can blame her for that, can they?"

—Spock and McCoy, on Natira
TOS / "For the World Is Hollow and I Have Touched the Sky"

"Hours can be centuries, just as words can be lies."

—Vanna to Kirk
TOS / "The Cloud Minders"

"Forget."

—Spock to Kirk, the gift of a mind-meld to help Kirk forget the pain of a lost love
TOS / "Requiem for Methuselah"

"Then tell me, what do you have to gain if we accept?"
  "Nothing but the knowledge that I have done what I believe in."

—Green and Surak
TOS / "The Savage Curtain"

"After all, a library serves no purpose unless someone is using it."

—Mister Atoz to Spock
TOS / "All Our Yesterdays"

"Self-expression doesn't seem to be one of your problems."

—Kirk to Saavik
The Wrath of Khan

"There are two possibilities. They are unable to respond; they are unwilling to respond."

—Spock to Kirk, on Regula One Station
The Wrath of Khan

"Remember."

—Spock to McCoy, mind-melding with the doctor
The Wrath of Khan

"Just words."
    "But good words. That's where ideas begin."

—Kirk and David
The Wrath of Khan

"'It's a far, far better thing I do than I have ever done before. A far better resting place that I go to than I have ever known.'"
    "Is that a poem?"
"No. Something Spock was trying to tell me. On my birthday."

—Kirk and Carol
Source: Charles Dickens, *A Tale of Two Cities*
The Wrath of Khan

"You okay, Jim? How do you feel?"
    "Young. I feel young."

—McCoy and Kirk
The Wrath of Khan

"The word...is no. I am therefore going anyway."

—Kirk to Sulu, on the attempt to save Spock on the Genesis Planet
The Search for Spock

"Yes, poor friend. I hear he's fruity as a nutcake."

—Kirk to Guard, on McCoy's recent strange behavior
The Search for Spock

"You're suffering from a Vulcan mind-meld, Doctor."
"That green-blooded son of a bitch!…It's his revenge for all those arguments he lost."
—Kirk and McCoy, on Spock
The Search for Spock

"You Klingon bastard! You've killed my son. Klingon bastard, you've killed my son…! You Klingon bastard!!"
—Kirk to Kruge, on David
The Search for Spock

". . . Jim…your name is Jim."
—Spock to Kirk, on the stirrings of strong memory
The Search for Spock

"Oh, joy."
—McCoy to Kirk, on getting to help build the whale tank
The Voyage Home

"Everybody remember where we parked."
—Kirk to crew
The Voyage Home

"It's a miracle these people ever got out of the twentieth century."
—McCoy to Kirk
The Voyage Home

"The rest of you…break up. You look like a cadet review."
—Kirk to crew
The Voyage Home

"Hello, Alice. Welcome to Wonderland."
—Kirk to Gillian
The Voyage Home

"I'm going to sleep this off. Please let me know if there's some other way we can screw up tonight."
—Kirk to Spock, on an unsuccesful dinner with the Klingons
The Undiscovered Country

"I tried to save him! I was desperate to save him! He was the last best hope in the universe for peace."

—McCoy to Chang, on Gorkon
The Undiscovered Country

"I don't see no points on your ears, boy, but you sound like a Vulcan."
    "No, sir. I am an android."
"Almost as bad."

—McCoy and Data
TNG / "Encounter at Farpoint"

"Well, this is a new ship, but she's got the right name. Now you remember that, you hear?"
    "I will, sir."
"You treat her like a lady and she'll always bring you home...."

—McCoy and Data
TNG / "Encounter at Farpoint"

"What's your name? Tell me you love jazz."
    "My name is Minuet and I love all jazz except Dixieland."
"Why not Dixieland?"
    "You can't dance to it."
"My girl."

—Riker and Minuet
TNG / "11001001"

"You've done well. A great starship—on the far reaches of the galaxy. It's everything you'd hoped."
    "Not exactly. Nothing works just as you hope...."

—Jenice Manheim and Picard
TNG / "We'll Always Have Paris"

"One is my name and the other is not."

—Data to Pulaski, on proper pronunciation of "Data"
TNG / "The Child"

"Data is a toaster."

—Phillipa to Riker, on summary judgment of Data's status as property or person
TNG / "The Measure of a Man"

"I dream of a galaxy where your eyes are the stars…and the universe worships the night."

> "Careful, putting me on a pedestal so high you may not be able to reach me."

"Then I'll learn how to fly. You are the heart in my day and the soul in my night."

—Riker and Guinan, demonstrating to Wesley the art of flirting
TNG / "The Dauphin"

"Tell me more about my eyes."

—Guinan to Riker
TNG / "The Dauphin"

"You're awfully young to be so driven."

> "Yes, I am. I *had* to be. I had to be the best because only the best get to be *here*."

—La Forge and Sonya Gomez
TNG / "Q Who?"

"There is no greater challenge than the study of philosophy."

> "But William James won't be on my Starfleet exams."

"The important things never will be."

—Picard and Wesley
TNG / "Samaritan Snare"

"Sometimes, Number One, you just have to bow to the absurd."

—Picard to Riker
TNG / "Up the Long Ladder"

"I don't bite….Well, that's wrong; I do bite."

—K'Ehleyr to Worf, on Worf being uncomfortable around her
TNG / "The Emissary"

"Men like us do not need holodecks, Wesley. I have played seasons in my mind. It was my reward to myself. For patience. Knowing my turn would come. Call your shot. Point to a star. One great blast and the crowd rises. A brand new era in astrophysics. Postponed one hundred and ninety-six years on account of rain."

—Stubbs to Wesley, on the concern that he may miss his opportunity to conduct the most ambitious experiment of his career
TNG / "Evolution"

"Conformity is not my style."

—Devinoni to Troi
TNG / "The Price"

"Oh, very clever, Worf. Eat any good books lately?"

—Q to Worf
TNG / "Déjà Q"

"He was the only member of my family who had a sense of humor. Except no one ever stayed around him long enough to realize it...but me. My mother tells me I remind her of him. And I probably do. The idea of 'fitting in' just repels me."

—Guinan to La Forge on her uncle Terkim
TNG / "Hollow Pursuits"

"You disagree with me, fine. You need to take it to the captain, fine. Through me. You do an end run around me again, I'll snap you back so hard, you'll think you're a first-year cadet again."

—Riker to Shelby
TNG / "The Best of Both Worlds, Part I"

"It's just that...ever since I was a child...I've always known exactly what I wanted to do—be a member of Starfleet. Nothing else mattered to me. Virtually my entire youth was spent in the pursuit of that goal. In fact...I probably skipped my childhood altogether."

—Picard to Troi
TNG / "Suddenly Human"

"He's still out there...dreaming about starships and adventures. It's getting late."
    "Yes...but let him dream."

—Marie Picard and Robert, on René Picard
TNG / "Family"

"If there's nothing wrong with me...maybe there's something wrong with the universe...."

—Beverly to herself
TNG / "Remember Me"

"I have become used to her."

—Data to Troi, on feeling friendship for Ishara
TNG / "Legacy"

"Not even a bite on the cheek for old time's sake?"

—K'Ehleyr to Worf
TNG / "Reunion"

"Is this how you handle all of your personnel problems?"
    "Sure. You'd be surprised how far a hug goes with Geordi
    or Worf...."

—Troi and Riker, on comforting her
TNG / "The Loss"

"I pity you. We live in a universe of magic, which evidently you
cannot see."

—Ardra to Riker
TNG / "Devil's Due"

"Jean-Luc, it's wonderful to see you again. How 'bout a big
hug?"

—Q to Picard
TNG / "QPid"

"That's one reason why I ran away. They're lost...defeated....I
will never be."

—Ro to Picard
TNG / "Ensign Ro"

"I think you've got a great deal to learn from Starfleet."
    "I always thought Starfleet had a lot to learn from me,
    Captain."

—Picard and Ro
TNG / "Ensign Ro"

"...That's it, follow your dreams. And write about them."

—Clemens to Jack
TNG / "Time's Arrow, Part II"

"You'll just have to read my books. What I am is pretty much there."
—Clemens to Picard, on not having the opportunity to get to know the author
TNG / "Time's Arrow, Part II"

"Throughout the ages, from Keats to Jorkemo, poets have composed odes to individuals who have had a profound effect upon their lives. In keeping with that tradition, I have written my next poem in honor of my cat. I call it 'Ode to Spot.'"

Felis catus is your taxonomic nomenclature
An endothermic quadruped, carnivorous by nature
Your visual, olfactory, and auditory senses
Contribute to your hunting skills and natural defenses.

I find myself intrigued by your sub-vocal oscillations
A singular development of cat communications
That obviates your basic hedonistic predilection
For a rhythmic stroking of your fur to demonstrate affection....

A tail is quite essential for your acrobatic talents.
You would not be so agile if you lacked its counterbalance
And when not being utilized to aid in locomotion
It often serves to illustrate the state of your emotion.

Oh, Spot, the complex levels of behavior you display
Connotes a fairly well-developed cognitive array
And though you are not sentient, Spot, and do not comprehend
I nonetheless consider you a true and valued friend...."
—Data reading his poem in iambic septameter
TNG / "Schisms"

"A deadline has a wonderful way of concentrating the mind."
—Moriarty to Picard
TNG / "Ship in a Bottle"

"Don't be afraid of your darker side. Have fun with it."
—Troi to Riker
TNG / "Frame of Mind"

"I've known I needed to do this for a long time. I just haven't been able to admit it myself."

"But you always said that being at the academy was the best thing that ever happened to you."

"I know. For a while it was."

—Wesley and Beverly, on Wesley's choice to leave Starfleet
TNG / "Journey's End"

"Now, you'll have to excuse me, Captain, I have an appointment with eternity and I don't want to be late."

—Soran to Picard
Generations

"You know you're causing a lot of trouble."

"I can't tell you how delighted I am to hear that."

—Sisko and Mullibok
DS9 / "Progress"

"Nothing makes them happy. They are dedicated to being unhappy and to spreading that unhappiness wherever they go...they are the Ambassadors of Unhappy."

—Bashir to Sisko on hosting several visiting Federation ambassadors
DS9 / "The Forsaken"

"It looks...ordinary. I've never cared to be ordinary. So you see, Odo, even we non-shape-shifters have to change who we are once in a while."

—Lwaxana to Odo, on being without her wig
DS9 / "The Forsaken"

"You are not at all what I expected."

"No one's ever paid me a greater compliment."

—Odo to Lwaxana
DS9 / "The Forsaken"

"Oh, I'm sure it isn't appropriate at all. But then, I hate to be 'appropriate.'"

—Dax to Arjin, on being on a first-name basis
DS9 / "Playing God"

"Will you stop talking and shoot them?"
—Dukat to Sisko, on the Maquis
DS9 / "The Maquis, Part II"

"I used to get a thrill just walking into that building. I'd look around at the admirals and think—'One day that's going to be me. One day I'm the one that's going to be making the big decisions.'"
—Sisko to Dax, on Starfleet Headquarters
DS9 / "The Search, Part I"

"Of course it's your fault. Everything that goes wrong here is your fault. It says so in your contract."
—Quark to Rom, on the replicator failure
DS9 / "Heart of Stone"

"They broke seven of your transverse ribs and fractured your clavicle."
> "But I got off several cutting remarks which no doubt did serious damage to their egos."

—Bashir and Garak, on the Klingon attack in the tailor shop
DS9 / "The Way of the Warrior, Part I"

"I'm not a writer yet."
> "Sounds like you're waiting for something to happen that's going to turn you into one."

—Melanie and old Jake
DS9 / "The Visitor"

"You mean your people are going to invade…Cleveland?"
—Captain Wainwright to Nog
DS9 / "Little Green Men"

"Stay back, or I'll…disintegrate this hostage."
> "With your finger?"
"With my death ray."
> "Looks a lot like a finger to me."

—Quark and Denning
DS9 / "Little Green Men"

"I do apologize. You must be incensed. In fact, if I were in your shoes, I'd...grab a bottle of champagne and shoot me."
—Garak to Bashir, on the doctor's earlier form of self-defense
DS9 / "Our Man Bashir"

"Sooner or later you're going to have to adapt."
   "Perhaps, in the end, it will be all of you that have to adapt to me."
—Dax and Worf
DS9 / "The Bar Association"

"You sentenced my wife to death."
   "Isn't that a coincidence? I was hoping you weren't married."
—Guard and Intendant
DS9 / "Shattered Mirror"

"*This* is important. You and I. Things change...but not this."
—Sisko to Jake, on the love between father and son
DS9 / "For the Cause"

"Fine. But I can't wait to get back to DS9 and see your face when you find out that I never existed."
—Bashir to O'Brien, on a potential predestination paradox
DS9 / "Trials and Tribble-ations"

"I guess the difference between you and me is I *remember this time*—I lived in this time. And it's...it's hard to not want to be...a part of it again."
—Dax to Sisko, on the twenty-third century
DS9 / "Trials and Tribble-ations"

"I had a feeling he'd become a doctor—he had the hands of a surgeon."
—Dax to Sisko on McCoy
DS9 / "Trials and Tribble-ations"

"You can't change a writer's words without his permission. That's sacrilege."
—Jake to Nog
DS9 / "The Ascent"

"I prefer the title 'gul.' So much more hands-on than Legate. And less pretentious than the other alternatives… president… emperor…first minister…Emissary…."

—Dukat to Sisko
DS9 / "Ties of Blood and Water"

"What are you doing in my closet?"
    "Conducting official FCA business."
"In my closet?"

—Quark and Brunt
DS9 / "Ferengi Love Songs"

"Welcome to Gaia, Captain Sisko."

—Miranda O'Brien to Sisko
DS9 / "Children of Time"

"This is the eighth run-through and you haven't been able to hit a single Jem'Hadar. And you shot Moogie."
    "I saw we weren't going to rescue her—so I put her out of her misery."

—Nog and Leck, on practicing for a rescue operation
DS9 / "The Magnificent Ferengi"

"You couldn't ambush a Bolian if he was blindfolded and tied to a tree."

—Nog to Brunt
DS9 / "The Magnificent Ferengi"

"Think of me as Morn. I can't believe I just said that."

—Quark to Larell, on joining a partnership that formerly included Morn
DS9 / "Who Mourns for Morn?"

"I read a lot of science fiction."
    "Bless you, my child."
        "The world needs more people like you."

—Darlene, Herbert, and Kay
DS9 / "Far beyond the Stars"

"What does fun have to do with Major Kira?"
    "I'll pretend I didn't hear that."
—Odo and Vic
DS9 / "His Way"

"I had a pretty good idea what this was the minute I laid eyes on it. That confirms it. It's a slab of stone with some writing on it."
—Dax to Sisko, on the ancient tablet brought up to the station from Bajor
DS9 / "The Reckoning"

"I just had this uncontrollable urge...to smash the tablet."
    "Oh, I get those urges all the time. Of course, I never *act* on them...."
—Sisko and Dax, on the dust and fragments before them
DS9 / "The Reckoning"

"Missing. The captain is missing. It seems I've found myself on a Voyage of the Damned. Very well. Please advise the highest-ranking officer who is not missing to see me at his earliest convenience."
—the Doctor to Neelix
VGR / "Time and Again"

"You're saying that somebody used his brain to send secret data to our enemy?"
—Minister to Tuvok, on Paris
VGR / "Ex Post Facto"

"Get the cheese to sickbay. The doctor should look at it as soon as possible."
—Torres to crew member
VGR / "Learning Curve"

"Barclay was part of the original engineering team that designed your program. He was in charge of testing your interpersonal skills."
—Kim to the Doctor
VGR / "Projections"

"From the day you came out of your mother upside down, I knew the spirits had chosen you to be a Contrary."

"No one chooses for me. I choose my *own* way. And if that makes me a Contrary, I'll have to live with it."

—Kolopak and young Chakotay
VGR / "Tattoo"

"Did anyone ever tell you you're angry when you're beautiful?"

—Q to Janeway
VGR / "Death Wish"

"But I've already prepared today's topic—'How to Keep Your Nostrils Happy.'"

—the Doctor to Neelix, on his health segment for Neelix's shipwide show
VGR/ "Investigations"

"'Roughing it?' Let's see....We have shelter, furniture, research equipment, tricorders, a replicator....It's too rough for me."

—Chakotay to Janeway, on having to camp out on a planet's surface
VGR / "Resolutions"

"Who are you people? And what is that thing in your pants?"

—Rain to Tuvok, on his tricorder
VGR / "Future's End, Part I"

"And *you*. Mister leisure suit."

"*There's* a name I hadn't considered."

—Rain and the Doctor
VGR / "Future's End, Part II"

"Foreplay with a Q can last for *decades*."

"Sorry, but I'm busy for the next sixty or seventy years."

—Q and Janeway
VGR / "The Q and the Grey"

"Never mind that. What are you doing with that dog? I'm not talking about the puppy."

—Q female to Q on Janeway, who's playing with the puppy Q gave her
VGR / "The Q and the Grey"

"Well? What are you doing?"
     "Enjoying myself?"
"Then show it."

—Torres and Paris
VGR / "Blood Fever"

"Careful what you wish for, Lieutenant."

—Torres to Paris
VGR / "Blood Fever"

"We have a saying, 'My course is as elusive as a shadow across the sky.'"

—Zahir to Kes
VGR / "Darkling"

"Who *wrote* this stuff?"

—Paris on the holoprogram
VGR / "Worse Case Scenario"

"I overslept this morning because I forgot to tell the computer to wake me…and then the acoustic inverter in my sonic shower blew out."
     "That'll make your hair stand on end…."
"So I didn't have time for breakfast, and when I got here two people were out sick so I had to cancel the fuel cell overhaul, and then an injector burst for no apparent reason and started spewing plasma coolant…."

—Torres and Paris, on "one of those days"
VGR / "Day of Honor"

"I haven't built any empires…and I can't say that I've personally defeated any enemies in battle. But you have to realize, I'm not living among warriors."
     "Then how do you expect to distinguish yourself?"
"I don't know. I guess I'm doing the best I can."

—Torres and Moklor
VGR / "Day of Honor"

"I can't imagine a time I wouldn't have found you fascinating."

—Paris to Torres
VGR / "Day of Honor"

"Duty calls."

—Neelix to Chakotay, on finding a reason to live
VGR / "Mortal Coil"

"Stop breathing down my neck."
    "My breathing is merely a simulation."
"So is my neck. Stop it anyway."

—the Doctor and EMH-2
VGR / "Message in a Bottle"

"Between impulse and action there is a realm of good taste begging for your acquaintance."

—the Doctor to Seven of Nine
VGR / "One"

"Well…what do you know? I finally got the last word."

—McCoy to Amanda
TOS / "Journey to Babel"

ACKNOWLEDGMENTS

My gratitude and appreciation:

To all the teachers, librarians, and booksellers who fostered my voracious book "habit" from an early age, especially my love of *Star Trek* books;

To Carol Baron for introducing me to Sandra Bettin, to Sandra Bettin for introducing me to Jonathan West, to Jonathan West for helping me get my résumé into the *Star Trek* offices, to Lolita Fatjo for finding my résumé on file and calling me in for an interview when a writers' assistant position was available, to René Echevarria and Robert Hewitt Wolfe for hiring me and letting me learn, to Bradley Thompson for being another joy to work for;

To Ira Steven Behr and Ronald D. Moore and Hans Beimler and David Weddle and Michael Piller and Jeri Taylor and Ken Biller and Nicholas Sagan and Michael Taylor and Lisa Klink, who encouraged and supported me, and to Janet Nemecek and Brannon Braga and Corey Weiss and Bryan Fuller and Pete Nicholls and Joe Menosky, who helped me get the scripts and the videotapes. My apologies if I've forgotten anyone!!!

Thanks to Paula Block in Viacom Consumer Products for encouraging me to pitch my idea to Pocket Books and for helping me find those last few episodes, and to Margaret Clark and

Scott Shannon at Pocket Books for helping me get this book published!

To my advocate and my cheerleader—my wonderful editor, Marco Palmieri—working with you on this book has been one of the best experiences in my life, thank you for being who you are.

And finally, to all the writers in the history of *Star Trek*, credited and uncredited, who conceived the thoughts, ideas, and dreams that give us all something truly wonderful to which we may aspire: I thank you.

INDEX